DREAM'S DARK FLIGHT

ROBERT CHAZZ CHUTE

EX PARTE PRESS

WHAT READERS SAY ABOUT ROBERT'S WORK

Chute sucks you in from word one and pulls you down his post apocalyptic rabbit hole! You will sleep with the lights on, covers pulled over your head and dust off the old teddy bear for comfort. Horrifically well written and engaging. There are other popular books in this genre, but after reading this there is nothing else that climbs to the heights of Chute's caliber. Chazz ranks among the top tier of our generation's storytellers. ~ Alex Kimmell, Author of *The Key to Everything*

Robert Chazz Chute is such a skilled spinner of tales that the reader is more than willing to suspend any possible disbelief to go along for the ride. ~ David Pandolfe, author of *Jump When Ready*

It's not very often one finds a writer with such a dark side that has such a great sense of humor. ~ Glenn Roberts, Amazon reviewer

The author has a definite talent with words and ideas. ~ Love to Read!, Amazon reviewer

His words lift and dance off the page, bringing the story to life. ~ Kindle Customer, Amazon reviewer

The world building is horrifically well done with twists and turns and deceit around every corner. ~ Wanda, Amazon reviewer

Nothing but sheer exhaustion could tear my eyes from the captivating dance of words choreographed by Robert Chazz Chute. ~ Halph Staph, Amazon reviewer

Wonderful action constantly holds your interest. ~ Sharon Finn, Amazon reviewer

The complexity and attention to detail throughout absolutely blow me away. ~ Kindle customer, Amazon Reviewer

Very few authors impress me with the their actual writing style, it's usually always about the story. But this author paints such beautiful vivid pictures with words that I found myself not only enjoying the story but enjoying the way the words created images in my mind. I know that sounds corny, but it is true. ~ B.H., Amazon reviewer

Chute gives us story worthy of Stephen King. A read both thoughtful and fun. ~ Linda Beer Johnson, Amazon reviewer

The author does an excellent job building the characters and getting you invested and involved. ~ Michele L. Hebert, Amazon reviewer

I just can't say in words what a powerful author this is! ~ Delinda L. Calkins, Amazon reviewer

Robert Chazz Chute writes so skillfully as to make the supernatural seem perfectly logical - and terrifying! There are twists, turns and surprises galore. You will be glad you bought this book - until you lose sleep because you can't put it down. ~ johligo, Amazon reviewer

When I want to read apocalyptic books or zombie stories, those books have to also be extremely well-written and something that I could recommend with zeal and confidence to everyone I know. Robert Chazz Chute's books are exactly that. ~ Mazie Lane, Amazon reviewer

He makes the stuff that is obviously fiction, believable. ~ W. Nickels, Amazon reviewer

I am a lover of paranormal, dystopian novels and depth of story as well as intelligence in writing style, and Robert has it all. Humor, wit, depth, intelligence and an awesome way with words/writing. ~ Amazon Customer, Amazon reviewer

Published by Ex Parte Press
Copyright 2015 Robert Chazz Chute
All rights reserved.
ISBN 978-1-927607-52-7 (Paperback edition)
ISBN 978-1-927607-43-5 (Ebook edition)

Media and rights inquiries should be directed to expartepress@gmail.com.

Dedicated to those who believed in us when no one else would.

Special thanks to Russell Sawatsky, Mazie Lane, Christina L. Rivers, Alex Kimmell, Tidal Ashburn and Dr. Janice Kurita for editorial assistance.

Fall now into Dream's dark flight.
Loose sprockets take their turn
in the factories of the night.
Grind gears of unknown origin,
as fire rises in lucid gyres of light.
Humanity's only sure cog and commonality:
we meet in mind and might.
All you thought was safe and true
will soon be banished in blindsight.
For you and yours and what may be,
we wrote this writ of right.
Flip the page and slip reality.
Pray we escape our waking fright.

1

B erkeley Campus, California
April 6

DR. CORA DANZIG'S yacht floated on a calm blue sea beneath a full
moon. Palms on the nearby shore swayed in a warm breeze made of
soothing whispers. Moonlight played over the gentle water and
reached into the shallows to cast shadows among schools of phos-
phorescent tropical fish. Cora looked up at the night sky and smiled.
The moon could not possibly be that big, nor could Earth's first satellite hang so low. Cora knew she was dreaming. The drug had
kicked in.

In this place, reality and imagination crossed paths and blended.
Cora returned to this lagoon many times in her experiments. She
sometimes referred to it in her notes as the Twilight Zone.

As Cora slipped off the boat's stern into the warm water, it was
like lowering herself into a bath. She floated on her back and stared
up at the night sky. Despite the bright moon, she could see the
constellations clearly. The city shine around Berkeley blotted out the
stars. Nor were these the same constellations visible from her home

in Emeryville, California. It was tempting to let go of her earthly bonds and slip up into the sky. She could hear the invitation from the blackness, the bell-like music of the spheres.

It was a tempting offer but tonight's experiment was meant for making decisions, not tourism through the cosmos. If Cora had taken too much N,N-dimethyltrytamine, she would indeed be transformed from psychonaut to cosmonaut. DMT was powerful but her recent experimentation with adding tiny doses of peyote to the DMT left her with more control of the experience. She dismissed the sky's siren song and turned her attention to her agenda. The trips could feel long but were usually short. In real time, they lasted no more than five minutes.

At fifty-six, Dr. Danzig was one of the few researchers, and the only one at Berkeley, who had logged so many hours micro-dosing DMT and peyote. Her aim was to reap the benefits of the psychedelic while maintaining control of her consciousness during sleep. She had trained herself to harness the power of the molecule through lucid dreaming. It was a difficult altered state to maintain but Cora was accustomed to listening to the messages bubbling up from her unconscious mind.

In a recent paper, she wrote: *It is as if N,N-dimethyltrytamine unlocks a door to another dimension of the human experience previously known only to a few shamans and explorers of the Mindscape. Through my sleep experiments, I believe I can prop that door open and access great mental health benefits. The potential for this research is as vast as the imagination.*

Her long dead mother had been a fearful woman, frequently convinced God was out to get her. If Cora showed too much joy and laughed too often, even as a child, her mother would caution her that bad things must follow. "It's the yin yang of things. You get too much of a good thing, God will level you out."

It was perhaps that indoctrination since childhood that spurred Cora to explore psychedelics in her own way. Other psychonauts tested their limits and took heavier doses for deeper mind trips. She set out to find the minimal effective dose of DMT. She was convinced that was the only way forward to general acceptance. To use DMT in therapeutic settings more widely, dosages must be codified and systemic.

What problems will I solve tonight? Cora asked herself.

First, one of her grad students was her closest assistant. Frederick Chambers was angling for a recommendation Cora felt she could not give. The Masters student was enthusiastic about the work. He was not, in her estimation, PhD material. Students entered this niche of neuropsychology for many reasons. Frederick, though exceptionally gifted, seemed primarily interested in getting high. Her decision would change the young man's life and not for the better. She couldn't imagine working with Frederick for another four years. He did not respect the sacredness of DMT or the seriousness of her work. It was Cora's hope that, with rigorous academic inquiry, she could take the stigma out of psychedelic research. DMT could help the dying cope with their end-of-life concerns. Psychedelic applications for PTSD treatments were also promising.

The soul of the molecule is compassion, she thought. *I will show Frederick compassion by refusing him this path so he can find a better one for himself and the world.*

Framing the problem in that gentle way eased Cora's mind. *Thank you, DMT.*

Next issue: Cora's father, Stephen Danzig, was ill with pancreatic cancer. He was receiving excellent care but the prognosis was poor. It wasn't legal for her to inject him with DMT to help him on his journey. However, as the warm water gently rippled over her naked body, she felt love and strength building in her chest. Before her father was gone, she would do the ethical thing — if not the legal thing. Cora would help her father with at least one DMT trip to ease his stress.

To Cora's surprise, distant thunder rumbled. She opened her eyes to see bright white meteors slash across the night's dark canvas. "Hello," she said. "Have you got something to show me?"

Many neurobiologists thought of DMT as a conduit to useless hallucinations. Cora was among the few practitioners who suspected the drug could be a being in its own right. She would never admit such superstition at a conference but, within the privacy of the lucid dream, she could admit that idea in safety. She often felt that she was not alone when she came to the Twilight Zone. That feeling now grew.

The first touch of a cold heavy raindrop spattered the middle of her forehead. This was new and unpleasant. If it continued for long, she would slip out of the Twilight Zone and wake up. This was not normal.

"What are you trying to tell me?" she asked the night.

In answer, the sky split in two. White light from above blinded her. A voice that was neither male nor female filled the sky. It filled Cora's head, too. "I'm telling you to stay away. This is mine. This is my place. When you see me again, I will be in your place. I'm coming for you. I'm coming for all of you. Ours is the army of the night."

Cora heard a sound she could not immediately identify: crackling and crinkling. Treading water, she looked around, frantic to see what was coming. The ocean, her sanctuary, turned cold. The tropical fish, so vibrant a moment ago, drained of color. They stopped swimming and floated to the surface.

Bad trip, she thought. She shivered as the cold enveloped her. *I've got to get out.*

Then the water began to turn to black glass.

Cora tried to swim to the safety of her yacht. Safety wasn't far, but she wasn't bathed in warm water, anymore. She was bathed in blood.

She awoke in darkness, screaming. Cora reached out, blind and desperate to pull the rip cord. Every movement was agony. Her mind was back at the lab but it seemed her body was still in the Twilight Zone. She expected splashing. All she found was pain. Finally, her fingers found the rip cord. An alarm sounded and red lights popped on inside her isolation tank.

"Frederick! Frederick! Come get me! Pull me out now! I'm burning! *I'm burning!*"

Her assistant yanked open the isolation tank's hatch. Humming white fluorescence dazzled her. Cool air rushed into the temperature-controlled environment as Frederick reached in to grab her beneath her armpits. "Easy! Easy! You're having a bad trip, Cora! It's just a bad trip!"

However, as he pulled her naked from the tank, his eyes told her he was shocked.

Frederick laid Cora on her back on the cold stone floor. His jaw went slack and he froze for a moment.

Cora's flesh was sliced open everywhere. Every wound stung from the 2,000 pounds of salt that had taken her out of gravity and into perfect buoyancy. She lay there, naked, helpless and shaking as she worked to pull in great gulps of air. "It feels like I'm on fire!"

As Cora's blood spread across the floor, Frederick fumbled with his phone to call 911. Before Cora lost consciousness, she grasped her assistant's ankle and whispered, "It's coming. It's coming for all of us."

That was the first psychedelic incident signaling the end of the world. It would not be reported in full for several days. By then, the apocalypse was already a growing wave threatening to consume us all. Some otherworldly force had found a new weak point to wend into our dimension. It crossed the barrier into our world. Its mission was to enslave and kill.

As Dr. Cora Danzig lay poised at the threshold of death, she debated whether life was worth the effort it took to breathe. A terrible invasion, she was sure, had begun. The only escape from searing pain was death...but maybe not even then.

CHAPTER 2

Fox Point, Wisconsin
April 8

The second warning sign that the world had changed, probably irrevocably, was missed by almost everyone. In a sleepy neighborhood on the edge of Milwaukee's suburban sprawl, twenty-three people were roused from sleep at precisely 2:28 a.m. to the sound of thunder. Or so most of them thought. Twenty-two of those twenty-three people grumbled and rolled over, content to let the storm pass as they slept. The weather service reported a clear night under a full moon. There was no storm.

In the morning, they would awake bleary and resentful of leaving their warm beds. Those twenty-two people yawned and stretched and scratched and showered and dressed. They prepared for their day, another Monday that seemed much like most Mondays. None was refreshed upon waking. They had vague recollections of a disturbing dream but the details were lost to the night.

By the time they'd made it to their front doors, last night's thunder was forgotten. They did not search for the rich, pleasant smell of spores rising from the earth after a hard rain. Those twenty-two people did not sense something was amiss until they opened their doors. They froze in shock when they discovered their front hedges and gardens and lawns had been destroyed.

But experiments have anomalies. Graphs have points that do not conform to the expected. Everything changes but not everyone conforms. The outlier that night was a twenty-six-year-old physio-therapist named Jennifer Daimler.

She was known as Jen to her friends and so she was Jen to just about everyone. Intelligent and excellent at her job, Jen appeared normal. With wide eyes and a ready smile, Jen was pretty yet approachable. Several young doctors and a couple of nurses had asked her out. She was determined to stay single for the foreseeable future. Gun-shy about dating anyone, she was still paying off credit card debt incurred by a bad ex-boyfriend. When the relationship got serious, she'd made the mistake of sharing an account with him. Jen had little time for leisure. She owed nearly $40,000 in student loans, plus the credit card debt. She worked double shifts at the hospital whenever she could. She wanted a dog. She pictured rescuing a sad-eyed beagle from the shelter. However, cooping up a pet in her tiny apartment while she worked all day wouldn't be fair to an animal.

Perhaps it was the stress of her life circumstances that stirred Jen more easily. Maybe the odd hospital shifts made her sleep restless and vulnerable. She did not take the rumbling through her neighbor-hood for thunder. Fox Point's one exception would prove of critical importance in the coming days. While others rolled over, content to slip back into a doze and forget, Jen dreamt of horses. For two full minutes, her mind spooled out an unlikely scenario in which she rode bareback on a black mare named Midnight. Unlike the others, Jen would remember the experience the next morning and for the rest of her life.

The dream was fun at first. Jen clung to the big horse with her legs until her quadriceps muscles threatened to cramp. Afraid she'd fall, Jen clutched at the horse's mane, the long hair in her fists. She tried to slow the beast but the horse was heedless.

Jen thought she was alone, but as she looked back, she found she was in the lead of a herd. Huge horses — whinnying and snorting — galloped at full speed behind her. Upon each horse sat a rider, as wild-eyed and helpless as she. If Jen had thought to count the number of other riders, she would have counted twenty-two. Despite the full moon, every horse was a dark shadow that reflected no light. Only their eyes and teeth shone white. Their teeth were longer than those of any horse on Earth, more like sabertooth tigers than a modern horse.

The dream devolved to terror as the herd plowed through everything in its path. Jen hoped the horses would leap the neighborhood fences. Instead, her mount led the charge and broke through wooden fences as easily as she might snap a lollipop stick. The mare, shiny with sweat, careened forward, forging a path of destruction. Jen's grip faltered. The horse bucked and rose in a high arc, its front hooves wheeling through the night air.

Jen's last cogent thought in the dream was, *this is a war horse.*

The stampede pounded by as Jen fell. Her bones and brains would have been dashed to powder and bloody slush under their sharp hooves but, when she fell, Jen landed on her own bedroom floor. Her thighs ached as if from prolonged exertion. Her hands were still tight fists, sore from overwork.

Jen hadn't fallen out of bed since she was a child. She lay on the hardwood floor in the darkened room. The sound of the herd's pounding hooves echoed nearby, drowning out the sound of her own shallow breathing. The noise retreated. In her fall, she'd knocked her alarm clock to the floor. The red digits swam in her vision. The numbers told her it was 2:32 a.m.

Jen almost laughed at the absurdity of the nightmare but the sound of heavy hoofbeats cut that impulse short. Sore and surely bruised from landing so hard, Jen staggered to her feet, leaned on her bed and almost fell on her way to the window.

Outside, she saw no mad herd of galloping warhorses bent on destruction. They'd already passed through her neighborhood. In the weak yellow cast of a streetlight, she could make out trampled gardens, flattened fences and many hoof prints. They had torn through both sides of the street.

Jen might have called someone, but what could she say? *A band of feral horses rampaged through my neighborhood and I heard them in my sleep and...what?* Had her brain pulled the noise from the real world and fit it to her dreams? That's what she told herself as she stumbled back to bed. As often happens when the world changes too quickly beneath our feet, she reengineered the information she had so it made more sense. Horses must have stampeded through her neighborhood. She had heard hoofbeats and her brain had fit the real world into her dream world.

Jen lay in bed for a long time, unable to sleep or even close her eyes. She finally fell asleep at 6:07 a.m., twenty-three minutes before her alarm was set to go off. When she awoke, still sore from her fall, she thought, *all dreams seem real. And nightmares, more so.*

There's a reason for that. She didn't know it then. Not yet. The apocalypse was still slowly unfolding, gathering strength.

CHAPTER 3

Belmont Plaza Hotel
  Dubai, United Arab Emirates
  April 9

In a panic, Nayla Garcia called for help from her hotel room. Mauro lay dead beside their bed. Though her husband was obviously beyond hope, she yelled into her phone in rapid-fire Spanish, begging for someone to come. It seemed the only thing to do, if only to share her grief.

Mauro married Nayla the same week he graduated from Argentina's National Technological University. He'd earned an engineering degree and won her heart with sweet words and unwavering affection. They'd never had a real honeymoon but, on their twentieth anniversary, Mauro took Nayla with him to Dubai. Mauro traveled for business but this trip was supposed to be romantic, too. The couple had arrived in Dubai the day before. Mauro knew a little Arabic. In Dubai, it seemed everyone at the hotel spoke English. Now Mauro lay sprawled on the floor in a pool of blood.

Calling for help, Nayla knew nothing of the local language and

her English was sparse. When the front desk staff failed to understand her Spanish, she yelled louder. "*Muerto! Muerto! Muerto!*"

Apparently, they understood that much or thought to use a trans-
lation app. A few minutes later, someone pounded on her door.
When Nayla rushed to open it, the grieving woman was surprised to
find a female police officer standing in the hall. She had assumed
Dubai's police force would be for males only. Instead of the familiar
green beret with a gold badge on it, the officer wore a headscarf.
Otherwise, the police woman was clothed in the olive uniform Nayla
had seen at the Dubai International Airport.

"What is the problem, ma'am?" the young woman asked in
English.

Distraught, Nayla spoke in Spanish again, crying and gasping
between bursts of words. The officer, Alma Nejem, watched the
woman impassively. She couldn't understand the middle-aged
woman but she had witnessed nervous breakdowns in the past.
Nejem raised her hands in a soothing gesture meant to get the
woman to slow down and breathe deeper.

Infuriated, Nayla stepped back and ran to the body on the floor.
Officer Nejem's nervousness rose when she spotted a pool of blood
beneath the still man. She scanned the hotel suite. The door had not
been forced. They were on the forty-second floor. The room's line of
floor-to-ceiling windows offered a commanding view of the city.
Besides the corpse, nothing else seemed out of place.

Insensible in her grief, Nayla knelt by Mauro and screamed at the
officer to help her husband.

That is too much blood, Nejem thought. *And that is no longer a man.
It is meat.*

The widow shook the body as if trying to wake her husband. But
the body did not shake back and forth as expected. The body was
mush. Nayla's hands sank into Mauro's chest. As she wiped her tears,
she covered herself in blood. It looked like she had donned war paint.

Nejem commanded the screaming woman to step away from the
body. The police officer stepped closer and gasped as she took in the

destruction. She had seen something like this before but never inside the hotel. The body of the middle-aged man was flattened against the floor as if he'd been crushed by a machine. *Terminal velocity*, Nejem thought. *This man looks like he jumped from a plane without a functioning parachute.*

The deceased was a small man, a little bloated in the middle. The officer estimated his blood volume at 5.5 liters. As the thick liquid spread beyond an elegant throw rug and across the hardwood floor, it looked like much more blood than that.

Following the officer's gaze, Nayla said in Spanish, *"He is a bloody rag, wrung out."*

The metallic odor rising through the room unsettled Officer Nejem. She didn't know what had transpired here. She prided herself on taking in problems at a glance and solving them. Nejem put a hand on the butt of the Sig Sauer at her hip. The feel of it soothed her. She gestured for Nayla to step back from the body.

"Mauro! Mauro! My poor man!" When she touched her face again, blood got in her mouth and she began to gag. She crawled to her feet and, arms outstretched rushed toward Nejem. Screaming in Spanish, Nayla continued to beg for help.

At that moment, Ibrahim Darzi appeared in the doorway behind Nejem. He saw the body on the floor and the woman covered in blood. He pulled his weapon, a Glock 17, from its holster. In Arabic, he screamed at the woman rushing toward Nejem, warning her to stop. He didn't get more than a word out before he began to fire.

Nejem wisely threw herself to the floor. Had she stood still, Darzi would have shot her in the back.

A Glock 17 holds seventeen rounds, but Officer Darzi didn't use them all. He got off seven shots before Nejem ordered the rookie to hold his fire. Darzi's first shot missed and starred the big floor to ceiling window. The next four rounds hit Nayla in the chest and drove her backward. The widow staggered back toward the cracked glass window. Darzi's last two shots sent her through it and over the balcony's railing.

Far below, the widow's body crashed through an awning and smashed through an empty table at the hotel's outdoor restaurant.

Nearby diners had just begun breakfast. Narrowly escaping injury themselves, the other hotel guests screamed, shuddered and vomited. Nayla Garcia's short flight ended with her body splitting and bursting as she arrived at her final destination.

Nejem would have covered for the rookie's impulsiveness if she could, citing some mitigating circumstance. She could have said the Argentinian tourist attacked her instead of looking for a hug. However, a cover-up was impossible. With all the blood, it was undeniable that Mauro Garcia had died where he lay. There was nothing in the hotel room — a bloody sledge hammer, for instance — that could have been used as a murder weapon. There was no blood trail out of the hotel suite.

Later, in her incident report, Officer Nejem noted the irony of the couple's deaths. In the end, Nayla's shattered corpse didn't look much different from that of her husband. Both had been turned to bloody mush.

Mauro Garcia did indeed look like he, too, had fallen from a great height. Nejem did not add so obvious a detail to the official report but the dead man could not have fallen farther than the height of his bed.

Darzi would suffer an investigation and be put on unpaid leave at the very least. If and when he returned to work, Nejem would knee him in the balls for nearly shooting her in the back. However, Officer Nejem did not get a chance to linger long over her report. She was still at the crime scene on the forty-second floor when the case (and the world) became more complicated.

More frantic calls for help arrived at the front desk. Fresh screams echoed up and down the halls of the Belmont. Twenty-two other hotel guests had died in the night. They all appeared to have met their ends in the same fashion: twenty-four bodies: one with numerous gunshot wounds.

All of them bloody mush.

CHAPTER 4

Cybersecurity Initiative Data Center
  Utah
  Comm Station Delta, Third Shift
  April 12

Fearful of starting a panic, Dubai's government quashed the story. The smashed bodies were quarantined. The international press was fed a story of a Legionnaire's Disease outbreak at the resort. Mystified, Dubai's General Department of Criminal Investigation sent out a highly classified yet vague query across Interpol's network, straight from the office of the UAE's Vice-president:

Alert: 23 dead in one night in a resort hotel, on eleven different floors spread wide apart. Any reports of terrorist organizations crushing bodies?

Nayla Garcia, quite rightly, was not counted among the dead. None of the victims was named in the Interpol alert. The report might have been passed over and filed away as a strange anomaly with no answer. However, the query piqued the interest of one analyst.

Stationed at the NSA's Utah Data Center, Thomas Reddy stared at his screen, reading the message several times.

Thirty-four, tall and gangly, Reddy appeared just short of malnourished. Unless he spoke of work matters, Reddy said little to fellow staffers. He preferred late shifts. Though the NSA desks were staffed with almost as many people at night, the office culture was different. The day shifts were louder. They captured more data but got less analysis done. Analysts on the graveyard shift were the NSA's workhorses and Reddy worked harder than anyone.

As Reddy reviewed the Interpol message, the words *twenty-three* and *dead* caught his attention. The query came in at 2:30 a.m., Mountain Time. The message contained twenty-three words, not counting the numeral 23 itself. Reddy typed *hotel deaths* into his search engine. He got several hits but discarded the links to numerous news stories reporting a killer earthquake that had leveled a hotel in Osaka, Japan recently.

The first story of relevance reported twenty-three dead from Legionnaire's in Dubai. The article mentioned a curious detail of a police shooting at the same hotel. The victim was identified only as an Argentinian national. The second bulletin reported twenty-three missing and presumed dead in the crash of Turkish Airlines Flight 46 near Nepal.

Forty-six is twenty-three times two, Reddy thought.

Nervous, he reached into his pocket and touched his key fob. The key ring held the keys to his car, his gun safe and his apartment. Nothing else. The key fob was a cheap souvenir given to him by his father, David Reddy. The plastic square contained an image representing the Baton Rouge Blue Marlins baseball team. The team had lasted only one season, 2001. Thomas Reddy was not a baseball fan nor was he sentimental about his dead father's gift. He found the cool, smooth feel of the plastic between his thumb and forefinger soothing.

He looked for updates on the Turkish crash but found none. The plane had yet to be found by rescue workers. Surely it would be found soon. In the meantime, the nonsense offered up in ensuing media frenzy included allusions to old movies like *Lost Horizons* and the one about the soccer team downed in the mountains, forced to become cannibals while they awaited rescue. Early speculation from the media, Reddy was sure, was ninety percent nonsense meant to fill time, not to enlighten.

Chatter in the Comm Traffic Monitoring Center suggested Flight 46 had been brought down by a powerful airborne hallucinogen. An aerosol concealed in the panels of the plane's filtration system could have been the vector. The panicked mayday from Flight 46's co-pilot was not public knowledge yet. The garbled message said something about snakes swarming the cockpit.

The part of the message the analysts played over and over was, "The pilot's asleep! I can't wake him! A python is coiled around his body! I am watching him...[inaudible]...he's getting swallowed head-first!" The transmission was suspended for five seconds. Then the co-pilot sent his last known message. "Cobras! Black mambas!"

Wait until the media gets hold of that, Reddy thought.

Macabre jokes were made at the data center, too, of course. The Comm Traffic staff prattled incessantly about the movie *Snakes on a Plane.* One of the women did a passable Samuel L. Jackson impression.

Everyone laughed except Thomas Reddy. He watched his colleagues speculate about the message as he jingled the keys in his pocket. His fingers found the cool plastic and he rubbed the key fob to calm his nerves. The woman with the Samuel L. Jackson impression looked his way, smiling. He smiled and nodded back but he worried he wasn't making the right facial expressions. He worried he was looking at his colleague too long. Then he worried he was not meeting her gaze enough. Was he too far or too close? What did his body language convey to her?

The key fob had not been enough then. He turned back to his computer screen and retreated to an exercise he used to calm himself. When he couldn't go running, Reddy used collective nouns to ease the tension creeping from his shoulders to his neck.

A flock of birds. A flight of birds. A pod of birds. A grist of bees. A swarm of bees. A drift of bees. An erst of bees.

The trick was to focus on something else besides the many variables that contributed to his social anxiety.

As he thought about the passengers on Flight 46 falling to their deaths, his stomach fluttered.

A bunch of butterflies is called a flutter, he thought. *When bullfinches gather, they are a bellowing. Wildcats are a destruction.*

He frowned as he reread the query from Dubai: Guests crushed to death in their hotel rooms without explanation, without a clue, without any terrorist organization claiming responsibility.

A murder of crows.

Reddy pulled the keys from his pocket so he could grip the Blue Marlins souvenir key fob. The plastic heated up in his palm.

The third hit in Reddy's search was a wildcard. The alert came from Flagler Beach from two nights before. The location hardly surprised him. Most of the weirdest stories seemed to emanate from Florida. There was the so-called bath salt zombie attack, for instance. Assorted crystal meth escapades at various Walmart stores were quite common. The case of the rocket-propelled grenade used to settle a domestic dispute had been a standout, too. However, the story on Reddy's screen was strange, even for Florida.

From the headlines, it seemed that this was a tragic case of a beach party gone sour. In the small hours of April 10, a group of students from Florida State had linked arms and walked into the ocean. Local newspaper reports conflicted with the official story. One witness reported that when the group — five women and eighteen men — walked into the waves, several of the men appeared to be snoring.

A spokesperson for the Flagler Beach Police Department, Sgt. Armand Rosamilia, announced in a press conference that not all of the bodies had been retrieved. Results from the autopsies would remain pending until the coroner for St. Johns County had time to process all test results.

"The Medical Examiner's Office will be overwhelmed for some

time, what with all the necessary analysis," Rosamilia said. "I have no names to release since we have not contacted all the relatives. There was one survivor, a young woman who was saved by a witness who prefers not to be named. The rescued woman was in critical condition at Flagler Hospital and has since been transferred via helicopter to Baptist Medical in Jacksonville. She has not regained consciousness. Detectives suspect that this terrible drowning must have happened because of some hallucinogenic — possibly acid or a new, deadlier variation on MDMA. Mix a stimulant like Molly with something like mescaline, for instance, and you could get mass psychosis. All of Florida is in mourning and the student community at Florida State in particular will be torn up emotionally. When we eventually release the names of those lost, I ask the media to refrain from turning this into a circus that multiplies the grief of the families involved."

When Sgt. Rosamilia was asked if any drugs were recovered from the scene, he answered, "No charges are being laid at this time. Our investigation continues."

Something fishy going on there. Reddy squeezed his key fob. *A deceit of lapwings.*

The bath salts zombie attack had been false, too. A crazed homeless man had bitten a man's face. The victim had been blinded and the attacker was shot dead by police. That much was true. Miami police blamed the brutal cannibal attack on bath salts. They had done so before a test for such a drug even existed. When the toxicology report finally surfaced, only marijuana had been found in the attacker's system. By then, the bath salts twist on the story had caught hold. The media perpetuated the bath salts myth and, when that faltered, the search for a cause had landed, quite ridiculously, on marijuana.

A pandemonium of parrots.

When Reddy glanced up at the time, twenty-three minutes had elapsed since he'd received the alert from Dubai.

He needed a label for a collection of unexplained deaths

involving the number twenty-three. The right word, he decided, must be *conspiracy*. Soon, he would amend that label to *beachhead*. Then? *Invasion*.

CHAPTER 5

Comm Station Delta, Third Shift
   April 12

Thomas Reddy's first call was to ASCWW. No one called the section by its full name: Altered States of Consciousness, Weapons and Warfare. The analyst chose to speak to Captain Harrison Frist in the NSA's Remote Viewer Section. Two branches of the military employed remote viewers in tenuous, underfunded projects. The most successful "Remote Joes" got recruited to the big leagues with the NSA and CIA.

There was a short delay as Reddy identified himself to the ASCWW's chat bot. His voice print matched. Reddy's security clearance was high enough to send a query to anyone below the Joint Chiefs of Staff. The call rang through.

"ASCWW. Captain Frist here."

"Good morning, Captain. It's Thomas Reddy from — "

"I know who you are."

"Very well. I expected to get an aide, sir. It's rare for me to catch someone of rank up at this hour."

"I knew you'd be calling."

Frist could be joking. Reddy wasn't sure. Humor often eluded him. He'd heard ASCWW's people tried to boost their reputations with double speak.

"We've had some events," Reddy said vaguely. "Has anyone in your section got anything for us?"

"You're talking about the snakes on a plane, right? Yeah, one of our Joes caught that. We're working on coordinates for the plane now. That what you mean?"

Reddy didn't want to lead the man. He suspected several of the staff in Frist's section were no better than carnival psychics who excelled at cold reading. "Anything else?"

"Bad dreams out of the Middle East. Deadly dreams. That's the signal I'm getting. Anxiety is climbing across the Mindscape. The barriers between nightmares and the waking world are thinner. I don't suppose that makes sense to you but I can feel it. I can almost see it. When I'm in the zone, I'm feeling around in the dark and I'm worried something's going to grab my hand. There are dangerous creatures there, Mr. Reddy. They're finding their way through the walls of consciousness, reaching into our minds and stirring things up. I think they plan to break through. I don't know where the enemy is yet, but something is wrong and it's coming our way. It's not clear yet, but when it gets close enough, I expect I'll see it and I'll shit the bed when I do."

The ASCWW officer could be a paranoid lunatic, Reddy thought, *but he sounded like a sincere lunatic.*

The story on the mass drowning in Florida had mentioned snoring. The bad dreams sounded like an interesting angle but the Middle East was always a hot spot. Reddy needed much more. "Can you give me anything specific?"

"I have three Joes asking for time off. They're having night terrors."

"What are they seeing?"

"That's just it. All they get is terror, no views. Something's not right. They get that trouble is coming. There's a rumbling through the *Unus Mundus,* is all."

"*Unus Mundus*? What does that mean, Captain? I'm unfamiliar —
"

"I'm referring to the collective unconscious. We are all one, Mr. Reddy. One mind, one being. Humanity is one eco-system. Isolation is an illusion. When we enter altered states, we access the ocean of information that all minds share. You surf the internet for a living. When we reach that place, we surf the waves of thought and navigate the shared currents of data, sussing out the echoes of chemical reactions and neurotransmitters."

Captain, Reddy thought, *you should slow down your delivery.* Frist's words sounded like a canned speech delivered so many times that the passion was sucked out of the poetry. *He probably lays that on every caller and all his recruits to the Remote Joe Division.* "What does that boil down to, sir? The *Unus Mundus* — "

"In short, Mr. Reddy, my guys sense a disturbance in the Force."

"I see."

"Do you? I think most people are blind. It's we who see."

"I see."

"Are you trying to be funny?"

"Not that I'm aware of. Perhaps that information is denied me by the *Unus Mundus.* Did your Remote Joes experience this disturbance while they were on duty?"

"No. Off duty. While they slept."

"And they reported these events independently of each other?" Reddy didn't want to bet on a claim made by a few odd soldiers angling for a weekend pass to Vegas.

"Two of them are in the same barracks. The third hates the first two. That's why I give it credence. I'm not giving them any time off. Something's going on. Don't doubt my people, Mr. Reddy. I know we're not taken seriously by some in the establishment but I'm doing serious shit here."

"Thank you, Captain. If you have anything more specific that seems relevant, please dial me directly."

"I'll keep you top of drawer." The officer clicked off before Reddy could say goodbye.

The analyst turned back to his computer and opened the OTS program. OTS stood for Over the Shoulder. The program's primary use was tracking the spread of viruses on a choropleth map. Each flu season, the more people got sick, the more they searched for remedies and diagnoses. OTS skimmed the search terms and translated it to a map of the world. As people searched for relief from their flu symptoms, OTS displayed the progression of the virus across the world's population. More searches equalled more infection.

Reddy experimented with various search terms related to sleep. It was, it seemed, a popular topic. Sleep apnea was more of a concern in developed countries so the map displayed bright red circles where the problem was more prevalent. Apnea seemed to plague those in urban areas more. Insomnia seemed fairly universal wherever people used computers. Those results displayed in cool blue circles with no pattern Reddy could detect.

Once Reddy had context, he opted to check up on Captain Frist's observation of a disturbed *Unus Mundus*. The analyst plugged the search terms *night terrors* and *nightmares* into the OTS. The results were more than he expected. Everywhere there were computers, it seemed these were popular topics and a lot of people wanted relief. Those results alone didn't tell him anything, however. He did a retroactive search, checking the same search terms one year previous. OTS went back to take a digital snapshot of those search results and translated them to the world map. Tiny navy blue dots appeared on the map. One year ago, these same search terms barely registered.

He tapped a new request in his keyboard and waited for the program to run checking the same search terms over time. A few seconds later, OTS showed Reddy the progression month by month. The skimmed search statistics stayed at more or less a steady rate. More people searched nightmares than night terrors, but overall, these were not major concerns across the world's population.

When OTS hit the current month, April, the map went red again. Large and small circles covered the world map just about everywhere there was a land mass and people were connected to the internet. In the last few days, a huge spike was evident. The hot map clearly indicated that people were now plagued with nightmares and anxiety about going to sleep.

"It is time to pay taxes in the United States," Reddy mused aloud. "That could bump up the stress but it's not tax time everywhere. And this time last year, the map was cool."

Curious, he ran the OTS search again, going backwards, day by day. The day before, the map's hotspots were not quite as large and not as red. The results steadily diminished. On April 8, the results were on par with the cold search terms throughout the previous year. The search terms appeared to heat up on April 9.

Reddy ran the analysis again, hour by hour, and noted a few spikes beginning on April 9, beginning at 7:30 a.m. EST.

He printed out a list of the geographic clusters. Apparently, hundreds of people had a terrible night's sleep on the night of April 8. They woke up to search for solutions early on April 9. The small red circles that signified the beginning of the spike in night terrors originated in Wisconsin, San Diego and Hollywood, California.

The analyst guessed that, if he could track prescriptions for anti-anxiety medication in real time, he'd see that consumption rate climb. OTS could handle such data but the medical system wasn't fully digital yet. Most practitioners still scribbled their notes and prescriptions on pieces of paper instead of entering medical data to the Cloud where the NSA could easily access it.

Reddy sat back, staring at his screens. He then refined his parameters, checking the peak hours when people used their computers for searches related to medical questions. He'd seen similar chart results with the ebola scare in 2015 and zika in 2016. The OTS choropleth map's dynamic display glowed bright red compared to those events. The media frenzy around zika and ebola had drummed up a lot of anxiety but the silent epidemic of night terrors appeared to be more widespread than either of those events. The difference this time was that no one seemed to know there was a new epidemic and it was spreading fast.

Reddy sat back again, his right hand worrying his key fob and making the keys jingle. *I don't know the cause. If it's a pathogen, I can't imagine the vector. Some parasites can influence the behavior of their hosts. It could be a mutant mite found in spinach, for all I know. But there seems to be some tenuous connection to sleep.*

The attack in Dubai had happened overnight when, presumably, hotel guests should be safe in their beds. Could Captain Frist's vague concerns about 'deadly dreams' have merit? How could the rise in night terrors across the world be related to a strange and inexplicable terrorist act in Dubai? The connection seemed like it could be a correlation but the logic was not linear. What others denigrated as mere intuition, Reddy called associative reasoning.

In Reddy's experience, people weren't really logical, anyway. They generally jumped to a conclusion. Then they reasoned backwards, supporting their quick assumptions with selective facts. He supposed he might be doing the same now but the OTS stats didn't lie. Something strange was happening to people each night and the night terror epidemic was spreading. The casualties in Dubai had apparently died in an unheard of way. Gunshots indoors were loud so Reddy deduced that, except for the Argentinian shot by police, the victims died in their sleep.

It was a leap to connect the facts to a cohesive whole, but only for smaller minds than that of Thomas Reddy. To get into the field and to explore this phenomenon further, Reddy would have to convince smaller minds he was on to something.

A group that works in an unimaginative bureaucratic hierarchy is a troop of baboons.

CHAPTER 6

Comm Station Delta, Third Shift
April 12

Reddy picked up his dedicated line. The comm rang through to his supervisor instantly. Section Chief Helen Warren answered on the first buzz. "What?"

"Chief, I have an Interpol query. I'd like to do the follow-up personally."

"What's that about?"

"I checked in with ASCWW. Captain Frist's people are having some unusual disturbances."

"Great. The flakes and nuts are on your side," Warren said. "What have you got that's concrete? What do we *know*?"

He paused, choosing his words carefully. "I understand your hesitation. This is something you don't want assigned elsewhere. Not yet, anyway."

"Is your spider sense tingling, Mr. Reddy?"

"You could say that."

"I wouldn't. It sounds ridiculous." The woman let out a long sigh. "Your analysis can be imaginative and useful but an action summary must be grounded in what we know and what we can prove. This sounds like another of your strange quests."

"Quests? No, I don't have a quest. I do have questions. If I'm right, this will be big and will be brought to a safe conclusion by a joint task force from Homeland...perhaps the DEA."

"The DEA? Uh...look...I know you want to get on track for field work, Tom, but your talents — "

"Please, call me Thomas. And I won't embarrass you, Chief. This is a need, not a want. I do have data to show you. May I join you in your office to discuss this?"

"Is this about the twenty-three enigma thing again? I saw the Dubai query come in. I knew you'd call me about this before end of shift."

"The Remote Joes — "

"I am not sending an analyst all the way to Dubai because Frist's got a remote viewer with restless leg syndrome who thinks she's a wiccan."

"Actually, I would prefer a flight to Florida, please. There are witnesses to interview."

"Witnesses? What the hell are you talking about, Tom?"

Reddy squirmed in his seat. It took great mental effort for him to refrain from correcting her again. He preferred Thomas to Tom.

A group of goldfinches is a charm. A kindle of kittens.

Reddy's breath deepened again. He slowly rotated in his chair to look back through the glass wall at the back of the room. Helen Warren sat at her desk staring back at him, waiting. He could hear her tapping a pen on her desk. "Could we meet in your office, please? I have a case to make. If I'm right, and I usually am, we could be on top of this before anybody on the day or evening shifts gets the scent."

Reddy waited while his supervisor gave a long pause.

"Plus," Reddy added, "you could get me out of the office for a day or two. Away from you."

Even at this distance, Thomas detected the hint of a smile at the corner of Warren's mouth. He wondered if he had made a joke.

"See me at the shift change. I'll give you two minutes. This better not be some *X-Files* shit. Your name isn't Scully or Mulder. Waste my time with nonsense and I'll send you down to Section G to peep on perverts through their laptop cameras. A month of keeping an eye out for sex offenders into BDSM grandma porn could get you focused on the right worries. You had a big hit once, Tom. That was good but I need more results on tangible ISIS threats. No woo-woo bullshit." She hung up.

A clattering of jackdaws.

Reddy sighed as he turned back to his screens to print out the dynamic mapping scans. He went over the data again and made a mind map of the commonalities. The witness in Florida had mentioned snoring. The co-pilot on Flight 46 said he could not wake the pilot. The message from Dubai said nothing about sleeping victims, only that twenty-three had died in one night. He was sure his Warren would say that connection was the most tenuous but, people slept at night. Not NSA analysts with OCD working the graveyard shift, but *normal* people slept at night.

Reddy made a list of the interviews he needed: Sgt. Rosamilia from Flagler Beach, the person who had saved the woman from the Atlantic and, of course, the drowning victim herself, if she regained consciousness.

His case for field work was shaky but he listed the mitigating factors which would aid his presentation. If he was correct, some new hallucinogen was being employed by someone for nefarious purposes. He knew if he used the buzzwords, "domestic terrorists" and the phrase, "international terrorist connection," he would have his supervisor's full attention. The results of the choropleth mapping would impress her most. If any case could be made to connect home-grown terrorists or the odd lone wolf to international terror organizations, Warren would gain prestige in the eyes of her superiors. She was very concerned with not only being right but also being among the first to spot a trend.

Reddy's talent for pattern recognition was well known among his colleagues. If he'd been more socially adept, he might have been promoted to Warren's level by now. Perhaps that was why she felt so threatened by his capabilities. At his annual reviews, she accused Reddy of relying on confirmation bias and selection bias. When Reddy joined the NSA, his psychographic profile was more to the point: socially awkward, apophenia, OCD, some paranoid tendencies, among other concerns. On their first meeting, Section Chief Warren had confronted him with the report.

Reddy didn't blink. "Some paranoia is a perfect attribute for a security analyst. Paranoia pays dividends."

"And the OCD?" she asked.

"I prefer the term detail-oriented."

"That's not the term the psychologist used."

"But I prefer detail oriented."

"You know what apophenia is? That's in the assessment, too."

"Apophenia is the tendency to see patterns where there are none."

"And you have that."

"I don't believe I do."

"The fact that you know the definition of the term suggests you do. An obsession with numerology is not something the NSA can use, Mr Reddy. What's next? Telling my future by...what? The bumps on my head?"

"I don't believe in phrenology. I know that term and its definition but I don't have that delusion, either."

"Well, that's comforting."

Reddy suspected she was being ironic. He was almost sure. "I reject the premise of the doctor's diagnosis. Perhaps I've identified patterns that others have not yet understood."

"We're a team here. Smugness doesn't help your case, Mr. Reddy."

"I'm sorry," he said. "I meant to be condescending. I don't think I'm ever smug."

"You graduated at the top of your class at Yale in Philosophy with a minor in Mathematics. You have to be smug."

"The practice of philosophy is mostly writing book reports about the ideas of dead philosophers. I came to no useful conclusions. I can be useful here."

Warren flipped through his *curriculum vita*. "Then you got a degree in criminology from a second string college — "

"My parents paid for Yale," Reddy said. "My father wanted me to go to Wall Street or into law. Criminology seemed close to my father's wishes so I tried that."

She looked him up and down. "If you became a cop, you'd get eaten alive."

"Then it's fortunate I'm not applying for a position as a police officer."

"Insolence is not useful, trust fund baby."

"Actually, I'm out of the will. My mother asked him to have mercy on me and find me a suitable job. Homeland Security could be a good fit."

"I'm sure you think so, Mr. Reddy. If not for your senator father, you'd be homeless."

"Quite possibly. That would be uncomfortable."

"And now, because of who your daddy is, you end up at my desk. How many strings did the Senator have to pull to get you through the door at the NSA?"

"Twenty-three," Reddy replied.

Warren was not amused but his other test scores and his connections required her to give Reddy a fair trial. Three months later, he was fairly fluent in Farsi and what he lacked in social skills he made up for in diligence.

The NSA came to value Reddy because he accurately identified an anomaly in scraped data that no one else picked up. The movements of a Russian container ship piqued his interest one night. Reddy noted that the ship had stayed in port too long. Coordinated with intelligence that Iraqi fuel dumps and weapons caches had been raided in the previous three months, he formulated a hypothesis. The Comm Traffic staff had scoffed at his warning of a terrorist threat. They told him he was seeing ghosts. Then satellite imagery confirmed Reddy's suspicions. That container ship in Kuwait City had been loaded with fuel and explosives. The ship was bound for Boston Harbor.

On February 3rd of 2012, an Ohio-class submarine, the USS *Henry M. Jackson* (SSBN-730) was dispatched to engage with the container ship. The encounter ended with the cargo ship's captain ignoring hails. The submarine destroyed the container ship mid-Atlantic. Based on the subsequent explosion, the Navy estimated that the terrorists had filled the target with enough explosives to destroy a city. Because of Reddy's warning and the CIA's subsequent intelligence gathering, a cataclysm was avoided. An explosion in Boston Harbor would have collapsed the US economy and started another war.

The official story was that the container ship had been lost at sea.

When Reddy was debriefed, the meeting with the brass should have been cause for celebration. Instead, Reddy embarrassed his section chief. Warren had handed Reddy a brandy snifter. He thanked her and put the glass down without drinking to the toast she offered.

An admiral in a business suit clapped Reddy on the shoulder and announced to the room, "Good job, boy! That was a tough catch and a good call."

Reddy shrugged and told the admiral it was easier than it appeared. He'd had no doubt of the mission's outcome.

"How's that, old son?"

"The USS *Henry M. Jackson* was a clue to destiny. The Navy hit the target on 02/03/2012. See? Two-three is twenty-three. Two and one plus two equalled twenty-three again. It was pre-destined. The universe pointed me toward the trouble."

He should have kept quiet about his superstition and used his triumph to greater advantage. Instead, as he shook hands with the directors of the CIA, NSA and the admiral, Reddy stared at the floor. He accepted a medal from the Chairman of the Joint Chiefs of Staff with a weak nod. When asked if he wanted to say a few words, Reddy replied, "No, thank you, sir. I should get back to work."

They all laughed but their laughter was cut short when he promptly exited the room and returned to his station. Before the door closed, he heard Helen Warren say, "Back to your nerd cage!" She brayed when she laughed.

Nest of vipers. An ostentation of peacocks. A trip of swine.

He'd saved Boston and all the terrible repercussions that would have resulted from its destruction, foreign and domestic. Despite Warren's dislike, Reddy's talents had built up idiosyncrasy points with his boss. It was time to cash them in on the Dubai mystery.

It was his NSA psychologist, Dr. Janice Kurita, who had explained the concept of idiosyncrasy points to Reddy. "You're a little weird, Mr. Reddy," Kurita had told him, "but if you are right and useful often enough, you get tolerated. If you're rude, you lose idiosyncrasy points. If you build up your positives, you will be forgiven your transgressions."

Reddy had frowned and shifted in his chair, crossing and uncrossing his arms. "Just as you have been kind to me in the past and built my trust, I will forgive you for calling me weird."

"Exactly," the psychologist replied.

"I never mean to be rude, Dr. Kurita."

"I know."

"But I think people are mean to me on purpose."

"Then they have to build up their idiosyncrasy points with you, don't they, Thomas?"

"No need. I can just cut them off from all unnecessary interaction and ignore them."

Dr. Kurita gave a slow nod. "That's another way to go with it, sure."

If Warren gave him enough time to explain, Reddy thought he might be let off his leash to pursue this new mystery of sleep and murder. Two minutes at the end of the shift might not be enough. She'd be too eager to leave.

The analyst wished he could review his strategy with the NSA psychologist before his meeting with Warren. He suspected that Warren's distaste for him might actually work to his advantage. She'd be glad to not look at the back of his head for a couple of nights. Besides, the case was too weird to assign outside the agency.

An alert flashed on Reddy's screen and he clicked on it. One of his keyword alerts was the number 23. His pulse jumped as he found the enigma had asserted itself again. There was no death associated with this story but it was no less strange than the others. A group of people using a sleep journal app in Chicago had recorded their dreams. They reported experiencing the *same* nightmare. The group numbered twenty-three, eighteen women and five men.

Reddy was sure the force behind the number 23 had set its agenda. A secret math worked the gears that turned the world. He didn't understand the patterns that formed the equation but he saw the results to the right of the equals sign every day. His boss would be helpless. She'd have to let him answer the call now.

Section Chief Helen Warren: her title and name had twenty-three letters.

His full name was Thomas Remington Reddy III.

Destiny, he was sure, had a plan.

With this new occurrence related to sleep, he was sure to be unchained from his satellite maps, eavesdrop traffic and recon screens now. Maybe the number 23 was a clue that revealed Simulation Theory was real and reality was a lie. Either way, he would need to talk to the owner of the sleep app. Private corporations did almost as much surveillance as the NSA. He might be able to use that resource for this case.

Though Reddy's father had been dead for several years, the senator had gotten his son into the NSA. Reddy's aptitude had earned him the right to stay on. Saving the world from a container ship full of explosives was just the preamble to a much bigger game. He would have to call on the experts in New York for this one, too. In a secret fortress in Brooklyn called the Keep, there were defense contractors and specialists who were used to dealing with strange and paranormal events. Before dawn reached Utah, he'd have to consult with them, too.

Section Chief Warren didn't understand him or the world. Existence is a mystery and 23 was a clue. The ubiquitous appearance of the number pointed the way to something great or something terrible. Reddy suspected that reality was a simulation playing out game theory. A game did not care who won or who lost, only that the game was played to a conclusive result.

Rubbing his key fob nervously, Thomas Reddy entered the game. *A pack of cards...a pack of lies...a cloud of dust....*

CHAPTER 7

Fox Point, Wisconsin
April 12

Jen walked along the path of destruction. The lawn in front of her apartment building was torn up. Insurance investigators had come to survey the damage and fill out the paperwork for claims. She'd seen people gather in twos and threes, shaking their heads and pointing at their damaged hedges and fences as if no one else could see for themselves. Several people up and down the street were filling in lawns with dirt and sod and spreading grass seed. They looked perplexed and miserable in equal measure. She spoke to several people in neighboring houses and apartment buildings. Everyone had questions. Where was the nearest horse farm? Did someone do this on purpose? If so, how? Who could do it and why?

One man walking his dog told her that it was a plot to lower property values and drive people out. "You watch. This is some kind of stunt to make money. The idea is to make people feel unsafe. Some big corporation will come in here soon and start knocking down houses and building those godforsaken apartment buildings. Condos, too, maybe."

The man apparently didn't know she was a resident of one of the block's rundown apartment buildings. Perhaps he didn't care. Jen gave him a nod to appear agreeable and walked on.

The hoof marks were not difficult to follow. Even as she tracked their course, Jen could see the dream unfold again. She heard the whinny of the horses. She could see the riders all around her, clinging to their mounts. When she closed her eyes, Jen could still feel the coarse horse hair of her mare's mane. She could still sense the smell of the beast's sweat. The horse had not been hers to ride. She had been a passenger, helpless to stop the throng. She may as well have been trapped in the hold of a ship during a ruthless storm.

Though several days had passed since the nightmare stampede, the police had not solved the mystery. Even the hospital's rumor mill was spinning but no culprits had been found. She'd watched online for news and listened to the radio, expecting arrests to be announced quickly. Nothing came of the police investigations.

The tracks turned left along East Hyde Way. Jen followed. It would be dark soon but, just like everyone else, she wanted to know how the horses could have disappeared. The trail ended among some nice houses close to the beach. The hoof prints simply stopped. It was as if the animals had grown wings and taken flight. She stopped at the last track and stared at it, waiting for an answer to the mystery. If only she could formulate the correct question, she was sure the puzzle would reveal its secret. Asking the right question was like placing the correct key in a stubborn rusty lock. But what was the question?

Two young boys approached her carrying skateboards. The first was short, about thirteen. "They aren't around here." His eyes were alive with intelligence and he had an easy smile. "We followed the tracks and they ended here, even the next morning, before the rain came. Those horses must have been heavy, like Clydesdales or something."

The second boy bobbed his head. "Totally!" Then he looked away, embarrassed. He was tall and lanky but Jen guessed he was about the same age. The boy would grow to be a handsome man when he filled out. He appeared accustomed to playing sidekick to his extroverted friend.

"They weren't like Clydesdales," Jen said. "They were formidable and strong, but...I don't know. They seemed much faster than that."

"You saw them?"

Jen shifted back and forth, uneasy. She'd spoken to no one about her nightmare. The only proof she had of the encounter was the bruise on her hip where she had hit the floor hard. *When I was thrown from the horse*, she thought.

"Miss?"

"Hm?"

"You saw the stampede?"

"No. I...I heard it."

"Was anybody riding them, do you think?"

"I couldn't say."

"Weird," the lanky one said.

"Totally," she said. They both looked at her and she felt awkward again.

"They must have been picked up here," the shorter one enthused, "but the better question is, where did they come from? We followed the tracks right back to where they started."

"And?"

"They start from nowhere and they end nowhere. No truck tracks. They stampeded and trampled my mom's azaleas and took off into the sky right here."

"Like Pegasus," Jen said.

"Yeah! That's what I said!" the short one said.

The sidekick nodded and looked off toward the ocean. "Wherever they came from and wherever they went, the police got no clue."

"How do you know that?" Jen asked.

The boy did not answer, as if he had not heard.

The first boy leaned closer and whispered, "His dad's a cop."

"Jeremy!"

"Whatever, dude. Chill. This is the most interesting thing to hit this town since...forever."

"We got the Rover Point Mall," the second boy said. "And that house designed by that architect."

"Frank Lloyd Wright," the first boy said. "Big deal. It's not even that cool. This is like, I don't know...."

"A Scooby Gang mystery, " Jen suggested.

Both boys looked at her, surprised.

"That's still on TV, isn't it?"

The lanky one cleared his throat. "My dad says whoever made this happen must have used construction equipment to cover their tracks. It only seems the tracks start and end nowhere."

His friend rolled his eyes. "Like that sounds much more real than horses with wings. Construction equipment means money. Who owns horses and construction equipment? Use your head. And where are the tracks from the construction equipment?"

"Maybe just one of those smaller tractors with a big brush on the front? Like a street cleaner that kicks up all that dust?"

"Nah, nah. Those hoof prints are *deep*, man."

"But why would they do this?" the lanky one asked. "What's the point? A prank?"

"Nobody put it on YouTube so it's no prank."

"Maybe it was an experiment," Jen suggested. "Or a demon-stration."

The short one looked at her skeptically. "Demonstrating what?"

"That it can be done, I think. It's someone's demonstration of power."

"Who?"

"Someone powerful. Someone playing us."

The boys began to blur. Jen gasped and blinked hard, trying to clear her vision. Then the world went black as she began to faint. The ground shifted under her and she fell forward into the short boy. Jen's last thought before losing consciousness was that she was close to asking the right questions.

She was about to be punished for that.

CHAPTER 8

The Unus Mundus
 Out of Time

Jen awoke naked on the floor of a white room. At least, she presumed it must be a room. She had no sense of the dimensions of the space. She began to orient herself by squeezing her eyes tight and crouching to touch the floor. It was cool and smooth as ceramic tile. She detected no edges. All was white light.

She opened her eyes again. The light was bright but she could not fathom its source. Everything except her body was white. She took a deep breath. Her lungs worked. She could hear her pulse pounding in her ears, as real as heavy hoofbeats. "Am I dead? I don't feel dead."

Laughter echoed from all directions. It was a woman's laugh, high and pleasant.

Jen could not detect where the woman might be. "Olly, Olly oxen free! Come out, come out wherever you are!"

The laughter halted. Then the echo stopped cold. Jen thought she heard something behind her, like the click of high heels on marble. She whirled to find a woman with short curly red hair standing before her in a long gown. The woman wore a platinum tiara. Her white dress was so diaphanous Jen could see the woman's pink nipples through the garment. The material was nearly indistinguishable from their environs so, if not for her plunging neckline and bright red hair, the newcomer might have melded into the endless white surroundings.

"Do you know what God said to Adam and Eve after they ate the apple?" the woman asked. "'Who told you you were naked?'"

"Where am I?"

"East of Eden, sugar plum."

"What?"

"You're black."

"Since birth."

"I didn't expect that. A black physiotherapist."

"Maybe you're racist."

The woman laughed. "I hadn't thought of that, either. I don't think so, though. Be honest. How many of your classmates were black?"

Jen made a sour face. "Three. There are more every year."

The woman circled her slowly. "*Mmhm.* For your information, I have several black friends. My accountant's son is black. Adoption, I think...or a stepson. Something...."

"If your accountant was black, I'd be more impressed. Where am I?"

"Somewhere between here and there. I'm figuring things out myself. I just found out recently that the world is much more complicated than I was told."

"Where are my clothes?"

"Oh, to be young and healthy. Enjoy it while you can. Everything goes away. Everything will go away soon. I have it on good authority."

"So, I'm here with no clothes on because — "

"A companion of mine requested that. Maybe he has an eye for the ladies...or humiliation."

Jen did her best to cover her breasts and crotch, suddenly self-conscious.

"Not that you should be ashamed, dearie. You have a lovely figure.

I'm jealous. All those everyday cares fade away in the end...too far before you reach your end. Much of the life I had amuses me now. You know, the thing about this place, the thing I love most? I'm queen. I had an interesting life out there, but in here? Even better. No noise you don't want. No taxes. No phone calls. Here, nothing exists that I can do without."

Jen looked around. "Your paradise is empty."

"Except for you, sugar plum. That was my point. I like the emptiness. I feel safe here. I haven't felt safe in a long time. Do you feel safe?"

"No."

"Smart girl. I wanted to find someone who would understand. I noticed you because you woke up and looked for my horses. Everyone else turned over and went back to sleep. You rode the night mare. I thought that was quite clever, didn't you?"

The woman's eyes were a startling blue, like the edge of flames. Jen studied the woman carefully. "Do I know you?"

"I get that a lot."

"Answer my question. Am I dead? Is this supposed to be...I don't know...heaven?"

"Oh, no. I don't think so. If it were, I don't think I'd be here."

"Hell, then?"

The woman looked around and smiled. "I'm sure Hell would be more crowded. Before you ask about Limbo, as a recovering Catholic, I can tell you, I don't think that's right, either. How about I ask a question. If you tell me the truth, I'll tell you a little something?"

"Fine."

"What's the last thing you remember?"

"I was talking to a couple of boys where the trail ended. The horses — "

"Yes, yes. I know all about the horses."

"Okay, then answer me, what was the horse dream about?"

"An experiment, just like you said. You're a clever one, aren't you?"

"That's it?"

"A girl has to feel her oats. I haven't felt my oats for a long time. I expect to conduct many experiments. It's so much goddamn fun, I can't tell you."

"How did you do it? Where did the horses come from?"

"And where did they go? Heh. Like I said, it's all new to me. I'm still getting used to dreaming things into existence. It's exhilarating."

"Dreaming into — "

"Funny how we spend a third of our lives asleep. Still, we discount the importance of dreams so easily. That's a lot of dumb denial, isn't it? You might say we're unconscious all our lives. Even when we think we're awake, who can be sure?"

"I need to hear a lot more about that," Jen said.

"Did you like my horses? I dreamed them. Weren't they wonderful? It's like Disney World but for adults. Here, you can do anything you want. It all feels so real, doesn't it?"

"I was terrified. It felt too real to me."

"Good. Good! You're smart to feel that way. Dreams feel so real, you can act out all your revenge fantasies. It's so...cleansing."

"Got a lot of vengeance fantasies to work on?"

"Oh, this is just the first reel of the movie. Wait till you see the climactic scene. It's going to be big. The whole world will stop and watch. That's the key. Everyone has to see what's coming. It will give them time for remorse."

"Enough games! Where am I?"

"Told you. You aren't here and you aren't there. You're somewhere to the East and I'm all the way West. I'm told this is one of those places where we all meet, at the edge of the possible. It's...so lovely and peaceful."

"That sounds like a bunch of nonsense."

"Oh, yes. Riddles and nonsense. True. But, anything new and unfamiliar seems crazy, doesn't it? Tell me, Jen, have you ever read a contract?"

"What?"

"You heard me. Have you ever? Especially financial contracts. People sign their lives away but they don't really understand what they're signing. They're just doing what they're told, hoping for a

better tomorrow. I know. I've done it myself with terrible consequences. Someone understands those things, I suppose, but the whys
and wherefores and what-have-yous are not for most mortal minds?"

"What's your point?"

"Life is a contract. The cost to enter the commitment is free. All
you need is a man's orgasm and an egg. A fleeting investment. But no
one counts the heavy cost of the balloon payment. If we're lucky, we
get two or three decent decades. Then the uncounted costs start to
pile up with interest."

"Your point?"

"I think I've found a way out of the trap. Life is a trap. Anyone
who doesn't think so hasn't lived long enough."

Jen stared at the woman's blue eyes, entranced. "What's
your name?"

"Mine is just one of those familiar faces you see everywhere," the
woman replied. "Thank you for your time. I'm still experimenting.
Why don't you relax? You'll probably wake up soon. I was feeling a
little lonely and had to share the unearthly experience with
someone."

"Unearthly?"

"Oh, don't worry. All will become clear soon...at least, that's what
my companion tells me. Soon will be too late but that's no concern of
yours in particular. Until then, just tell yourself this was another bad
dream. Or that this was a silly work of imagination. No one will
believe the truth. They hardly ever do. You think anyone really
believed Alice when she came back from her trip through the looking
glass? Toodles!"

"Wait! How do I get out of here?"

"My friend will send you back from whence you came, sugar
plum. Thanks for the chat! You'll see me again in dreams and nightmares, I'm sure! Everyone will."

The woman turned to go but Jen grabbed her arm. "Why are you
doing this?"

She looked into Jen's eyes, her face softening. "Imagine owning a
car for a long time. It breaks down and you have to walk. Then you

have to crawl. Suddenly, you're given a Ferrari. Wouldn't you want to take it out for a test drive at the track and shove the accelerator through the floor?"

"I don't get it. Talk plain."

"When you've been powerless for a long time, dearie, it's good to feel powerful again. I'm back and Big Daddy gave me the keys to the Ferrari."

"What's your plan?"

"Oh, I just want tiny acts of vengeance. It's Big Daddy you have to worry about, I think. He doesn't tell me everything."

"Who's Big Daddy?"

"My companion. The monster under the bed. The eyes behind the walls. The thing that goes bump in the night. The Boogeyman. You'll all meet him soon enough. I have other fish to fry."

"What are you?"

"Hey, chick! I don't *own* this car. I'm just taking it for a spin!"

Jen held the woman's forearm tight. She gasped as her hand emptied. The woman's arm sifted out of her grip like sand in a high wind.

The woman's laughter echoed even after she vanished into whiteness without dimension. Then the white light began to fade. In a moment, Jen stood in alone in empty twilight.

The darkness began to swallow the remaining light. As blackness stole over her, she cried out, "Wait! Hello? Is anyone there?"

From close by, a deep rumbling voice replied, "I am here."

"Who — "

"I am the Darkness Visible."

Jen turned this way and that, searching for the source of the voice. To her left, she saw a strange silhouette in the dim light. What little light still shone illuminated a tall, broad shouldered figure. It was black except for a few gleaming edges on its armor. It could be a large man in a strange suit. It could be the black carapace of an impossibly large insect. It was the silhouette of horns on its head that transfixed her.

Her pulse pounded in her ears and her breath came fast. Jen thought she might be sick. "What's happening?"

"Which would you rather?" the thing asked. "To be alone in Limbo or to be alone in the dark with me?"

"Who are you?"

"I am an emissary. You didn't answer my question."

"I don't even know where I am. What could I possibly say that would satisfy you? You're obviously trying to scare the shit out of me. Mission accomplished."

"But you aren't defecating. That's a strange metaphor. I didn't use to understand human metaphors. Your cultures are interesting, though very idiosyncratic."

"Talk to me," Jen said. "It's getting dark and that won't be just a metaphor in a minute."

The thing laughed. "You, I like. Your kind will ask about your experience here. Don't tell them anything. They'll throw you in an insane asylum. It's happened before."

Something in the monster's right gauntlet burned bright orange and threw sparks. It was a symbol of some kind Jen did not recognize. It could have been cyrillic or a runic letter.

"What is that?"

"It is the symbol of my house. This symbol tells others of my kind that you are mine, to kill or to use. I am your master now."

"I don't have a master. Never will."

"Brave words spoken from a slave's lips are tiresome."

"I am not your slave. That was done to my ancestors. Never again. You don't know what you're asking."

"I do not ask. I tell. You speak of slavery of your ancestors. I speak of all humans, everywhere and soon." As the last of the light leaked away, the thing rushed at her.

Jen screamed as she reeled back. She fell and kept falling. For a moment, the thing coiled its thick arms around her neck. Somewhere in the dim recesses of her mind, Jen knew what the pain between her shoulder blades meant.

Her last word before losing consciousness again was, "Never."

CHAPTER 9

Orthopedic Hospital of Wisconsin
   Glendale, WI
   April 12

Jen awoke screaming. She lay in a bed in a familiar place. Breathing so fast she feared she would hyperventilate, she was soon surrounded by nurses she recognized. She was in her own workplace. She had spent little time in the emergency room and had never seen it from a patient's perspective. The white sheets were rough. After being in the White Space, the overhead fluorescents seemed dim by comparison. Jen trembled, cold and terrified.

A man she knew in passing, Dr. Ralph Davies, asked her if she knew where she was and the name of the president. As Jen's breathing began to slow she answered his questions correctly.

"And what's the date?"

"How am I supposed to know that? How long was I out?"

It was still April 12, 8:15 p.m.

"How are you feeling, Jen?" Marisa Gustafson, the triage nurse, asked. "Do you remember what happened?"

If she had been taken to a different hospital, Jen would not have been so honest. However, she felt she was among friends. She told the truth, starting with the night she rode a nightmare. She ended on her conversation with the boys on the road by the beach. She was not ready to share the story of the Woman in White. That, she was sure, would get her confined and committed to a psych evaluation. They might even use restraints to tie her to her bed.

"Night terrors," Dr. Davies announced. "That's my diagnosis."

Jen supposed he meant to sound confident. Instead he came across as self-important. "Night terrors? Isn't that just for little kids?"

"Usually between ages four and twelve, but a tiny percentage of adults get them, too."

"But what about the hoof prints and the property damage? That's real, unless my whole neighborhood is dreaming."

"I heard about that," Davies said. "Everyone has. Sounds like mass hysteria based on a clever hoax. For all the reports, no one seems to actually have seen a herd of horses pass through."

Jen tried to disguise her frustration. She was sure she failed in that endeavor.

"Jennifer?" Davies said softly. "When you went for your walk this evening and met those two boys, are you even sure you were awake? Is it possible you were somnambulant? Do you have a history of sleepwalking?"

Jen frowned. "Well, yeah, when I was a kid, I did sleepwalk a little. I dressed myself and got ready for school in the middle of the night a few times. But I was awake when I left my apartment and followed the tracks — "

"How can you be sure?"

Exasperated, Jen raised her voice for the first time. "How can you be sure you're awake right now? That's a ridiculous question."

"Okay. Here's what happened," Davies said. "A few nights ago, you heard something while you slept that you integrated into your dream state. You heard the horses gallop by. The confusion you feel is basically your left brain trying to make sense of an info dump from your right brain while you were asleep."

"I thought left brain, right brain stuff was debunked."

"Yes and no. The larger point is, have you been sleeping well since the incident?"

"Hardly at all. I'm...I'm afraid to. Especially now."

"Have you been under a lot of stress lately?"

She thought of the money she owed, the boyfriend she'd kicked out and the extra shifts she'd taken in the physio clinic without a break. "Yes. I've been under a lot of stress."

Whenever doctors don't know what's going on, she thought, *they blame the patient and call it stress.*

Davies began filling out the box on the chart on his iPad where, Jen knew, he'd made his conclusions and written his diagnosis. "We'll do some further investigations, if you like. Given that you lost consciousness, I'd suggest we set you up with a halter monitor to check heart function. A CAT scan wouldn't be out of order, either, but my preliminary clinical impression is you need more rest and we should get you down to the sleep clinic for an evaluation. I'm going to give you a prescription for Ambien. Don't worry about a thing, Jennifer. You're one of us. We'll take care of you."

Dr. Davies was about to open the curtain when he turned back to her with what she recognized as a practiced casualness. "Oh, and one more thing. Have you seen Dr. Paola Harvey? She's excellent. It would be a good idea to check in with her. Just to help with some strategies to deal with the stress."

"That's a good idea," the nurse enthused.

"Harvey? The shrink?" What she was waiting for had arrived. Davies and Gustafson were giving her the courtesy of a less formal psych evaluation, trying to make Jen think it was her idea.

The nurse patted Jen's arm. "Think about it. After my husband was diagnosed with MS, I had a few sessions with Dr. Harvey. I thought it would be all talk, talk, blah de blah and Valium. Instead, Paola got me going to the staff yoga class. Helps me. And she's really kind, Jen."

She considered telling them about the Woman in White but, looking at Dr. Davies, Jen couldn't trust anyone with the full story. She didn't mention the monster, either. It sounded like a crazy hallucination. She kept her mouth shut and lay back in her bed, shivering in her paper gown.

Jen's silence did not matter. Davies had recorded enough on his tablet that a threshold was breached. Thomas Reddy's algorithm to scrape relevant medical data on patients with unusual sleep disorders was tripped. Within seconds, Jennifer Daimler's name and address was at Big Data in Utah and on Thomas Reddy's phone.

She didn't mention the alien symbol branded into her back. Jen didn't even know it was there. Not yet.

CHAPTER 10

Hollywood, California
   Pinehurst Road
   April 13

The agent's name was Dennis Flanagan but everyone called him Desi. The man, late middle-aged and feeling every year lately, stood on his back patio. He stared at the fence that bordered his small yard. He swirled the ice in his glass of Elijah Craig. The fancy bourbon was two or three hundred dollars a bottle but money wasn't a problem for Desi. He could afford Elijah Craig. People were Desi's problem. Age, status, murder, curses and moving house preoccupied him this night (in no particular order.)

He owned fifteen percent of several successful stars and a string of B-listers. Most of his clients could get some work as character actors, do voice overs or get some national commercials. Stars rose and fell. Agents stayed. Hollywood agent was the perfect job for Desi. He scheduled three lunches a day, typically taking meetings at Bouchon. Desi spent his days on the phone handholding casting directors, actors and assorted wannabes. He couldn't imagine what else he might do if he didn't have his stable of artists and connections.

Sometimes he wished he still agented musicians, but that was a younger man's game. Hollywood best suited his talents now. Rounds of golf were more Desi's speed. Staying up all night macking on rejected groupies, endless travel and doing cocaine with strangers was too much to ask now. Only a couple lines of booger sugar would kill his night's sleep and ruin the next day's work.

Still, life in Hollywood was not as grand as he'd prefer. A man of his talents should be living larger. Everyone who was anyone seemed to be driving a Prius now, even guys like Leonardo Di Caprio. Bentleys were out of fashion. It was harder to tell who the real ballers were anymore. Desi preferred the eighties. That was a decade for driving a Bentley. Ostentation had become a social crime.

Desi's biggest problems were, in his estimation, twofold. As he poured his fourth glass of Elijah Craig in half an hour, he watched Butch, his Pembroke Welsh Corgi, pee on the azaleas. The dog's name was Butch but the animal thought his name was Little Shitter (due to his master calling him that so often).

First priority, Desi thought. *I have to do something about that fence. Cameras and an alarm aren't enough. What good will blurry pictures of burglars do after they've killed me for my baseball cards? The Ty Cobb alone wasn't quite mint, but it must be worth well over a million by now.* He worried the concrete barrier was neither high nor foreboding enough. His neighbors would not approve of a topping of razor wire. Maybe he could get his gardener to glue some broken glass along the top of the wall.

In 2001, a girl had been stabbed to death by a serial killer just down the street. Desi hadn't known about the killing when he bought his house. His divorce had been a fresh wound then. He'd been looking for a quick move. He'd only meant to live in this house for a year but business preoccupied him more than domestic concerns. He never felt like he had time to deal with moving.

The hell of it was, Desi had only recently found out about the grisly murder two doors down the street. Three days before he'd been blissfully ignorant. Then he met with a writer who thought he was the next Judd Apatow. Somehow, just to break the ice, they'd begun talking about Hollywood murder stories. Then the truth spilled out. The murder hadn't happened in his home but it was too close for Desi's comfort. The agent believed in lucky streaks, bad luck and curses.

Desi was known for wearing one color of tie: green. Green meant money and money was lucky. Desi had always been a superstitious man. While he was unaware of the nearby murder, it couldn't affect him. Now that he knew, he had to move.

The victim had been Ashton Kutcher's girlfriend. The actor found the poor girl when he came to pick her up for a post-Grammy party. She'd been stabbed thirty-seven times.

"Bad voodoo," Desi told Butch. "I have a bad feeling. Something bad is going to happen."

The dog looked toward his master a moment before going back to sniffing around the azaleas.

That was the second problem. First he would make his property more secure. Then he'd have to put the house up for sale, anyway. "We haven't stopped to smell the roses, Butch. Well...maybe *you* have. But what have you got to worry about? Little Shitter! Stop peeing on the azaleas!"

The dog ignored him and marked his territory.

Desi sighed and ruminated on the tasks ahead. He'd have to get someone to pack the house up and put his stuff in storage. To get a better price, he'd need painters to freshen up the place, maybe do some minor repairs he'd ignored for more than a decade. Surveying his house and lawn in the moonlight, he said aloud, "I deserve better than this. I don't even have a pool!"

A real estate agent had told him a pool was less attractive to buyers than it once was. Desi suspected that was a fly-over state delusion. Anyone who worked in show business needed a pool, if only for the look.

"Butch!" Desi called out. "The next house will have a big backyard for you to shit in and a big pool, too. Long past time we moved. I should be hosting big parties. We'll get a place with a view. Don't shit in the pool, though. You're going to have to commit to that and I'll hold you to it."

The dog looked back at him, his ears perked.

"What's a matter? You hear an intruder? A serial killer? A mountain lion coming to eat you up?" Desi loosened his tie and poured himself his last drink. "I like the look of Beachwood Canyon, you know? Think you can handle a hoitier and toitier mansion? I sure could."

The dog began to whine and cower. Desi paid little attention. Elijah Craig was for sipping and appreciation after sealing a deal, not guzzling and rambling to his pet. "I'm drunk. C'mere! Let's get some sleep!"

Agitated, the dog barked louder.

"*Sh!*"

Butch kept barking.

"C'mere!" Desi called. "You'll wake the neighbors!"

The Corgi went silent and slunk into the shadows beneath the plants along the bottom of the fence. Butch had disappeared from view but he kept growling.

Desi couldn't remember Butch growling like that. He let out a low whistle. "Dammit, what's gotten into you?" Then the man heard a sound he could not identify. As Butch snarled, Desi looked around, confused. What had that sound been? "Hello? Is anyone there?"

The sound came again but from a different direction, like a fluttering of wings.

"I've got a gun!" Desi called. He did, too, but it was in a desk drawer in the house, unloaded and unused for years.

The agent looked up. His jaw dropped. His eyes went wide. "Can't be real," he said. "I haven't drunk that much."

Sharp winged shadows blocked out the moonlight. Large birds, predators all, attacked from all directions. They moved as one, swarming him until he disappeared amid scratching claws and beating wings. They took Desi's eyes first. When he opened his mouth to scream, one of the birds dove down his throat and the next went for his tongue.

The wings were leathery, like those of bats. The birds' long beaks were cruel knives, razor sharp, hooked and serrated. No ornithologist on Earth could have identified these creatures. The birds ripped through his clothes and tore his flesh into long strips before burrowing for his organs. They ate voraciously and, in minutes, rose from what was left of the body as suddenly as they had appeared.

A woman's cackling laughter melted into the night air, finally tapering to silence.

Butch waited a few moments, sniffing the air. When the dog was sure the predators were gone, he cautiously emerged from his hiding place. The Corgi slunk toward his fallen master. Then Butch AKA Little Shitter bent to lap up Desi Flanagan's blood.

CHAPTER 11

Walter Reed National Military Center
Bethesda, Maryland
April 14

Dr. Mikola Kallaste had hardly slept for two nights and he didn't know why. Insomnia was commonplace all of a sudden. Even those who said they slept did so fitfully. Though sleepy, he strode into his outer office in a hurry. His two o'clock appointment was already waiting. Kallaste's assistant, Jill McCafferty, tapped her wrist before handing him a patient file. She wore no watch, but the gesture was meant to remind him to stay on time. He had a seminar to attend immediately after meeting with his patient.

"Communications are a little wonky," McCafferty said. "Good thing I wrote down your seminar time. I can't access your Google calendar on the laptop."

"Google's not working?"

"My cell doesn't work at all."

"Have tech support look at the laptop," Kallaste said,

"It's not the laptop, Mik. A lot of people are having tech problems. Nobody seems to know why. Anyway, you're late. Better get to it."

Kallaste shrugged and turned on a smile as he greeted his patient. "Lt. Francis Grundy! Hello, again."

A large man whose arms were covered in tattoos, nodded from his seat across from the doctor's desk. The patient sat in silence.

"Sorry I'm behind schedule. Pleased to meet you."

Grundy nodded and shook Kallaste's offered hand with two perfunctory pumps before pulling away. "What did the test say?"

Kallaste sat at his desk and scanned the patient's chart. He unfolded a long graph to decipher the lines and squiggles. "Good news and other news. The other news is you are not sleeping as deeply as you should. The good news is, we can treat it. According to your sleep study, you stop breathing quite a bit. At several points, you stopped breathing for forty-eight seconds. It's definitely sleep apnea, but we can help you with that."

"You sure that's accurate? I don't think I slept at all during the test."

Kallaste looked up from the paperwork and smiled in a way that he hoped was reassuring. "I know. Everyone feels that way when we do a sleep study. You're not in your own bed and it's unfamiliar and uncomfortable — "

"Uncomfortable? *Ha!* I was hooked up with so many damn wires, the only shut-eye I got was when I blinked."

"I understand. However, the numbers don't lie." The doctor sorted through the file to look at Grundy's questionnaire. "Even without the sleep study, I could tell you these results are not surprising. Are you still falling asleep at stoplights?"

"I only did that once or twice."

"Exhausted all the time?"

"I've been exhausted since Afghanistan." Grundy's mouth was a hard line.

Kallaste put down the file and stared into his patient's eyes. "Irritable?"

"Yup!"

"Pissed off your wife yet?"

For the first time Grundy gave a grudging smile. "You could say that. She can't sleep in the same room with me anymore. When I'm not choking in my sleep, she tells me I snore like a jet engine."

"Then let's fix you up with a CPAP. The machine will open up your airway while you sleep. Are you familiar — "

"I've seen them things. I don't know how I'm going to get any sleep with that thing on my face all night. I'll hang myself with the air hose, won't I?"

"It takes some getting used to but when the machine's white noise replaces the snoring, you won't disturb your wife's sleep anymore. You'll feel much better and put less strain on your heart."

"But how do people sleep with that hose and all?"

"We call the air hose your leash but it's six feet long. You'll be fine. No one has accidentally tied it into a noose yet."

Grundy's face softened. "Is there anything I can do besides wearing a mask and hooking myself up to a breathing machine?"

"No guarantees but losing weight often helps."

Grundy glanced down at his midsection and reddened. "Yeah. Guess that's what I should do, anyway. Got lazy since I lost my leg. Since I got out of rehab, I haven't been keeping up with my PT so much. Mostly, I watch the Sox and drink Pabst."

"But that's not your highest aspiration, is it?"

Grundy shook his head. "The Sox suck this year."

"It's still way early in the season."

"For me, everything sucks right now."

"Let's get your breathing and sleep back on track. Then maybe you'll lay off the Sox."

"I'm not sure what 'on track' would look like."

"You handled the stress of defusing IEDs, Lieutenant. You saved lives. Now it's time to save your own."

"I...uh...I hadn't thought of it that way."

Kallaste looked at the chart again. "The anti-depressants you're on don't mix well with Pabst Blue Ribbon. No beer helps with weight loss."

Grundy chuckled. "Okay. I got it. Message received, doc."

"You can handle this, Lieutenant. It's going to be all right. Things are going to get better. It'll be hard at first but you've had to do lots of things that were hard at first."

The big man nodded. "Yeah. I just feel so...ground down. Like I can't take much more."

"You thought it would be easy once you got home, right?"

"Easier, yeah. I did."

"And now that you're back home, you're thinking, is this all there is?"

"That's about right."

"Sir, every day I meet men and women just like you who feel the same way. I follow up with those same people and, after a short adjustment period, they all get more energy. They feel better. You will feel better. There's more room for what they want to do with their lives. The worst is over now. You know that right?"

"No one in Virginia is trying to blow me up, so there's that."

"Then don't you do it. Once you get your energy back, set a goal to lose about forty pounds. That's your next mission. My assistant, Jill, will get you a referral to a nutritionist."

"Forty pounds? That's not going to be easy."

"You're a man who gets things done. Don't expect it to be easy. Accepting that it will be hard and doing it anyway is what makes you who you are."

"I think I've forgotten that guy. I'm not sure I can be that guy, anymore."

"Sure you can. You didn't run away from live bombs. You can deal with a diet. Our nutritionist will get you cooking up a lot of vegetable soups and making salads. No calorie counting, no portions. Lots of food. Sound good? You made it through boot camp, went to Afghanistan, got your leg blown off and survived. You telling me you can't handle this?"

Grundy laughed and his shoulders dropped a little as he relaxed in his chair. "You're a confident guy, Dr. Kallaste."

"I only treat the best so I get the best results. Guys like you rise to challenges. That's what makes my job easy." Kallaste came around the desk to shake his patient's hand. "Jill will set you up for an appointment for another sleep study with a CPAP so we get the air pressure right. Sound good?"

Grundy leaned on his cane as he rose and accepted the doctor's hand. "Thanks for your time, doc. You're right. I've been acting like my war is over. It never really is, is it?"

"Expect great things, Lt. Grundy."

As Grundy limped out of his office, McCafferty appeared in the doorway. "Two gentlemen to see you, Doctor."

"I have to be at that seminar by three."

A tall gangly man in a dark suit stepped in front of Jill and flashed his credentials. "Agent Thomas Reddy." The ID told Dr. Kallaste he represented the National Security Agency.

Behind the agent stood a round man in a blue hoodie. His long blonde hair hid half his face. "This is Mr. Cahill," Reddy said.

Cahill shaved his wispy beard in a way that reminded Kallaste of Robert Downey Jr when he played Tony Stark in the *Iron Man* movies. He looked like no law enforcement official the doctor had ever imagined.

"I'm afraid you're going to miss your seminar, Dr. Kallaste," Reddy said. Cahill bounded in and the agent closed the office door.

"What's this about?" Kallaste asked. "I don't even have any outstanding parking tickets so...are you going to tell me my country needs me? Something like that?"

Cahill and Reddy glanced at each other. Reddy did not crack a smile. Cahill looked miserable and maybe a little frightened.

"Oh. This is serious and you guys are sure you're in the right office?" Kallaste retreated behind his desk. He gestured to the two empty office chairs but neither man accepted his invitation. "What's up, guys?"

"We need your expertise, doctor," Reddy said. "There's a sort of virus — "

"I'm a sleep medicine specialist."

"We don't have someone like you at the Center for Disease Control to call on."

"I'm not surprised. The CDC is underfunded and — "

"I'm told you're the guy to get," Reddy said.

"Flattering, but — "

"We need you now. There's a helicopter on the roof. We'll brief you on the way."

"What the hell is going on?"

Cahill put both hands on Kallaste's desk and leaned close to whisper. "It's *invasion*, man."

"An invasion? By whom?"

Reddy cleared his throat. "We worried about the Chinese hacking all our software and the North Koreans detonating an EMP. We thought ISIS would get hold of a dirty bomb or the Russians would lose track of a nuke that would wind up in San Francisco or New York. At Homeland Security, we're always trying to anticipate the next development in terror tactics. However, humans frequently worry about the wrong things. As a species, we're incompetent at risk assessment."

"I worry disco will make a serious comeback," Cahill said. "Just goes to show."

Kallaste glanced at Cahill. "He's interesting."

Cahill tilted his head toward Reddy. "He's weird. Talks like Joe Friday. You won't get used to him. Come with us and I'll tell it to you straight. For the first while, you won't believe a word. Then the story will seem more and more plausible. After that..." Cahill shrugged.

"After that, what?"

"When I tell you about the invasion, you'll be scared to sleep," Cahill said. "Then you'll shit your pants."

"Please excuse Mr. Cahill. He is given to raucous hyperbole," Reddy said, "though, if my assumptions and predictions are correct, a certain amount of anal leakage would not necessarily be entirely inappropriate."

Cahill laughed. Reddy didn't crack a smile.

CHAPTER 12

Tourtour, France
April 14

Francois Dufour was born in Lyon on August 18, 1939. On September 3, France and her allies declared war on Germany. His mother and father fled to New York before the month was out. Despite his name, Francois spoke with a Brooklyn accent and had forgotten all the French his mother taught him. By design or happenstance, Francois had slipped past every war safely. Until now.

At noon, he walked to the center of the village of Tourtour and sat at a little outdoor cafe. He sipped strong coffee and read from tour books. He ate little but tipped generously for the privilege of keeping his table. Francois had brought Aldous Huxley, George Orwell and Albert Camus with him. He'd planned to read the books he'd loved as a young man. His dour mood killed that nostalgic notion. Mostly, Francois watched the day wane and the locals pass by.

If this is the end, he wondered, *is that all there is? Shouldn't there have been more?*

He'd once been a very handsome man. Some elderly women of his acquaintance looked to his full head of silver hair and strong jaw and told him he looked regal. They said his white hair gave him a distinguished air.

Screw that. I want to be sexy.

Age had a way of making a person invisible. He still appreciated the pretty girls who walked by. Francois had no delusions that the young women might return his admiration. Ageism annoyed him, though he supposed he'd been guilty of it, too, long ago. A man his age had to be circumspect around the opposite sex if the woman was far younger. He had no interest in being thought a dirty old man, or worse, cute in that way that suggested he was harmless. His body had grown old, true. Francois felt sure that his mind was remarkably unchanged since he was twenty-two. Old people were supposed to be wise but, in his experience, most people didn't change much. A fool didn't get smart just because he was older.

And this old fool still loves a tall woman with long shapely legs. Oh, to have a woman's legs wrapped around me again.

As the day's light began to fade, Francois became the cafe's last patron of the day. The beginning of the busy tourist season was at least a month away. The villagers seemed a little weary of his ilk. When he glanced her way, the establishment's sole waitress made a show of looking at her watch. Still, Francois lingered. He sipped his cold *cafe au lait*. In San Diego or New Orleans, he could order this drink and a waitress would bring him a cup as large as a soup bowl. In Tourtour, the *cafe au lait* came in tiny cups meant for unhurried, dainty hands. The French sipped. They never guzzled.

This thought amused Francois. If his family hadn't fled France, assuming he survived the bombings and the Occupation, he might still have ended up in this same chair. Everything might be the same except he wouldn't even notice the size of the cups.

Also, a crazy woman would not be threatening to murder me in my sleep.

The air was too cold for an old man without a light jacket or sweater. Francois preferred discomfort. The weather and the espresso kept him awake. He dreaded the return to the little boarding house up the lane. Dufour knew the waitress wanted to go home. He wanted to go home, too, but his lovely house overlooking Solana Beach was not safe. He had fled to France to get lost. He could never go home again.

He'd come to the village two days before. The brochure reported that Tourtour was "the village in the sky of Provence." That sounded peaceful, like a little bit of heaven. It was hard to imagine anything bad happening in Tourtour.

Francois arrived with two bags stuffed with hastily packed belongings. The bed and breakfast up the hill turned out to be a boarding house with a broken water heater. The mattress was so uncomfortable it might have been stuffed with straw, but Francois didn't mind. He was glad to be an insomniac now.

The old man finally stood and nodded to the waitress. He removed all the money from his wallet, put it on the table and placed the empty cup atop it so the rising wind could not whisk it away. Francois slung his bag of books over his sloping shoulders and walked up the lane toward his lodging. Two young women no older than twenty passed him on the way. The wind pulled at their short skirts and pressed their clothes tight to their bodies. They were lovely, red-cheeked and curly haired. They did not even glance his way.

He wanted to turn and yell after them, "I directed major films! I've taken starlets to bed! I'm a man! I'm *still* a man!"

He turned in time to see the girls disappear around a corner. He did not call after them. Instead, he whispered to himself, "I am already a ghost." The wind swallowed his words. No one heard him.

If what the Woman in White says is true, I'm a ghost two times over.

CHAPTER 13

Tourtour, France
   April 14

Tired from his walk uphill, Francois sat by the wood stove in the front room of the boarding house. Most of the rooms were empty. No one disturbed him as he stared into the flames. The fire warmed his feet. He began to relax a little. All that espresso would surely keep him up through the night. He was of that age when a man had to get up at night to urinate frequently. That suited him fine. Francois was sure he'd do no more than slip into a light doze. He doubted he'd sleep enough to dream. In the morning, he'd be up and out the door again. The Woman in White would not find him in Tourtour.

A knit shawl made of creamy yarn was draped across the back of the couch. He pulled it over his shoulders and crossed his arms. His new residence was a bit dreary but it was quiet. He hadn't realized until he came to the little French village how cacophonous his retirement had been. Loud people, relentless news reports, constant traffic and sirens. Back home in San Diego, people were overstimulated. Tourtour was nearly as silent as a tomb.

"Shall I put another log on the fire, *monsieur*?"

His elderly hostess, Madame Giroux, stood in the doorway.

"No, I'll be going upstairs in a moment. I'm sorry. This must be yours." He began to take the shawl from his shoulders but she gestured for him to stop. He nodded his thanks. "Just a minute more. No need to burn another log for me. Just resting. My mother used to say, 'Up the wooden hill,' when it was time for bed. The journey up the stairs feels like a long, intimidating journey at the moment."

The fire crackled and a cinder sparked a memory. He'd once heard that sound every day. It was a warm feeling. He let his shoulders drop as he pictured his mother and father in front of a kitchen stove. They teetered forward and back in twin rockers. Mother would sew or knit and listen to his father read the news from the newspaper. Perhaps he didn't need Huxley or Orwell or Camus to revisit earlier and better days. Any wood stove felt like home.

"How long do you intend to stay, *monsieur*?" Madame Giroux asked.

He looked up, startled. He hadn't realized the old woman was still standing in the doorway. In that unguarded moment, he admitted, "I expect to die here."

The woman touched her hair, fidgeting as she regarded the American with the French name. Her English was flawless, but somehow, she was sure, the old gentleman must have misunderstood her question. "Most tourists only visit Tourtour for a day and a night. The mill, the church, the fossil museum — "

"I'm an old fossil," Francois said. "I think I belong here, don't you? I was born in Lyon — "

"It is early in the season but I'm sure you would enjoy a wine tour. We have lovely views, but you must see Var, *monsieur*." She cleared her throat. "Before you die."

"Thank you, Mrs. Giroux, but I think I'll hide in Tourtour a little longer."

"Hide, *monsieur*?" The old woman laughed. "Are you on the run from the law?"

Francois gave an unconvincing laugh in return. "Not from the law...from justice."

Francois gathered himself for the steep climb up to his room. His knees ached all the time now. He'd forgotten to pack the cream he used for the pain in his aching joints. He struggled to his feet and let the shawl slip back to the couch.

"Are you alright, *M'sieur* Dufour?"

"Do you know, in entertainment circles, it is commonly accepted that the most boring thing in the world is for someone to tell you his dreams? Is that just an American thing or have you heard that here? French cinema does tend to demand more of its audience. Pardon me for saying so but I never understood the allure of French art films beyond showing more sex."

The woman looked confused. "Dreams?"

"Being boring, I mean, yes. As a storytelling device."

"A dream would make for a bad movie. Dreams have no consequence in the real world. They are..." She fluttered her hands in the air in a gesture Francois took to mean intangible and frivolous.

"Ah, but what if they did matter in real life? Dreams and nightmares are a mysterious level of consciousness. I've received many good ideas from dreams. It's the brain leaving clues, staying busy, telling you who you are. Lately I've discovered dreams can be so much more. Dangerous even."

"I'm sorry. I don't understand," Madame Giroux said.

"My parents feared cancer," he said. "Pancreatic cancer killed my father. He felt fine and then one morning he complained of a sore stomach. His skin turned yellow. We took him to the doctor. Within two weeks, he was dead. My mother died of melanoma but it took her so long to go, she wished for pancreatic cancer."

"Terrible," Madame Giroux said. "Simply terrible. I am sorry for them."

"Thanks, but my point is, my parents both got what they feared most. Maybe they could have died of something else if they hadn't worried so much. I think if we focus on something, it expands to fill our minds. We may even manifest it in our bodies if we think about it enough."

"You may be correct," she said. "There are several religious sects who never speak of illness for fear of taking it into their bodies. They believe illness begins as a mental infection."

"If I had known that," Francois said, "I would have been much more careful what I thought about. I used to make horror movies."

Madame Giroux smiled. "How nice."

Francois looked into the old woman's eyes. She was agreeable but she was humoring him. "What I mean to say is, what we fear defines us, Madame."

"And what makes you afraid, *monsieur*?"

"When my parents died, it was like watching someone rot from the inside out. A terrible thing to witness. Since both my parents died that way, I worried for years that I was cursed to die like that."

"You won't die that way," Madame Giroux said.

"Thank you," he said, genuinely touched by her compassion.

The old woman's blue eyes slowly clouded to white.

"Madame Giroux? Uh...are you feeling well?"

Her skin yellowed. Her cheeks became drawn. She opened her mouth to speak but her jaw flopped open as if it had somehow become unhinged. Her small teeth turned black before his eyes. The woman looked blind but she appeared to stare at him. She did not make a sound. The veins beneath her skin darkened in rivers of dark twists and tributaries. Her yellowed skin thinned. The black blood in her veins wriggled like worms just beneath the surface.

Francois DuFour screamed for help. Then, horrified, he screamed long vowel sounds.

Madame Giroux's abdomen swelled and the buttons of her white blouse burst. The alabaster skin of her belly darkened to blue. The skin became shiny as it tightened against the pressure building from within.

Francois stepped back, still screaming. To his relief, someone was coming. He heard fists pounding on the front door of the house. "Come in! Come quick! Something — "

Madame Giroux's belly split and her intestines fell out as her knees buckled and she dropped to the floor. Her eyes had split, too.

The fluid from her corneas drained away but the empty eye sockets still seemed to stare up at him.

Francois staggered back against the wood stove and burned the palms of his hands on its hot edge. He bent forward to vomit. He had little to give. Throwing up ended in long strings of spit from his chin to the floor.

He heard the front door burst in but he was sure help had arrived too late. His vomit was bloody. Whatever virus was killing Madame Giroux, he'd got it, too. His guts roiled. It was as if he had swallowed eels equipped with spikes for dorsal fins. Francois stared down at his belly as the pressure built.

When he looked up, villagers streamed into the living room and crowded around the door. Each of them looked like a rotting corpse. He saw the young women who had passed him earlier. Their heavily lipsticked mouths were caked in bile and their long curls peeled back from their scalps as they shambled toward him. They looked angry. They moaned as they reached for him slowly.

Francois pissed himself. Despite his aching knees and sore belly, he wanted to run, to throw himself out of the front window. That route was blocked, too. Villagers congregated at the windows, slapping weakly at the glass and woodwork with open palms, leaving bloody smears.

Francois recognized his waitress from the cafe among the throng. Her shoulders were uneven and her neck was at a crooked angle. She drooled blood. As his belly split, the stench of rot reached his nostrils. He tried to hold his intestines in but his organs slid out, greasy with slimy shit and cloying blood.

A tall man stumbled toward Francois. His movements were uncoordinated. One of his eyes hung down his cheek, swinging from the optic nerve like a fleshy clock's pendulum.The man opened his mouth and maggots swirled across his tongue. His speech was thick and slow but he spoke in English.

The last words Francois Dufour heard were accusatory. "*Idiot! You...fell...asleep!*"

CHAPTER 14

En route to Reagan National Airport
   Washington, DC
   April 14

Mik Kallaste's thighs and buttocks clenched involuntarily as the helicopter lifted off. He preferred aircraft with wings. At least in an airplane there was a chance of gliding to safety if the engine quit. During the short helicopter flight from Bethesda to Reagan National Airport, Agent Reddy busied himself with his phone.

The clatter of the helicopter rotors made conversation difficult. Reddy forbade Kallaste from asking any questions on his headphone mic. The NSA agent pointed to the pilot and shook his head. "Not cleared."

"But I don't know anything yet!" Kallaste said. "Am *I* cleared?"

Reddy ignored him and returned to his phone. Then the agent's head jerked up and he turned to Dr. Kallaste with an urgent look. "Do you have a dog or cat at home that needs to be fed?"

Kallaste shook his head. Assured he had no starving pets at home, Reddy looked relieved and retreated back to his work.

"I thought the NSA knew everything about everyone."

"We do. I just want to be sure your information is up to date."

Kallaste searched Reddy's face for a hint of humor. If the agent was mocking him, his delivery was remarkably deadpan. Kallaste assumed Reddy was working. The agent never tilted his screen. The doctor couldn't get a glimpse of what absorbed him so.

If I catch him playing Candy Crush, I'm going to chuck him out the door, Kallaste thought.

Cahill leaned close to Kallaste's ear and yelled over the din of the rotors. "Just wait. Secrecy is standard. It's all about operational security."

"What does that mean?"

"If you don't need to know, you never know."

"How can I help with anything if I'm kept in the dark?"

Cahill shrugged and stared out the window. With nothing to do, the doctor stared out the window, too.

As the landscape slid beneath them, everything seemed smaller. It also seemed fragile. It had taken very little to disrupt the doctor's organized life. Reddy simply showed up with credentials that allowed him to do anything. All the agent had to say were the magic words: *national security*. Kallaste was bound to do as he was told.

When the helicopter arrived at Reagan National, Kallaste bided his time until he was alone with Reddy and Cahill. In the end, it was Cahill who did the talking. He revealed what little they knew about the incident in Dubai as Reddy had told it to him. When Cahill was done, Kallaste went over it in his head for a moment before saying a word.

"How many dead again?"

"Twenty-three crushed victims," Reddy said. "There was a another but that death is not relevant."

"Crushed!" Cahill said. "We're not in Kansas anymore, Toto!"

"There's a little more," the agent said. "Many of the twenty-three were in bed beside a spouse or a lover. None of the people on the other side of the bed knew what had happened to their bedmate. They woke up and found their partners dead on the floor."

"Incredible," Kallaste said.

"And nobody has any ties to terrorist organizations, no motives, no...anything, really," Cahill said. "The government is bringing us in as a Hail Mary."

"Uh...what do you do?" the doctor asked Cahill.

"I'm an app developer, a civilian, and I eat a lot of cornbread. I *love* cornbread. It's cake but you don't feel bad if you eat it for breakfast."

"Tell him about your relevant role, Mr. Cahill," Reddy said.

"I've been working on sleep apps, tracking and enhancement. Everybody wants and needs more sleep. I'm working on Apple and Android apps to compete with Sleep Cycle right now — "

"We believe night terrors are linked to the violence perpetrated on the victims in Dubai," Reddy said. "We just don't understand the connection yet."

Kallaste looked at both men, dumbfounded. "This is ridiculous. People dream every night. It's just the brain keeping active."

"More active than when we are awake, in many cases," Cahill said.

Kallaste waved him away. "We mine our dreams out of shared experience. If I dream I forgot the combination to my high school locker while I'm late for a math test and I'm also naked, so what? There's going to be a surprising number of people who have a similar dream and have probably experienced it several times."

"There's nothing easily dismissed with what happened in Dubai," Reddy said sharply. "Statistically, more than seven hundred people die falling out of bed each year. None of them will be crushed to a gelatinous pulp. That happened in one night in one hotel. Twenty-three dead."

"Why link it to dreams, though?"

"The link was tentative at first. Then I did some research — "

"And since then there's much more to go on," Cahill said, "thanks to me."

Reddy gave a curt nod. "Mr. Cahill developed a sleep journal app. Two days ago, a cluster of users in Chicago recorded having the same dreams. Last night, clusters of users in Rhode Island, San Diego, Delaware, Atlanta, New Orleans, Montreal and Belgium all reported experiencing the same dream. The effect seems to be spreading."

"It's still in beta," Cahill said. "Most of my subscribers are in the Midwest." He tried to sound casual and failed. Cahill was obviously very proud of his software programs.

"A bunch of people had a similar dream. So what?"

"The people in Chicago all dreamed of losing their teeth," Cahill said.

"You can find that in any dream dictionary, I'm sure," Kallaste replied. "I'm guessing it means their in-laws are coming for a visit or they're under stress and it's a mortality dream. More likely, like all dreams, it's just the brain cleaning house. At worst it means they eat too much sugar and need to use a toothbrush. The brain wants to be active all the time. That, poor diet and not enough exercise are at the root of most sleep issues. A dream can't crush bodies."

"You don't get it, man!" Cahill insisted. He looked agitated and red in the face. Kallaste took a step back from him.

"Doctor? May I call you Mikola?" Reddy asked.

"Call me Mik."

"Mik. The Chicago cluster lost them all. Every tooth fell out in the night. They're calling it the Tooth Fairy Virus."

"Impossible."

"The impossible is what we're tasked to deal with," Reddy said.

"Ooh!" Cahill exclaimed. "*Impossible Missions Force!* You're good-looking, Doc. You be Tom Cruise. I'll play fat Simon Pegg! I love *Mission Impossible* movies!"

Ready gave Cahill a sharp look and put a finger to his lips. "Restraint, please, Mr. Cahill. We've discussed this."

Kallaste looked back and forth to each man, searching for a hint this was an elaborate prank. "Were they...old or something? A lot of people grind their teeth and...." Kallaste's voice trailed off when he realized he was grasping at straws in the face of the incomprehensible. "What about last night? Belgium and Montreal and...all those places?"

"The other reports on my app? Worse than needing a full set of dentures, Mik. Much worse."

CHAPTER 15

Reagan National Airport
 Washington, DC
 April 14

Reddy and Cahill watched Kallaste pace the private airport lounge.

Cahill leaned against a wall. "Give it a minute, Mik. It is a lot to get your head around all at once. In a few minutes, teeth falling out will sound good and merciful."

"Tell me the rest, then."

"The other users reported seeing a massive firecane in their dreams," Cahill said. "Most woke up screaming and couldn't sleep the rest of the night."

"What the hell is a firecane?"

"I had to look it up," Cahill said. "You ever hear of a fire devil or firenado, Doc?"

Reddy cleared his throat. "Mr. Cahill is speaking of what's more commonly known as a fire whirl or fire tornado."

"Tornado plus fire. Soon to be a major motion picture, I get it," Kallaste said.

"A firecane, until recently, was a theoretical phenomenon," Reddy said. "Meteorologists posited that a hurricane's lightning crossing an oil spill could ignite a fire storm and cause mass destruction."

"It was just an idea," Cahill said. "No one had ever seen it."

"Was? C'mon, guys. What's going on?"

"The phenomenon has been reported in Micronesia," Reddy said. "Most of Guam and the Marshall Islands were spared."

"Heh. *Phenomenon*, he says! It happened! In real life!" Cahill said, a little too loudly. "It was never seen before and now it's here! All predicted by my users! Who knows how many other people dreamed of firecanes last night? They'll all have to buy my app to find out... after I release the premium version, of course."

"Maybe Mr. Cahill's users predicted these disasters," Reddy said. "Perhaps they *caused* the phenomena."

Cahill frowned but said nothing.

Dr. Kallaste took a seat and drew long slow breaths. "This is lunacy. *Science* — "

"Can change in the light of new facts," Reddy said. "If science does not change as the world changes, it becomes religion. I understand your inclination to lapse into denial. Denial is a powerful force."

Cahill patted his belly. "Denial is what keeps me thinking I'm a little chubby instead of obese."

"It is my hope, Mik, that you will transition through this phase to understanding quickly."

"You guys...is there a camera somewhere? Is this a joke? How come I haven't heard about these firestorms?"

"You will soon," Reddy said. "International aid is already being mobilized, mostly through our base in the Marshall Islands. Estimates are that over 100,000 have already died. Thousands more will perish from their burns. This is as serious as a nuclear strike. We want to get the relief airlifts well under way before it becomes general knowledge."

Kallaste's eyes narrowed. "You can't keep it that quiet, can you? With cell phone cameras uploading to YouTube — "

"My phone is coded to work through the Dark Net. For now, all the public knows is that these remote areas have been hit by devastating hurricanes. We aren't allowing media in or out and we're jamming commercial communications internationally."

"How?"

"It's a remote area made up of more than 2,000 islands. We're blaming sun spots and destruction on the ground for the lack of communications. The world doesn't know about firecanes yet and not one in ten Americans could point to Micronesia on a map."

"You can't sit on news this big, surely," Kallaste said. "Why would you?"

"Panic hurts economies, throttles stock markets, leads to suicide cults and hoarding."

"The Russians and NASA kept the alien signal from us for a year." Cahill blurted.

"That's a separate issue."

"You sure? Alien signals from deep space — "

"*Possible* alien signal singular," Reddy said.

"The possibility of an alien signal from space doesn't seem to have had much impact beyond Facebook," Cahill grumbled. "The powers that be still kept it from us as long as they could."

"And in the end, there was no panic," Reddy said. "Our strategy worked. Now people generally assume that story is another piece of fake news. Please, Mr. Cahill, let's stick to the crisis at hand. I believe we are under attack but I do not suspect it's an alien invasion from Alpha Centauri."

"You can just throw a blanket over worldwide communications?"

"We're the NSA," Reddy replied, as if that explanation was sufficient.

"But how?"

"Since the firecanes hit, we have invoked national security to shut up MSNBC, CNN, Fox and the like. I'm sure they're preparing scary graphics and they'll all believe in climate change now. However, they won't release any story about this until we allow it."

"All those networks are owned by defense contractors," Cahill said. "If they want those juicy military contracts to keep coming, they play ball, right?"

Kallaste shook his head. "But the internet — "

"Again, we are the NSA. We don't just dip into the information stream and monitor it. We regulate it."

Cahill's face reddened. "*Regulate* it? Ever hear of a little thing called freedom of speech?"

"I often wonder how the populace can be so naive," Reddy said. "They see our effects but think nothing of the cause."

"Yeah, tell us about it, but be as condescending as possible," Cahill said. "That will get me on your side."

"Very well," Reddy said. "Everyone knows that Adolph Hitler's attack on Russia was an insane military move that lost him World War II. If he hadn't opened a conflict on two fronts, Germany would have won the war. People never think to look to the causes of things."

"You mean that Hitler was crazy?" Cahill suggested.

"Superficial analysis, sir. Hitler's mother Klara died of breast cancer at the age of forty-seven. Hitler was only eighteen when his mother died. He was terrified of cancer. Hitler invaded Russia when it was tactically inopportune because he feared he would die of cancer before his legacy was complete. Even the mentally ill have reasons for the evil things they do. Everything has a reason and a cause. Things do not simply happen. There is a chain of events to follow back to the origin — "

"Agencies like yours are filled with bureaucrats who think they know what's good for us." Cahill's face was red with anger.

"We've kept the wolves from the door fairly successfully."

"Except for 9/11."

"I wasn't working at the NSA then, Mr. Cahill. In any case, conspiracies abound and a few of them are real. Society works better when we have cozy lies to comfort us."

"You think we can't handle the truth! You treat us like children."

"Statistically, that's true. Climate change has become a political football, for instance, but the one agency that takes the ramifications of climate change most seriously is the Pentagon. Meanwhile, the voice of the people is a muddled mob shuffling toward self-destruction. It's up to the bureaucrats to keep order. That's the way the world really is. In many ways, the world is asleep and we'll only maintain peace by keeping you that way."

"Enough politics!" Kallaste said. "Between dying in their sleep and setting countries on fire, people are going to wake up to how the world works. They'll realize how vulnerable they are. They'll be afraid to go back to sleep."

"It's my job to prevent that from happening," Reddy said. "We've got to get everybody back to sleep — to use your analogy, Doctor. If we fail, our national security will be compromised. What if the President falls out of bed and turns to mush tomorrow morning? We have to solve this mystery and do so as quietly as possible."

Cahill's mouth twisted into a sneer. "Ha! Bud nipped and best forgotten, huh? Can't happen. Once news gets out — "

"We're going to solve this problem and it will all go away."

His words carry resolve, Kallaste thought, *but he speaks with no more passion than a text-to-speech program.*

"There's no way!" Cahill said. "I don't care how huge Big Data gets. News of this will get out."

"And it will evaporate and be dismissed just as quickly. Few in North America remember the big tsunami that hit the Philippines a few years ago. All horror fades. It's how we get up and go to work each morning."

"You're a cocky bureaucrat," Cahill said.

"Cocky?" For a moment, Reddy looked away from Cahill. "No one has ever called me that."

Kallaste caught a look in the agent's eye that made him wonder if Reddy's mask had slipped. The doctor thought the man might cry.

The moment passed and Reddy straightened. "The so-called magic bullet theory has been explained many times. The CIA and the mafia were both large organizations motivated to kill President Kennedy. Still, most people believe Oswald acted alone because it's the official story. And consider his brother's assassination. There were more bullets fired at Robert Kennedy than could be held in

Sirhan Sirhan's gun. Still, people believe comforting lies of lone assassins."

"That was all before the internet!" Cahill said. "How are you suppressing information now?"

"Please sit and lower your voice, Mr. Cahill. Your tantrums are as unhelpful as Dr. Kallaste's denial." Reddy looked around the empty lounge, apparently to confirm they were alone. He appeared to have regained his composure.

"Answer my question," Cahill demanded.

"Along with a few other tricks, we can suppress information using the SEME."

"For the MD in the room, what the hell is that?" Kallaste asked.

"He's talking about the Search Engine Manipulation Effect," Cahill said.

"That's a thing?" the doctor asked.

Reddy nodded. "It is. And since it's not particularly germane, that's really all I can say. Should either of you decide to share anything I've discussed with you, you will be held without trial indefinitely. You know how we deal with whistleblowers."

"You take away the whistle and bury the blower," Cahill said.

"And that's only the whistleblowers you know about," Reddy said.

Kallaste and Cahill looked to each other. The doctor mouthed the word, *Gitmo*. Cahill took a seat and stared at the carpet.

Reddy looked at his phone for a moment. "So help me, gentlemen. Micronesia. Why do you suppose the firecanes struck there? What's the strategic value of those targets to a terrorist organization?"

"You said these weird weather phenomena were as serious as a nuclear strike," Kallaste said. "Our first experiments with nuclear weapons took place in remote areas: the Nevada desert, underground, the Bikini Islands. If your crazy hypothesis about what's happening is correct, Micronesia is a test."

"Or a demonstration." Cahill paled. "More to come."

"Interesting," Reddy said. "To see the truth, all we have to do is come to the data innocent, free of preconceptions."

"Preconceptions?" Kallaste grimaced. "You mean like how we understand how the world works?"

"A minute ago, you didn't believe the NSA could control the mainstream media. You'll be more useful to me if you work with the facts as presented instead of fighting me. Cognitive dissonance is not helpful."

"Yes, sir," Kallaste said.

"We'll both be well-behaved soldiers," Cahill said.

"I know you'll try, Mr. Cahill, though that's setting a high bar for you. Please do not shout at me again. You disturb my mental equilibrium when you shout."

"Disturb your...do I turn you on? Are you coming on to me, Mr. Reddy? I'm flattered!" Cahill winked at the doctor. "Yeah, he likes me."

Reddy gave a long-suffering sigh. The agent turned his attention to his phone, his knees bouncing up and down nervously. As he worked, the NSA agent muttered, "A beam of rays...a bench of judges...a cluster of nuts...a clique of schemers...a choir of angels...a choir of singers..."

"A barrel of monkeys?" Cahill suggested.

Reddy shot Cahill an angry look and spoke with real heat. "Don't mock me, Mr. Cahill. I've got a process and you're interfering with it. Remember the terms of our agreement and hope I don't change them so you go to jail."

Cahill sat back in his chair red-faced. He whispered to Kallaste, "Didn't think he had that much Darth Vader in him. I'm beginning to see why he is what he is."

His whisper had not been so soft that Reddy did not catch it. The agent wheeled on the big man. "I have difficulty dealing with people on a social level. You have no idea how hard.... Look, if I seem strange to you, consider that you, Mr. Cahill, are as exotic to me as any unfamiliar animal in a zoo defecating on the viewing glass. I have a job to do and I will do it. You — "

Kallaste cleared his throat. "Agent Reddy? May I ask, respectfully, when you aren't using your relaxation cue...the grouping words — "

"The collective noun device, yes?"

"When you aren't using that, who are you pretending to be when you're around people?"

Reddy looked at the doctor, startled. In a moment, his face softened and his shoulders relaxed. "So you understand?"

"Yes. Not from my training or at the hospital. I've seen it in my own family. A cousin. If you don't mind me asking, who is your avatar for your coping strategy?"

"Humphrey Bogart."

"Ah. That makes sense now. For a person in your position, that's a solid choice."

"Computers are my special interest but a therapist helped me to focus, to approximate — "

"You don't have to explain. Your history is your business. But may I ask one more thing?"

"What?"

" Any particular movie of Bogey's?"

"*The Big Sleep.*"

The doctor chuckled. "That title kind of fits, doesn't it?"

Reddy nodded. "Yes, I suppose it does."

"What the hell are you guys talking about?" Cahill asked.

"Irony," Reddy replied. "And like the man said, this is my business. Your business is to lay off and do as you're told."

"Yes, sir! Spoken like Sam Spade," Cahill said.

"Shut up, Cahill," Kallaste said.

"Yeah. Or I'll bust you right in the mouth," Reddy added.

The big man wisely shut up, at least for a while.

CHAPTER 16

Reagan National Airport
   Washington, DC
   April 14

Dr. Kallaste waited for Reddy to look up from his screen. When Reddy was at work on his device, it was as if he and Cahill did not exist. Finally, Reddy looked his way. "What do we do next?"

"We'll go to our base of operations. We've set up a post in California at Berkeley."

"Why there?"

"It is my supposition that someone has harnessed a force derived from altered, unconscious states to manifest real world events."

"You're talking telekinesis, telepathy," Cahill said. "Magic. It's all kind of *Nightmare on Elm Street*, isn't it?"

"I am not familiar with the details of that movie," Reddy said. "As for magic, I'm still formulating my opinions. I believe that word is commonly applied to illusions and things that are not yet explained. Explained phenomena cease to be called magic. Anything we label magic is something we must explore until it ceases to be unexplained. To that goal, we're setting up a sleep lab to help us identify who is behind these events. We need to change the location of the battlefield and make bad dreams remain in altered states of consciousness."

"Who's at Berkeley?" Kallaste asked.

"We're collecting witnesses and asking them to participate in sleep studies in a lab on campus."

"Okay, but who is heading the medical team?"

"You are, Mik."

Cahill laughed. "Shouldn't we get everybody together at Fort Bragg or under a mountain in Colorado with NORAD or something?"

"There is equipment at Berkley which is integral to our research and counter-attack."

"Counter-attack?" Cahill fidgeted. "What if it's the Chinese or North Korea? What if it's Kim Jong-un who figured out how to get us to lose all our teeth and set us on fire?"

"One disaster at a time, Mr. Cahill. We have to trace the source of these phenomena first."

"Like tracking ants back to the nest to kill the queen," Kallaste said.

"In our sleep," Cahill added. "Sure, that'll be easy. I'm hoping for a super villain with a Fu Manchu mustache and claws for hands."

"With a head office under a volcano?" Kallaste suggested.

Reddy sighed. "It will be someone who appears much more mundane, I'm quite sure. Evildoers don't have fortresses like in comic books, sir. They're young college students with extreme libertarian fantasies or disgruntled loners who barely hold on to part-time jobs. That's how they profile, typically."

"Given the strangeness of these terrorist acts," Cahill said, "why would you think anything about the terrorists will be typical?"

"That," Kallaste said, "is a good point."

Before Cahill and Kallaste could ask another question, a far door opened. Two men in fatigues entered, side by side.

"Our crew is here, gentlemen. We have a C-130 on the tarmac."

"We're in the Army now," Cahill said sourly.

Reddy frowned. "As far as anyone is concerned, you and Dr.

Kallaste aren't here. When this is over, you will return to your usual routines and never speak a word of this. On the plane, I have documents for you to sign to that effect. Stopping these phenomena is not enough. It must remain secret. Come. Much to do. Little time."

The pair of recruits trailed behind the NSA agent. "He's fun, isn't he?" Cahill asked. "When he picked me up for this little safari into weirdness, I noticed he doesn't carry a gun. I asked him about it. The guy holds up his phone and says to me, 'I mostly use this.'"

"Interesting." Kallaste said it in a way that told Cahill he wasn't at all interested.

"Anyway, don't try to make small talk with Agent Reddy. He sucks at it."

"I noticed his flat affect."

"I hope you're better at conversation," Cahill said.

"I have a feeling you'll carry that weight for both of us."

Cahill grinned. "Great! I'm the plucky comic relief on this sci-fi adventure."

"Is that what this is?"

"Mm. Maybe supernatural. Anyway, I'll be the funny guy who somehow survives. You play the dashing doctor who would have gotten the girl except you nobly sacrifice yourself. You'll probably do something heroic and stupid to save all mankind."

"I'm not wild about that," Kallaste said. "Did you rehearse that in your head a lot or — "

"Nah. All improv, man, plus I watch a lot of Netflix."

"I haven't decided whether I like you yet," Kallaste said.

"Same," Cahill said. "Reddy's a stiff, but you got a lot of starch up your ass, too. Doesn't matter. When you're electrocuted by some huge piece of scientific equipment, I'll be there to comfort the girl you won't live to marry."

"Thanks, Cahill. I appreciate that."

"See? You feel better already."

"You're an app developer, right?"

"Yeah."

"That explains it."

"What?"

"Lots of time alone, poor social skills — "

Cahill grinned. "Does not share toys. Does not play well with others. Problem with authority. I've heard it all since elementary school, man! But every class needs a clown. Without me, you'll think too hard about your inevitable doom as we confront whoever kills people in their dreams."

CHAPTER 17

Neither Here Nor There
  Out of Time

The Woman in White hovered above a beach in Kiribati. This had not been a place for tourists. The beach was littered with ashes and, below her, a long-abandoned hotel sat crumbling. The firestorm had swept through and then back out to sea.

"Something troubling you?" the disembodied voice asked the Woman in White.

She could feel the deep rumble of his words in her chest. The redheaded woman considered her words a long time. "It doesn't seem real, Big Daddy."

"Reality is a slippery thing."

"Really? I thought there was only one."

"If no one can agree on one reality, there can't be just one, can there?"

She shrugged and stared down at the burnt bodies absently.

"Everything is real somewhere. It always was. Ours is a multi-verse, of mind and body, time and space. Soon, the separate realities will no longer be confined to their old boxes."

"I feel like I've been living in a small box for a long time," the woman said.

"Do the bodies disturb you?"

"They aren't pretty anymore."

"If Death be not beautiful, why do we stare into Her face so long?"

"Huh?"

"It's a poem from my people," the voice said. "Whenever we see death, we cannot look away. We tell ourselves we shouldn't look but we stare at the body. Some of your rituals even make a ceremony of viewing the body at the funeral."

"The bodies. Are they real?"

"They serve as an announcement to the world that I am among you again."

"I'm sure you'll make a big splash, Big Daddy."

"You have questions, do you not?"

The Woman in White shook her head. "The bodies are...interesting."

"They do bother you."

"There's a song. It's called *Strange Fruit*. When I see these people burnt up, I feel like I'm listening to Billie Holiday sing it again."

"Yes. See? Both sad and beautiful."

"The twisted limbs. That is...um...what do their deaths say, Big Daddy? Teach me."

"Their last gestures tell stories of anguish. They're off to explore new realities now. I set them free."

"I've never been good at reading people. I'm worse at reading dead people. What's next?" she asked.

"Bored already?"

"More like excited to get out of the box and away from here. I don't know why you showed me this."

"I want you to know how powerful the tools I've given you can be. So far, you have thought small."

"You think so? I've already exercised more power than I ever had. This doesn't feel real. I don't know what's real anymore. Not since I went to sleep...or since I woke up. I'm not sure which is which. Is any of this real?"

"There are forces in the world," the voice said, "that try to make things stay the same as long as possible. They praise stability and pretend it is not stagnation."

"Time to shake things up, huh?"

"We will."

"I'm going to fly some more. I love to fly."

"It is glorious, isn't it? Such pleasures should not be confined to the likes of birds and bats, should they?"

"You've never told me your name, Big Daddy," she said. "Tell me your name."

"It's a secret."

"Tell me."

"Very well. I am Cord."

"That's kind of a lovely name for a strange-looking fellow."

"Thank you, but where I come from, I am not strange."

"Why did you choose me, Cord?"

"Because I think you're lovely, too. You were chosen."

"You chose me?"

"You came highly recommended. Your loved one wants you to be free and free of pain."

"My loved one. Yes...he's a good boy. And you are generous. It is so good to finally benefit from generosity. Thank you, Cord. Thank you so much."

"Your pains and problems are all in the past as long as you stay by my side. You are special. You know that, right? "

"You look scary, but under all that, you're a man, aren't you? That's the sort of thing men say to women. I'm not some stupid girl. I know a line when I hear one. I've heard quite a few sweet talkers in my time."

"I am not a man."

"Then I like you even more now, Cord."

"We'll teach the world new ways. We have to make them see and feel the power."

"Is it magic?"

"Is nuclear power, a steamship or fire made of magic?"

"Okay, I get it. I'm not saying you're wrong, Cord, and I appreciate all that you've done for me so far. I really enjoyed what happened to Desi. Still, down there...." She pointed to the burnt bodies of casualties who had tried to make it to the sea before the fire consumed them.

"You worry about the dead?" Cord asked. "They no longer have concerns."

"You tell me I have no concerns. Am I dead, too?"

"No, child. You're learning how to live."

The Woman in White looked troubled. "Desi deserved to die. But there are kids down there. They burned alive for a while before they died."

"This is my way. Most died of smoke inhalation. Most of the rest died from suffocation as the fire consumed the oxygen."

"Yes, but — "

"People change very slowly or not at all. They must be pushed. There is no more time for slow change. In order to appreciate all the possibilities of their new reality, we must grab their attention. That is what this is. They only respect power if it can hurt them. We will teach them respect. They will come to worship you."

The Woman in White smiled before she floated away on a breeze. "As they should. Thank you, Cord."

"No, no. Thank you. I have chosen you as my conduit to a new world. I am your Adam. You are my Eve. We will build a new world together that is worthy of our highest dreams."

"You talk like the Devil," she whispered as she rose higher into the colder air currents.

"I am not a man. Nor am I a devil."

"Cord...Big Daddy...so many names. Are you God?"

"Certainly not, but...." The clouds parted to reveal the smoking remains of Kiribati. The Woman in White heard delight in Cord's disembodied voice. "I can see why you might make that mistake. It is your God's nature to show them might. Each of their deities is a mirror. They look to gods and find their own reflection. Yours is a warlike people so your gods must be warlike."

"What should I do now, besides fly away?"

"Whatever you want, of course. If the ashes of my enemies disturb you, go find some enemies of your own. Go save someone if you want to. What is the opposite of burnt and destroyed?" Cord let out a deep rumbling chuckle. "I've forgotten what life without pain is. Humans taught me that."

"I'm sorry."

"It is their way."

"I think I'll go try to balance the scales somehow, for those below and for you."

"Do whatever you like, as long as you stay asleep, nothing can hurt or burn or kill you. Yours is the sleep of the deathless."

"Deathless. I like that. I *love* that! Call me Deathless."

CHAPTER 18

C-130 leaving Washington, DC
    April 14

On the flight west, Cahill and Kallaste sat beside each other in uncomfortable jump seats. The military plane was packed with equipment, all in boxes marked only with barcodes.

Kallaste regarded his seat mate. "How did you become an app developer?"

"I did it like I do everything else. I stumbled into it. I'm a high school dropout."

"Why a sleep app?"

"It's where the money is." Cahill chuckled. "I was a hacker in high school. I couldn't see the use in most of what I was learning so I went straight into business. The only thing I missed about high school was senior prom. By the time a kid graduates from university with a computer science degree, he's deep in debt and most of his knowledge is already outdated. I started earning early and put out half a dozen sleep-related apps."

"And somehow, Agent Reddy found you."

Cahill shook his head. "My tech is proprietary and my user list is encrypted. Reddy is in a hurry so he recruited me instead of sweating me and just taking my stuff."

Kallaste checked his watch. "Flying west, we're gaining a few hours but losing orientation time. Not long before New York is asleep and vulnerable."

"A good chunk of the planet is already dark and sleeping, Doc. Whatever is happening is a *global* disaster."

"Sorry," Kallaste said. "I wasn't thinking about the rest of the planet. Every disaster movie I've ever seen except old Godzilla movies is kind of oriented toward the United States under siege."

"That's because those movies sell big abroad. A lot of disaster movies show the White House getting blown apart. Give the people what they want to see — "

"But this disaster scenario seems kind of...personal. There's no place to hide. It's not like we can move to higher ground to avoid the flood or move out of tornado alley. Everybody sleeps and everyone dreams."

"Everyone?"

"One in 250 think they don't but they do. They just don't remember."

"Let's think outside the box. What could the mechanism be for the killings in Dubai? Telepathy?"

"As far as I'm concerned, those were deaths. I don't know if they were killings, not yet."

"You're a pretty committed skeptic, man."

"I just don't know what's going on and I can't explain it. That doesn't make me a skeptic. It means I don't know enough to say, yet."

Kallaste wished he could use his phone, if only as a distraction. However, Reddy had taken his device from him when the doctor signed the NSA's non-disclosure agreement. He'd barely read the document but he guessed he didn't need to. If he turned into a whistleblower, he'd be considered a traitor and fall under "severe penalty of law." When he'd scanned the NDA, that phrase had jumped out at him.

"What kind of name is Mik Kallaste, anyway?"

"My father was from Estonia. It's a small country south of — "

"Finland. Yeah, I know," Cahill said. "I'm one of the few who can find Micronesia on a map, too."

The doctor reddened. "Sorry, I didn't mean anything by it. Most people I meet aren't familiar with Estonia."

"I only know it because that's where Skype and Kazaa started. Paypal, too, I think."

"Oh. I didn't know that."

"Skype was originally called Skyper, as in Sky Peer-to-peer. That domain name was already taken so now we have Skype. You still have family there?"

"Distant relatives. I've never been. I was brought up in New Jersey. My father teaches chemistry at Princeton."

"Still?"

"Yeah. He's old but still sharp and spry."

"You gonna call him when you can? Warn him?"

"What would make sense to my dad? Should I tell him to wear a sweater? This isn't the sort of problem where it will help to go hide in the basement beside a pile of canned goods."

"No, I guess it's not."

"You got anybody you could call if the phones worked and Reddy let you keep your cell?" Kallaste asked.

"A few exes, but I've never managed to part with an ex on the best of terms. What about you? No girlfriend, boyfriend or fiancee?"

"I had a fiancee."

"Had?"

"She had a good job in New York. I had a good job at Bethesda. Couldn't get past that. Now she's on Wall Street and I'm...actually, until this afternoon, I knew what I was doing."

"The exciting stuff happens in uncharted waters, doc."

"Call me Mik."

"Please call me Cahill. It's not that I'm being unfriendly. I hate my first name. Everybody calls me Cahill."

"Now I have to know."

"Eugene."

"Condolences, Cahill. That's just tragic and your parents are mean."

"I've just decided to like you, Mik."

The men exchanged glances and chuckled.

Reddy emerged from the cockpit. "Gentlemen, we have another incident I suspect is relevant."

"What happened?" Cahill asked. "Are Superman and Batman joining the team?"

"It happened in France. We don't know the strategic value of the event but this one is radically different."

"How?" Cahill and Kallaste chorused.

"I have video."

CHAPTER 19

C-130 over Nebraska
   April 14

Reddy turned the sound up on his phone. Kallaste and Cahill leaned closer to peer at the screen. The grainy video was jerky. After a moment, it became obvious that the recording was taken by a helmet cam.

"Where is this?" Cahill asked.

"Tourtour, a small village in Provence."

Several men in Hazmat suits carrying weapons came in and out of a shot as they exited the back of an armored personnel carrier. Bodies littered the street. The number of corpses increased as the team turned to approach a yellow house. The domicile, tall and angular, stood in a tight cluster of homes along a narrow street.

Kallaste glanced at the NSA agent. "How many dead?"

"Six or seven hundred. We don't have a confirmed body count yet."

The team tasked to explore the scene was calm and professional at first. The camera picked them up in the periphery until they formed a line. For a moment, white hazmats with yellow reflective tape filled the screen. Two technicians carried what looked like sample kits. Several men carried MP5s. "Are the weapons necessary?" Kallaste asked.

"They don't know what they're getting into," Cahill said. "Just like us."

The exploration team kept their comm channel clear most of the time. The cam's mic picked up a few curt commands and cold observations in French.

"What are they saying?" Cahill asked.

"My French is rusty," Kallaste said, "but I have the gist. They're talking about the possibility of nerve gas and contagion. The commander of the squad just radioed to the uh...*Gendarmerie Nationale* to push the quarantine zone back another ten kilometers in all directions."

"Not too rusty there, huh?" Cahill said.

"I had a French Canadian girlfriend and a couple of summers in Montreal."

"I had a Canadian girlfriend, too," Cahill said, "but she was made up." No one laughed. Self-conscious, Cahill asked a serious question. "Why are they focused on this one house?"

"It's the epicenter," Reddy said. "The villagers appear to have converged on this one address."

Vague, grainy shapes littered the ground as the camera man turned his head too fast. The helmet camera picked up its user's breathing, fast and shallow. The man's breath doubled as he encountered a corpse up close.

They glimpsed a dead child as the cameraman looked down. The man turned away and moved on quickly.

"Reminds me of old pictures of Jonestown or Waco," Cahill said.

"Tourtour is a tourist town," Reddy said. "There are no cults on the watch list from the General Directorate of Internal Security."

The cameraman must have forced himself to look at the next body. The view lingered and the details were gory. The twisted corpse had once been a man, perhaps in his forties or fifties. It was difficult to tell. The body's putrefaction was too advanced to be sure of its age.

Exposed bone and muscle showed through where the rotten flesh had been torn or burst from expanding gases.

"According to the supplementary reports, a little tour bus comes through the village each morning," Reddy said. "The tour guide swears everything was normal yesterday."

"Can't be," Kallaste declared. "For this atrocity, someone dug up a graveyard."

Reddy shook his head. "A graveyard that uses no preservatives? Hundreds of bodies that weren't there yesterday? Doubtful. The logistics alone —"

"They aren't from a graveyard," Cahill said. "I've seen every zombie movie. When the dead rise from their graves, they'd all be dressed up in their favorite dresses and Brooks Brothers suits. That's what's wrong with most zombie movies. They don't have the budget for the formal wear."

"This makes no sense. I've done cadaver labs. That body must have been dead for months," Kallaste said, "and exposed to the elements."

"That body was identified as the village baker. The tour guide swears he bought pastries from that man yesterday."

"Impossible."

"As impossible as human flight or a manned trip to the moon or sending robots to explore other planets?" Reddy asked.

"That's a specious comparison."

"Easy, Mik," Cahill said. "Who are you going to believe? Agent Reddy or your lying eyes?"

"I'll reserve judgment until I can come up with an explanation that makes sense. So far, my whole day looks like an elaborate prank."

The camera turned and focused on more bodies. The cameraman never paused long but the images were just as disturbing each time. When the technician looked up, the view was a brief wide shot of the side of the house. Bodies were piled on top of each other. Under a broken window a mound of people lay dead.

"It's...as if...." Cahill didn't finish the thought.

"As if the villagers were trying to get into the house," Reddy said.

"Or out," Kallaste suggested.

"No. The reports found the broken window glass was inside the house."

As the team got closer, the cameraman took a more circuitous route around the bodies at his feet. Soon, the frame bounced back and forth in a clumsy and chaotic motion. The man's breathing became fast and ragged.

"Lousy camera work," Cahill said.

"He's climbing over bodies," Kallaste said.

When the cameraman looked down, the view confirmed the doctor's guess. Team members were indeed stepping on bodies to climb to the porch. There appeared to be an argument between two investigators.

"What are they saying?" Cahill asked.

Kallaste leaned even closer to the small screen. "Too fast for me to catch. *Sh.* I think the door is blocked by too many bodies."

After a moment, the leader gestured for his team to enter the house through a window instead of trying to breach the front door. The camera's view showed a battering ram being passed from hand to hand. As the point man smashed a window, the team's chatter ramped up. The leader raised an arm to signal to everyone to shut up and listen.

"They're scared," Kallaste said.

"Aren't you?" Cahill asked.

"Yeah."

"You know what the dead look like, Mik. Those cadavers...it's like in the movies."

"I know what you're going to say, Cahill. Don't."

"Doc — "

"Eugene."

"Zombies," Reddy said. "They look like zombies."

All three men remained silent as they watched the cameraman's progress. Inside the house, the dead had fallen in a circle. Every corpse lay with arms outstretched, jaws wide. In the center of the circle, an old man sat slumped on a couch. He'd draped a white shawl over his shoulders.

"The palms of that man's hands were so burnt the skin was shriveled black," Reddy said. "His guts were ripped open and his entrails stretched across the floor. Several intestinal loops were wrapped around the television set."

"Look at the way the other bodies...like they're reaching for him," Cahill said. "The old man must have been the zombie messiah."

Reddy pulled his phone from the doctor's grasp and slid over to a jump seat to send a new batch of emails. "There's something personal about this attack. No one else's colon was tied to a TV. Other than the abdominal trauma and burns, he looks like he could be asleep in front of the wood stove. I think that old man was a cause or a catalyst."

"Then he's a clue," Kallaste said.

"Oh, my, yes, Mik," Reddy said without looking up from typing madly on his screen. "I thought that was obvious. However, I'm glad you're finally over your denial and are ready to deal with the new reality."

Kallaste opened his mouth to object but Cahill put a gentle hand on his arm. "Just go with it, man. We're on the crazy train and we've got tickets to the end of the line."

CHAPTER 20

En route from Linares, Mexico to
Phoenix, Arizona
April 14

He had a name but the sixteen people in his charge knew him only as
Coyote or "the coyote."

One young mother carried an infant in a sling. The father looked
young and broad shouldered, but the mother was a slight woman and
could not have given birth long ago. She should have crossed the
border while she was still pregnant. Coyote worried most about the
infant. However, the cool air and the steady swing of the walk
through the night often kept children quiet and sleeping.

Most of his charges were used to work and hardship. Their shoes
were broken in and their hands were callused. Still, how long could
he push the group until they pleaded with him for rest?

Coyote went through everyone's bags before he let them climb
into the back of the old van. He threw to the ground anything he
deemed useless weight.

"Carry one picture of your family and keep the rest in your

memory," he told one man. "By dawn, a three pound photo album will feel like thirty pounds too much."

Coyote had crossed the border into the United States many times in many places. Border Patrol had arrested him several times, but mostly, he got his people through. Coyote didn't know this was the night that would change his life.

They started out late in the day, all sixteen packed in tight. They knew better than to complain. As the immigrants came close to the border, they would have to get out and walk through the darkness to the light. It would be hard. It was always hard.

The oldest man was in his late sixties and crossing the border was a young person's quest. The man's spine was deformed in some way, as if he carried a turtle shell on his back. Besides the mother and new baby, the old man was the group's weakest link.

Coyote would tell them when to drink and, when they did, they would have to control themselves. They would have to sip to make their water rations last the length of the journey. If they thought they were thirsty early in the night, they didn't know real suffering. By dawn, they would know what real thirst was.

A walk across the border at night was not the same as a stroll down a long road. The terrain was uneven. Snakes, twisted ankles, falls and getting caught were constant worries. Most of all, Coyote led a race against the sun.

The Border Patrol had grown more harsh recently. The hike across the border was necessarily longer than it used to be. Coyote had occasionally sent stragglers back rather than lose the whole group. Some stragglers died. Such sacrifices were not memories he cherished but Coyote could not let his failures go, either. People got lost in the borderlands. They died of thirst. There are fewer worse fates but, this night, he would see worse.

When the terrain was rough and his feet hurt and people began to complain, Coyote thought of his brothers. They worked far to the south. South was safer.

At the resorts, the gringos came to drink and carouse. The cartels stayed in the North. There were no beheadings near the resorts where the white people's cruise ships docked. Their failed drug war was invisible to them. Those tourists didn't see the mutilated bodies hanging from bridges in Juarez.

Coyote knew bad men who did this work. He hated them. Circumstance had made Coyote a hard man but he was a pragmatist, not a sadist. His job was getting people where they needed to be. Besides, his work was better money than he could earn bowing and scraping and serving drinks to fat tourists.

They planned to cross the border west of Laredo tonight. As they marched to their fate, Coyote walked farther than any of them. Though he was in his late forties, he was quick. He knew heat, cold and exhaustion. He kept moving. Mostly, he led the way but he would double back periodically to check on the slowest of the group. Sometimes he would encourage them. More often, he would berate and threaten them. Everyone responded differently. None of that mattered as long as he arrived at the rendezvous point with the same number of people who had paid their way in Linares.

None of them would thank him for being their guide when the van arrived to take them farther north. He didn't need their thanks and he didn't need them to like him. But the young mother, the baby in the sling and the oldest man with the strange spine? They worried him.

Coyote had just checked his compass and assured himself all was well when his night's work turned to shit. Headlights popped on. They ran, but the border patrol was ahead of them, too. The group was trapped along the edge of a deep gully. Nowhere to run. If there had been, the patrol would have just run them down. Tonight's long walk was over.

Coyote ordered everyone to sit. He remained standing, his hands high in the air. Officers began shouting. They pointed their guns at him. He never traveled into the United States armed. Few coyotes did. He would surrender and he would speak to the men with guns, calm and sweet.

Usually, capture, arrest and processing was routine. A bus would come eventually. Coyote could rest his aching feet. He wouldn't have to worry about the young mother, her baby or the old man. He would give the Americans a false name and, in a month or a year from now, they might capture him again. Getting people back and forth across the border was a game. Sometimes it could be an expensive game with risks and gambles and tragedy, but it was just a game.

His people understood the risks. No one liked the coyotes but they did not blame him for this kind of failure. The people blamed their own government for their impotence. They blamed the Americans for their selfishness. But tonight was not like other nights. The Border Patrol was not playing according to the usual rules of the game.

One of the officers was a young man with swagger. Coyote recognized his type immediately. Some men need liquor for artificial courage. Others need a badge. The officer waded into the huddled group, breaking them up. He lined up the would be immigrants, forcing everyone to their knees. When the old man did not kneel fast enough, the officer kicked his legs out from under him. The old man landed hard on his turtle back.

The border patrolman laughed. Worse, there were six more standing in front of the headlights. They all laughed.

On his knees with his hands behind his head and his ankles crossed, Coyote searched the silhouettes for a female officer. He found none. That was a bad sign. Female officers took the wind out of macho sails and de-escalated situations. Left to their own devices, young officers like this turned situations into problems.

Coyote could feel the tension building among the officers, like a bowstring pulled taut and quivering with potential energy behind an arrow. The way they laughed and looked to each other, egging each other on, was unprofessional. None of his group had resisted capture. The border patrol's victory was complete yet they wanted more. They wanted to make something happen. Something bad.

"Hey, beaners!" the young man announced. "No free ride tonight! You gots to pay the toll." He repeated himself in broken Spanish. None of Coyote's group seemed to understand his exact words, but they got the gist.

He saw no mercy in their eyes. Coyote had seen the same look among *Federalis* sometimes. Something had gone wrong with these men. Sometimes, when men had seen many bad things, they took their suffering as license to impose evil on others. To get their jobs, they probably spoke of duty and love of country. They might bray about sacrifice and law, but somehow their work made them monsters. Now they loved power.

Coyote looked back to his group. All lowered their eyes and were silent. Two women cried. A couple of the men were pretending not to, trying to look brave.

Brave makes no sense out here. There are no rules among these men.

Coyote's throat was dry but he spoke, meek and gentle. "We surrender guys! You win. These people are tired. Let's call it a night, eh, *amigo?*"

"Sure, *amigo!*"

Coyote saw the hit coming but not fast enough to duck or roll. He'd been hit across the face with a flashlight before but never this hard. He fell into the dirt. He tasted the grit of sand first, then blood. He ran his tongue over his teeth. A couple were loose and his gums bled.

The young man stood over him, crowing and cackling. Coyote didn't dare spit out the sand in case the officer took that as an attack.

Another man, an older officer, walked down the line with an air of authority. He flashed his light in each person's face, blinding each for a moment. He seemed amused at the young man's antics. He chuckled as he paced back and forth. The border patrol's laughter rose again, contagious among them.

The officer who had struck Coyote moved on. His gaze fell on the young mother. She knelt beside her husband. He held the baby. Husband and wife stared at the ground, praying in urgent whispers.

"Hey! Pretty *señorita!* That your baby? That's a sweet baby! Still asleep. You be good and he'll sleep all the way through, huh?"

The woman began to choke and weep. Her husband's jaw tightened in fury. Coyote hoped the young father would do nothing to provoke their captors. Coyote's hope was answered as the father, more mature than his years, begged for mercy for his family.

The monsters have proven to each other that they are powerful, Coyote thought. *The bus will come soon. They're just goading us. We have played our role. We are sheep. Surely, that's enough.*

He was wrong. The monsters just cackled harder.

"Hey, *señorita*, I have some questions. You come with me in the back of my Jeep. If you're good this won't take long at all. Let's have an interview."

No better than the cartels, Coyote thought. Rape for mercy. It would not be the first time it had happened along the border. Any time men had power over others, this happened.

If people knew this horror, they would think, that's terrible. Oh, well... what can I do? Then they'd turn the page of their newspaper and wonder, *why isn't there ever any good news to read?*

Coyote slowly pulled himself back up to his knees, showing his open empty hands. "Leave the girl alone. We are human beings. Treat these people well."

He told the young Border Patrol officer to do things. For that, the thug stalked over and hit Coyote across the face three times with the long handle of his flashlight. The last blow opened Coyote's forehead and hot blood blinded his left eye.

Coyote did not fall into the dirt this time. Instead, he stared up into the young man's face. "You do this because you want to do this. You do this because it feels good."

"So?"

"I have done bad things but not because it feels good."

"So?"

"So stop."

"Why?"

"Because sometime maybe you'll have to pay for it."

The monster was just a silhouette in headlights to Coyote. However, Coyote was sure he knew what the monster's harsh laughter meant. He stiffened his spine and waited for more strikes from the heavy flashlight full of nine D batteries. He was surprised to see the officer raise his pistol instead.

Coyote closed his eyes. He wondered what price he would have to pay in the next life. Did it matter if a man sinned for good reasons? Would the bastard who executed him suffer in a worse hell one day, or would they burn together, side by side for eternity?

Grinding metallic thunder, unearthly and fearsome, split the night. The cacophony spread out, echoing to the horizon. Coyote trembled. At first he thought the sound was what a pistol shot to the head seemed to a dead man. When he dared to open his eyes, Judgment Day had come.

CHAPTER 21

San Francisco, California
  April 14

The C-130 landed at San Francisco International twenty minutes before midnight. Two FBI agents in a black SUV met the plane. The man, an agent named Burke, told Reddy the drive to Berkeley would take forty minutes without traffic, "so, over an hour." Agent Burke did not speak again.

Reddy did not look up from his phone. "Plenty of time for a briefing and emails."

A tall Asian woman opened the back door of the SUV. "I'm Agent Karen Shin. We'll get you where you need to be. Mr. Cahill, please get into the far back seat of the vehicle."

"You already know my name?"

"Apparently, sir."

Kallaste paused to speak to the agent. "You're FBI? I didn't think the NSA and the FBI and all those alphabet agencies cooperated with each other."

"It's a new Homeland Security, Dr. Kallaste. It seems there's a lot riding on our mutual success."

"Since Tourtour, I'm getting lots of cooperation upstream and downstream," Reddy said absently.

"Yeah, the zombie apocalypse gets everyone's attention," Cahill said.

"Don't use the z-word," Kallaste said. "It sounds too stupid."

"Don't say anything," Reddy ordered. "It's Agent Shin's turn to talk. I still don't have any autopsy results from Dubai or from the French. Have you got anything for me in that regard?"

Shin shook her head. "The French coroners are overwhelmed. They're getting help from labs all over the EU. They're looking for a poison. The locals in France are sure it's some new toxin."

"And Dubai?"

"That roadblock seems to be composed of secrecy combined with lack of cooperation. Some of the bodies were buried immediately. Others were sent to their home countries and are still in transit. None has been released to our medical examiners for autopsy."

"The first thing they should check the Dubai bodies for is something that induces extreme osteopenia," Kallaste said. "I can't imagine how else anyone could break that many bones without a sledgehammer."

"Thank you, Doctor," Reddy said. "We thought of that but it doesn't explain how their flesh turned to jelly. Do you have news about the man in the shawl, Agent Shin?"

"The French authorities identified him as Francois Dufour. He's an American citizen."

"With a name like Francois Dufour? Gotta be fake," Cahill said.

"His California driver's license was upstairs in his room at the boarding house. He lived most of his life in California," Shin said. "Retired. Married three times, two divorces. His last marriage ended with the death of his spouse. Natural causes. No priors."

"I don't know any Americans with names like Francois Dufour," Cahill said. "Still sounds suspicious to me. If the guy had an Arabic name, the government would already be sending in the drones and hellfire missiles."

"I'm not interested in misdirected xenophobia, Mr. Cahill," Reddy said. "Agent Shin, please continue."

"His birthplace was listed as Lyon, France but his family emigrated when he was a baby. The French are checking for relatives in Tourtour."

"Dufour stayed in a boarding house," Reddy said. "Few people travel around the world to stay at a boarding house when they could stay with relatives. That's likely a dead end."

At the edge of the tarmac, a TSA agent pulled back a gate. The SUV rolled out of the airport at high speed. The driver didn't use a siren but the vehicle's blues and reds strobed through the windshield and by the headlights. Some drivers — not all — pulled out of the way. Traffic was thick. The driver slowed as they hit the highway.

"What did the zombie messiah do for a living?" Cahill asked. "I'm gonna guess, evil scientist, maybe a mastermind chemist whose own bio-weapon caused his undoing. Add a secret lab guarded by his private army and we've got a new Bond movie."

Shin looked at Cahill for a long beat. "A lot of people died, sir."

"I know, Karen. I saw the recording and I'll never forget it. I take it I won't be easing the tension with my trademark levity this evening."

Shin turned back to Reddy. "Dufour was pretty vanilla. He was a filmmaker."

"Any political message in his movies?"

"Romances," Shin said. "No politics."

"Wow! Just...wow," Cahill said. "Maybe you should check his library card for subversion and perversion."

Shin ignored Cahill. "We're digging through his tax records and talking to his neighbors. No red flags raised so far. His last projects were directing a few short films and one independent movie more than ten years ago. The biggest star he worked with was John Cusack."

"How is that actor relevant?" Reddy asked.

"Uh...he's not. I just happen to like John Cusack," Shin said.

"Me, too," Kallaste said. "*Grosse Point Blank* is one of my favorite movies."

Reddy pressed on. "Where did Dufour live precisely?"

"He moved to San Diego from Burbank in 2007. I checked Google maps. He lived in a gorgeous place not far from the beach."

Reddy sat back and closed his eyes. "When did Dufour fly to France?"

Shin had been reciting what she knew. She reached into her jacket and pulled out a notebook that was marked with small yellow Post-Its. She found the information she was looking for quickly. "He flew out of LAX on the evening of April 9."

"There was a spike in night terrors early on in the case. San Diego was a hot spot."

"How the hell could you know that?" Cahill asked.

Reddy ignored him and tapped on his cell phone for some time before speaking. "Tell your people to keep on Dufour's trail, Agent Shin. Someone connected to him is a person of interest. They either warned him or maybe the terrorists came after him in San Diego."

"What makes you so sure?" Shin asked.

"The man died on a shabby couch by a wood stove." Reddy turned his screen to show a big house in San Diego. "Dufour lived in a palace. Why run away to France when he could be living here?"

"Flimsy," Cahill said.

"Entertaining flimsy suppositions is how I came to head this investigation," Reddy said. "Observation plus imagination divided by facts times thought equals detection."

CHAPTER 22

San Francisco, California
  April 15
  Last Day

"The French are looking for traces of some kind of biological residue that would account for what happened in Tourtour," Shin said. "The rapid putrefaction — "

"There's more going on here than something that mimics one apocalyptic fantasy," Reddy said. "I know the French reports are dramatic but it's not all about zombies. What else have you got?"

Shin looked to her notes. "Someone in the CIA's Psy section observed that some people with multiple personality disorder change their physiology as they change personalities. The person they become who claims to have diabetes, for instance, actually changes his or her blood chemistry and the pancreas stops working the way it should. In rare cases, scars can come and go depending on which personality rises to the surface."

"That's kind of cool," Cahill said, "but what does that have to do with this?"

"They're proposing that this could be some sort of induced mass hysteria. They're saying the agent could be a hallucinogen."

"People can talk themselves into exacerbating symptoms, even give themselves strokes and heart attacks with their own anxiety," Kallaste said.

"In their sleep?" Reddy shook his head. "Keep in mind, this is the same division of the CIA that's working on a bomb to turn opposing forces gay."

Cahill burst out in a high-pitched giggle. "Really?"

"While it's true that people can create their own symptoms," Reddy continued, "that's doesn't fir the facts. How would a drug that can't be detected induce mass hysteria in strangers in separate rooms in a vast resort hotel in the middle of the night? And why wouldn't it affect others in the hotel?"

Shin shrugged. "We're looking at Chinese fringe groups and North Korea, of course, but most of our intelligence resources are focused on activities of extreme jihadists, sir. Considering Dubai — "

Reddy's eyes narrowed. "Dubai is smack in political hotspot territory, I grant you, but — "

"It's none of the above," Kallaste said.

Reddy gave the doctor his full attention. "Tell me why."

"It can't be the usual suspects. Firestorms? Hundreds of rotting corpses that were alive and well yesterday? People shattering every bone in their bodies by falling out of bed? Besides being weird, what do those manifestations have in common? Nothing besides they all sound like supermarket tabloid hoaxes."

"It is the very novelty of the attacks that link the disparate events," Reddy replied. "When the impossible happens in several places in the space of a few days, it's reasonable to assume one malignant force is behind it."

"But no terrorist group has claimed responsibility. We can't be terrified if it all stays a secret. If any known terrorist group could do all this, they'd be bragging about it."

"Maybe they will once the word gets out," Cahill said.

"But what did innocent people in a little village in France ever do to anyone?" Kallaste exclaimed. "That doesn't sound like terrorists to me. It's a small village. When 9/11 happened, the media had cameras all over it. If this were jihadists, they'd fill Times Square with bodies. Or Paris. Not...where was it again?"

"Tourtour," Reddy said.

Kallaste bobbed his head. "When the terrorists get a new way to attack us, don't they stick with that one strategy? I never thought of terrorists as particularly imaginative. You got teeth falling out here and countries burnt up there. Kind of all over the map, aren't they?"

"Interesting, Mik. Thank you. I'll consider that in full."

"It was something Cahill said that made me think of it, comparing the attack to a zombie movie. This is violent and as terrible as any terrorism, but the events are so strange, we shouldn't be looking only at the usual suspects. They still haven't managed to get hold of a dirty bomb."

Cahill gave the Kallaste a grateful nod. "True. People still working on indoor toilets are unlikely to suddenly jump to psy warfare that defies physics."

"Then, thank you both." Reddy turned back to Shin. "Has the FBI interviewed the people who predicted the firecanes?"

"My *customers*, you mean?" Cahill said. "There goes their hope for privacy. The reviews on my app are going to plummet. This is what I get for cooperating."

"Mr. Cahill," Shin said, "if a person predicts where they think a body might be found using voodoo psychic powers, I know I'm talking to the murderer. So, yes, we're talking to everyone who wrote in your sleep journal app about fire tornadoes. We can't find any connections among the users so far, except that they all used your app, of course."

"What's that supposed to mean?" Cahill sounded more surprised than angry at Shin's implication.

"Relax," Kallaste said. "A bunch of psychic warriors doesn't need an app to connect them."

"That's right. They could simply have a nap and meet in the *Unus Mundus*," Reddy said.

Kallaste looked at the agent curiously. "The *what* now?"

"We can discuss that later. Agent Shin," Reddy said quietly. "Do you have the supplies for which I called ahead?"

"In the bag beside Cahill."

"Mr. Cahill? If you would?"

Cahill passed a black cloth bag to Reddy who unzipped it.

The agent pulled two phones from the bag. "These will work. They are for communicating with me or Agent Shin only."

"No idle internet browsing?" Cahill asked.

Agent Shin shot him a sour look. "I've already reviewed your browsing history, Mr. Cahill. Better you stay on task. Idle hands and all that."

Cahill reddened. "Damn."

"The warning screen does say we can still see you, even when you set your browser to incognito."

"Yeah, I just never thought I'd be talking to federal agents about my...curiosities."

Reddy handed Kallaste the black bag. "I have several prescriptions for you to choose from, Mik. I'll leave the choice and dosages to you, of course. In this regard, everyone on this project is your patient."

Kallaste reached up to flick the dome light on and pulled out a handful of small plastic containers. "I see. You don't want us to fall asleep."

"Sleep is the war zone," Reddy said. "We don't want you to become victims of a manifestation. And there are the night terrors."

"Night terrors?"

"They're becoming more and more common. If the progression continues along the extrapolated course, we'll all be having night terrors soon. It will take all our perspicacity and sagacity to solve this before the attacks affect everyone."

"Have you always talked like a machine, Agent Reddy?" Cahill asked. "Did you come out of the womb that way or were you made in a factory?"

"My mother used every dinnertime to correct my grammar, to sharpen my mind and to expand my vocabulary. I'm sorry you were not so blessed."

"I read comics in front of the TV, played video games and had fun," Cahill replied. "I'm sorry you were not so blessed."

"I had an event," Agent Shin said. "Night terror. I saw my whole family drowning."

"Are they okay?" Kallaste asked.

"So far." She looked haunted.

"I'm sure that was frightening," the doctor said. "Glad they're okay."

"It's not all okay. Dreams and nightmares feel real at the best of times. Mine felt so real because I woke up in the bathtub, choking... drowning. I'm afraid to fall asleep again. Maybe ever."

"Who drew the bath?" Kallaste asked.

"I suppose I did."

"Somnambulation. Had you sleepwalked before?"

"Never."

"Pardon me for asking, but have you entertained any suicidal thoughts?"

"Homicidal, never suicidal. Why would you ask that?"

"I was wondering about the possibility of post-hypnotic suggestion," Kallaste said, "but you can't make anyone do something while they're hypnotized that they wouldn't do when they were fully cognizant."

"Nope," Shin said. "In fact, I really want to live. I nearly didn't make it last night. Drowning woke me up."

Cahill brightened. "Okay. Staying awake sounds really good now. I don't want to miss a minute. This is history in the making and I've been running on adrenaline. I'll burn out soon, though. My usual drug of choice when I'm coding is energy drinks packed with caffeine."

"Those are terrible for you," Kallaste said.

"Yeah? That's news. I had no idea except for the way it makes my heart pound after the twentieth hour straight at the keyboard. What have they got for us, Doc? Some kind of super soldier drugs to keep us hyper alert?"

Kallaste considered the labels on the medications. "The usual. You might feel a bit super for a while, before the crash of exhaustion kicks in."

"Bennies? Have you got those? I've always wanted to try bennies."

Kallaste nodded. "We do have benzedrine, actually. My compliments to your pharmacist, Agent Shin. Dexamphetamine...Adderall. Nice, but I suggest we try the Ritalin."

"Why?" Cahill asked.

"Always go with the tried and true. When everything else is falling apart, it's important to hold on to something tested and familiar. Vitamin R helped me get through med school."

"Do you have ADHD?" Cahill asked.

Kallaste smiled. "No. It's just that med school is insane. Half my senior class was on Ritalin to get through seventy-two hour shifts in the ER. Same as every med school and law school on the planet. You go to any emergency room anywhere, somebody in a white coat is high, guaranteed."

Shin's phone vibrated and she checked a text. "We've got what looks like another manifestation. It happened three days ago but the LA office found a possible connection to the dead man in France. An agent is dead."

"An FBI agent is dead?" Cahill asked.

"No. A Hollywood agent."

"Ah. The worst kind. What happened to this one? Lose all his teeth and turn into a werewolf?"

Shin frowned. "I have pictures." She turned the phone to show Reddy.

"Send a helicopter and tell the local LEOs it's coming. Fetch the corpse," Reddy said.

"The LA office is all over it. The remains are already ahead of us on the way to Berkeley, sir," Shin said.

"Good. I need solid data. Get the coroner to the lab so she's ready and waiting as soon as the body arrives. The autopsy shouldn't take long. There's not much left to examine."

CHAPTER 23

Berkeley campus
   Last Day

Berkeley was not what Dr. Kallaste expected. The alphabet agencies had taken over an old library building on Berkeley's campus. "Why aren't we on an army base somewhere?"

"My investigation turned up an incident here," Reddy said. "As far as we can tell, the first relevant event occurred in a sleep lab in the basement. It happened April 6, three full days before Dubai. We didn't connect the Berkeley manifestation until the Dubai incident yielded greater contextuality."

"A manifestation in an old library?" Cahill looked elated. "Ooh, this sounds very *Ghostbusters*! Anybody get slimed?"

"Easy, Cahill," the doctor said. "The Ritalin's got you excited."

"The manifestation happened in a lab downstairs," Reddy said. "Professor Cora Danzig was conducting experiments in an isolation tank. Berkeley has several such tanks."

The trio passed pairs of guards, all in camo and carrying sidearms. None of the guards wore any insignia or rank designation, just American flag patches at their right shoulders.

"Apparently the equipment is so heavy," Reddy continued, "the administration chose the old library for Dr. Danzig's laboratory. The floors are reinforced to hold the weight of thousands of books."

"I use a Kindle," Cahill said. "Hardly any weight at all."

"Thank you, Mr. Cahill. You're always so helpful," Reddy said. "I hope you'll be of more aid soon. I have a work station for you in the conference room so you can monitor and report your app's results in real time."

"As long as I'm reimbursed for my time and my app remains proprietary, I'm glad to help."

Reddy sighed. "We thank you for your patriotism, altruism and cooperation."

Cahill shot the agent a sour look. "That's how the government talks when they're screwing you over."

"You didn't serve, did you, Cahill?" the doctor asked.

"Nope, though I did work at a Denny's one summer. Did you serve, Doc?"

"Yes."

"Was it worse than working over a hot grill cooking up grand slam breakfasts and Moon over my hammy?"

"Thank you for your service, Eugene."

Kallaste and Cahill trailed after Reddy through a dimly-lit corridor to a spiral staircase. As they descended into the gloom, the NSA agent looked ill in the pale glow of his phone.

"Why is it so damn dim down here?" Cahill asked.

The disembodied voice of a man answered. "Because bright lights stimulate melatonin. Down here in Dreamland, we do our most inspired work when we're sleepy."

When the trio reached the bottom of the spiral staircase, the silhouette of a lanky man with frizzy, curly hair appeared. "Welcome to Berkeley, gentlemen. Mr. Reddy has told me all about you. I'm Frederick Chambers. Call me Freddy."

Cahill and Kallaste shook the young man's hand as Reddy typed on his phone. "We're told the first manifestation happened here," the doctor said.

"As far as we know," Freddy said, "but I doubt it was the first manifestation."

"Why do you say that?" Cahill asked.

"There's plenty of weirdness in the world. Who knows how long this has really been going on? Is Bigfoot alive? The mountain gorilla wasn't discovered until 1902. Or what about the New Jersey Devil? Is that real? And what's with the big bloop in 1997?"

Reddy looked up from his phone. "The what? What was that last one?"

"The bloop. There are a bunch of unexplained sounds from the ocean's depths. The bloop was a gigantic sound traced to the southern tip of South America. Some say it was an ice quake but many scientists say it had to be organic. If it was a creature, it would have to be enormous. Some even say it's H.P. Lovecraft's Cthulhu."

Cahill's face was shiny with sweat and his eyes were bright with curiosity and Ritalin. "What's a...what was that?"

"Cthulhu! Monster octopus. Could be a dragon or a god," Freddy said, unable to contain his glee. "It's dead but it still dreams. That captures the imagination, doesn't it?"

Kallaste stepped closer. In the dim light, it was hard to tell if Freddy's eyes were red or unnaturally dilated. He was sure the young man was high on something. He wondered how long Freddy had been awake.

Reddy went back to texting. "I can assure you, the New Jersey Devil is not real. Bigfoot is, despite the claims of Sir Richard Attenborough, highly unlikely. Someone would have hit a sasquatch with a car by now if it existed. I don't know about the bloop."

"Okay, what about Marfa?"

"Who's she?" Cahill asked.

"Not a she, man. Marfa is a *where*. Marfa, Texas. Who can explain the lights in the sky over Marfa? That's gotta be UFOs."

"I could explain the lights over Marfa, Mr. Chambers, but it's classified," Reddy said.

Freddy stared at the agent for several beats before breaking into a grin. "This guy! I'm never sure when he's joking but I'm beginning to think it's all the time."

"Please show Dr. Kallaste to the lab."

"Right this way, Doc!" Freddy beckoned as he marched quickly down the dim corridor. "You're going to love it!"

Reddy leaned close to the doctor and whispered. "Keep an eye on him. He's self-medicating." Kallaste nodded but the agent squeezed the doctor's forearm, holding him back a moment more. "Let's try to keep Cahill and Chambers apart. I fear they'll be a bad influence on each other. I don't trust people to whom everything is a joke."

"I heard that," Cahill said.

"You were meant to."

CHAPTER 24

Cancun, Mexico
   Last Day

Coyote sipped the cold *cerveza preparada*, savoring the hot sauce on his tongue. As he looked into the eyes of his two brothers, he wondered if they could believe his story. He'd showed them the fresh wound on his forehead. That was almost all the evidence he had.

"Tell it again," his older brother, Juan, said. "Tell it again, from the beginning."

"It was West of Laredo, just after midnight, when that man put a gun to my head," Coyote said. "The noise from the sky stopped time like a smashed clock."

When he tried to describe the sound, he pictured metal on metal scraping together in a piercing shriek. "Remember those old Japanese monster movies? Godzilla attacking Tokyo? Remember Mechagodzilla? It was like a noise the robot Godzilla might make as he was chewing up a train car. The noise filled the sky."

Juan sat with his arms crossed, measuring every word for the weight of lies. His younger brother, Albert, leaned forward in his seat, wrapt and wide-eyed.

When Coyote told them about the border patrol, they nodded in recognition of the truth. They all knew the occasional excesses of some law men. By the way he shook when he spoke, they were sure Coyote had been through a traumatic experience. The evil that men do surprised none of the three. However, the appearance of the Woman in White was too much for Juan and he said so.

Albert defended Coyote. "You go to church twice a week. Every night, you're on your knees, Juan. Now Coyote tells you one prayer got answered and you want to piss all over it?"

Juan appeared unmoved. "Tell your story again. I need to hear it again. Then I will decide what to do."

Coyote took a deep breath. "When the metal sounds came, she appeared above us. She floated in the air, maybe thirty feet above the ground." He pointed up, as if he could still see the woman in her long flowing dress. "As soon as I saw her, I shouted, '*Madre de Dios!*'"

"*Madre de Dios,*" Alberto echoed.

Juan's eyes narrowed. "But she was a white woman in a white dress?"

"*Si*, and beautiful like an angel."

"Go on."

"First, the pistols got steaming hot. Every officer squealed and shouted as they dropped their weapons. The man who hit me? I saw his gun hand. The pattern on the pistol grip was burned into his palm."

"What did you do then?" Alberto asked.

"I saw the steam rising from the pistol. It had just been pointed at my head a second before," Coyote said. "I would have picked it up but it just got hotter. It glowed red, as if it had just come out of a smelter. His weapon *melted*. The sand around the barrel bubbled and turned to glass."

His brothers looked to each other but said nothing. "What then?" Albert prompted.

"The lady in the sky said nothing. I knelt in the dirt and stared up at her with one eye. The other was covered in blood but I didn't even think of it. I just stared up at her. I felt no pain then. Just...safety. Strange safety."

"You weren't afraid?" his oldest brother asked.

"Not of her. The sounds from the sky made me want to wet my pants, but she saved me. I'm the only one who saw everything. My group was already on their knees and when they saw the lady, they shoved their faces in the dirt and prayed louder than I've ever heard anyone pray in church. My group, they were moaning and shouting to God."

"And the bad men?" Albert asked. "Tell us about them again."

"Each suffered a different way. The one who would have touched the young mother went down. He tore at his own face with his fingernails. He pulled out his own eyes, screaming the whole time. It was as if his fingers were not his own. The worst was...he turned away from me, as if to show the men he came with...."

"What?"

"He dropped his pants, reached between his legs and...he tore himself."

"I'm not sure — "

"Like papa used to do with the rams, but without a knife. With his bare hands, he did it."

The brothers stared, horrified. "No one can do that," the oldest brother said. "I mean, it's theoretically possible, I suppose, but — "

"I saw it."

"What did the lady say?" Juan asked.

"Nothing. The noise from the sky kept grinding, on and on, like some kind of huge eating machine whose jaws did not work right."

Juan rolled his eyes. "Mechagodzilla. Right. You said that."

"I said it all before. You're listening for me to change my story. Nothing has changed. I know this is hard to believe — "

"No. I *want* to believe," Juan said. "We both want to believe you have changed. But you are my brother. I know you."

"What then?" Alberto asked. "What happened to the other men? Tell us that."

"The young man collapsed in the dirt but he did not pass out. He writhed like a snake caught in a trap. That's when the officer in charge spoke up. He yelled up at the Woman in White. He asked for mercy. He crossed himself and kept doing it, in case once wasn't enough, I guess."

"Catholic?"

"Must have been. Maybe. I don't know. Maybe after seeing what happened to the first man, instant conversion."

Albert chuckled but one hard look from Coyote cut his laughter dead.

"The man in charge said the young officer was just one bad apple. He said there were six more good officers who'd done nothing wrong. That's when I yelled. I told her there were no good men among them. I told her how they had all laughed at us when we begged for mercy."

Juan's gaze bore into Coyote, daring him to foul a single detail.

"The officer in charge went next. A wind came up out of the East. The wind howled and it seemed to be...this sounds crazy...the wind seemed to be *aimed* at him. The dirt was kicking up hard at him and sticking to him in clumps. Not for me or the others. I was not ten feet away but all I felt on my cheek was a soft warm breeze."

When Coyote closed his eyes, he could still see the man turn to sand. The officer's legs went first. He fell to the ground. Once his legs transformed to sand, the wind whipped his limbs away. The officer tried to pull himself toward his truck by his elbows but he was a sand sculpture before he got twenty feet. Then he was dust in the wind, sifting away to nothing.

Coyote couldn't describe the horror of that to his brothers. It seemed too strange to give voice to, so he didn't try. Not that the rest was any easier to believe.

"The other men tried to run to their trucks. They didn't get one step closer to their vehicles. One turned to glass. That one became a statue. It sounded like it hurt. He stared at one outstretched hand, screaming. For a moment, I could see his insides — the organs, I mean."

"But you said it was dark, right?" Juan asked.

"He stood in the headlights. He had just enough time to know death was coming. When the noise from the sky hit again, he shattered."

"Jesus!" Albert said. "I wish I'd seen it."

"No," Coyote said. "No you don't." A single tear slid down his cheek. He took a gulp of his beer and knuckled the tear away.

Juan's face softened. "Take your time."

"Another man burst into flame. He started running. That one sprinted flat out and fell down into the gully behind us. He set fire to some bushes as he rolled down the hill."

Coyote paused, gathering his thoughts. "The largest man among them fell to his knees and clutched his heart. Maybe that wasn't the doing of the flying lady. I think he saw the impossible and his heart stopped from seeing it. Maybe. I don't know. My heart was hammering pretty hard, too."

"And no one else saw this?" the oldest brother asked.

"Like I said, they had their faces in the dirt, crying and praying."

"Good Catholics all." Juan counted on his fingers, making sure Coyote had not forgotten a detail. "What happened to the last two?"

"One shot himself in the head. I don't know if the lady made him do that, either. Could be, he was just being sensible. He might have seen that he was probably next in line, marked for death."

"That leaves one more by my count," Albert said.

"Swallowed. He sunk into the ground like he was on a slow elevator to hell. He cried out for Jesus to save him as he went down. Then the ground filled his mouth and he was gone. No trace. All that was left was his hat, his cell phone and his gun. The pistol was still steaming when the angel disappeared."

Coyote sat back in his chair, sweating profusely. When he looked up into his brother's faces, he knew the older one thought he was a liar and a poor one at that. His younger brother believed every word.

"That was the last group I'll ever take North. They went on to Phoenix. I drove a Border Patrol Jeep to get back. Then I got a plane ticket and came straight to you."

"And now," the oldest brother said, "you want a job at the hotel. You don't need to tell a story like this, you know. We are your brothers. We'll find you a place but, after so many years as a coyote, are you sure this is the place for you?"

"Brother," he replied. "I have endured a lot. I know how to suffer. I can stand on my feet for hours and not complain. I can go without sleep and keep working. I can serve the tourists with a smile and they will never know what I really think of them. I can make less money and I won't think a life of service is beneath me. I need no thanks and I need no one to like me. My long walks are over."

Juan sighed. "Good. I can get you a job. Nothing fancy but steady."

"Thank you. You'll never regret it. I swear." He reached for his dirty old backpack. As soon as he got a place, he would shove his pack into the back of a closet and never use it again. He was home to stay.

Juan stood and touched Coyote on the shoulder. "I can get you that hotel job but take me seriously about this. No one will believe you. They'll take you for a drinker and a liar or worse. Never tell that ridiculous story again."

Alberto nodded. "Sounds harsh, but Juan is right."

"Of course, I am. The hotel manager won't appreciate a man with imagination as we do, Coyote."

"Coyote is dead. We must bury that name. I am Raphael again and for the rest of my life."

He stood. "One more thing, though." He pulled something from his pack. "We should bury this where it will never be found, just like its previous owner."

"I will never tell this story again, but I don't want my brothers to think I'm a liar." Raphael held out the dusty brown hat of a United States Border Patrol officer.

CHAPTER 25

Berkeley campus

Last Day

Piles of boxes filled the library basement's darkened corridors. "Please excuse our mess, Mik," Freddy said. "Since the feds moved in, they brought a lot of boxes."

"What is this stuff?"

"Food and some medical supplies mostly, I think. They seem to be planning for a siege. New guards show up and they don't leave. They hang out upstairs and play a lot of poker. It's all Defcon 1 down here but they keep a low profile on campus. Don't want too many questions asked, I guess."

"What do you do here, Freddy?"

"Grad student. Neurophysiology now but, before I'm dead, the university will have a faculty dedicated solely to psychonautics. I'm going to be in charge around here someday."

"Is that what brought you to Berkeley? Psychonautics?"

"World domination later. I'm writing my masters thesis on formalizing edibles now."

"Come again?"

"The problem with edible medical and recreational cannabis is the variable potency. A pot brownie in the same batch can be mild or it can put you on one of Jupiter's moons. Find a reliable way to standardize the dosage and there will be a lot less drama about edibles. The transition is inevitable. We're going to have dispensaries everywhere. Edible marijuana sales are going to push back the limits of human consciousness. We'll explore our true potential. Like Aldous Huxley said, 'Dream in a pragmatic way.' A brave new world isn't far off."

"I see."

"You're a cynic, aren't you?"

The doctor shrugged. "I'm a skeptic. And wasn't *Brave New World* a dystopia?"

Freddy smiled. "Maybe the so-called problem is the solution. You ever think of that?"

Kallaste shook his head. "Anyway, as far as drugs go, I don't even drink so — "

"Apples and oranges, doctor. Edible marijuana is the most underrated psychedelic. It's processed differently when digested instead of inhaling the smoke. Eating it is much more powerful than a joint but safer than just about anything. I could be researching mushrooms but the government propagandists would get people worried about confusion with poisonous toadstools. Marijuana is the way forward. With work like mine, libertarian liberation will come sooner."

"Okay. Is that what you're high on now? To stay awake?"

"Nah. Weed makes me sleepy and quiet and thoughtful. I went with a heavy stimulant."

"What drug are you on?"

"I'm using the same drug the government packed in soldiers' rations in World War II."

"Coffee?"

Freddy gave Kallaste two thumbs up. "Bingo! I am so high on caffeine right now, I've got the nervous system of a squirrel. Pardon my chatter."

"How many espressos can you do in a day before you burn out?"

"Greek coffee is a finer grind so the caffeine content is higher than espresso. If I get too jittery and my nerves can't take more, I'll switch to caffeine pills and see how far that gets me. I'm supposed to talk to you about being my candy man if I need to switch to heavier drugs."

"You know what's happening when people fall asleep. Take it seriously."

"Yeah, I know. I've seen it. Strange and dangerous things go bump in the night. Step into the office and I'll show you where the first known manifestation occurred."

A desk and two chairs almost filled a small booth. An ECG, EEG and an intercom rig sat beside a computer with a microphone stand and recording equipment. Through the booth's glass, Kallaste peered at four huge isolation tanks.

"You ever see *Altered States*, Mik? William Hurt played the scientist who was also kind of a dick. In the movie, he sort of turns into a monkey but not really. Remember that?"

"Never saw it."

"Too bad. That movie got me interested in this research. Never thought we'd break through Huxley's doors of perception this hard or this fast."

"Doors of perception?"

"Yeah. 'There are things known and there are things unknown, and in between are the doors of perception.' That's Huxley. If he was alive, I'd tell Reddy to get him on our team. When you're out to save the world, you should have a philosopher on the case. You guys will have to settle for my genius."

"Okay."

"You laugh — "

"Only on the inside, deep down."

"Nice. But this whole thing started like a scene from the movie and I was right here at the beginning. The incident here was nothing compared to Tourtour! Reddy forwarded the French zombie footage to us. Did you see it yet?"

The doctor nodded.

"That got kind of George Romero, didn't it? This thing is much bigger than one mind getting blown in an isolation tank. This is, like, global."

"So...were you the first victim? In one of these isolation tanks?"

"Hello, Dr. Kallaste. Agent Reddy told me you were coming." A middle-aged woman stood at the door. She wore a blue lab coat with the sleeves rolled up. She stood on crutches, her legs wrapped in white bandages. Red scars, both thin and thick, wound through her exposed skin. Her face was a roadmap of pain. "I'm Cora Danzig. I prefer not to be thought a victim, please. Also, you called my pretties, 'isolation tanks.' I prefer the term Lilly tanks or flotation vehicles. We're striving to reach beyond the stigma and preconceptions of the isolation tank cliches."

"Pleased to meet you, Dr. Danzig. Call me Mik."

"Cora." Danzig gave her assistant a sour look. "And please, Freddy, *Altered States* was 1980. Let's move beyond those cliches, too."

Kallaste made an effort to stare into Danzig's eyes. He didn't want to seem like he was staring at her scars. "Flotation vehicles?" he asked breezily. "That's new to me."

"Psychonauts fly through the Mindscape, Mik. Until recently, I never crashed. It seems we are not so isolated in those tanks, after all. Something else is out there waiting for us. I think the entity attacked me so I could not dismiss the experience as a mere hallucination."

"I don't understand."

"Neither do I, really. I had an experience in the tank. The room is soundproofed so Freddy didn't hear me screaming. I couldn't seem to get to the intercom but I found the alarm button eventually. When Freddy pulled me out, I was bleeding to death. The water had turned to glass shards."

"The water in the tank?"

"The water in the Mindscape. I was dreaming lucidly. Everything was fine until it was not. I believe this was a warning, sending us a message that there are dangers, even in the Psychonautic Sea."

"Psychonautic Sea?"

"The Collective Unconscious. I've also used the term Twilight Zone though, after my experience, I see that was disrespectful and flippant. Some call it the *Unus Mundus*. It's where our consciousness goes when we dream."

Freddy crossed his arms and leaned against a wall. "Psychonautic Sea is also the name of the boss's next book. I prefer Mindscape." He turned to Dr. Danzig. "I still think you should rethink that title, Cora."

Kallaste sensed tension between them and pressed on. "So what you experienced...the glass...it was confined to the dream, right?"

"The glass was in the dream, yes. The effect was not. If a shard had penetrated half an inch to the left instead of the right, my femoral artery would have been cut. If not for Frederick's assistance and the EMTs, I would certainly be dead."

"So maybe your experience wasn't a message."

Danzig raised her head. "How do you mean?"

"Whatever it is, it almost killed you. You don't kill the messenger if you want the message to get out."

Freddy nodded vigorously. "An experiment gone awry. Or an accident. This could be a benign force that doesn't know what it's doing, yet."

"It told me clearly it was coming for us," Danzig said.

Kallaste scowled. "Us? Us who?"

"At the time, I took it to mean everyone. The threat was clear. The voice told me it was coming. Freddy dubbed the enemy The Voice, capital T, capital V. Freddy is...colorful."

"I'm sure Cora means to say I'm the genius who saved her life."

Before Cora could reply, Freddy's phone made a sound like a sonar ping. Reddy's voice came over the device. "I have evidence of the enemy here. Please join me in the conference room, Freddy. Dr. Kallaste and Dr. Danzig? I'll need you, as well, of course."

"He knew we were all together," Kallaste said. Then he patted the pocket that carried the phone the NSA agent had given him. "Oh."

"That's Big Brother and Santa Claus for you, man," Freddy said. "Always watching."

"My goal, Mr. Chambers," Reddy answered, "is efficiency."

"Huxley said the second worst enemy of life is total efficiency," Freddy said.

"What was the worst?"

"Total anarchy," the grad student answered. "If you look around, that's pretty much what we've got now, anyway."

Reddy sounded annoyed. "Please show Dr. Kallaste the way to the conference room now. I have a concrete manifestation and the victim was not asleep this time. The effect may be growing as we waste time."

"C'mon," Danzig said. "This way. Mind the boxes." She lurched forward deftly, accustomed to her crutches.

"Do those crutches hurt your hands?" Kallaste asked.

"Oh, a bit. But the pain keeps me awake. I'm not ready to go back into the tank. Not for quite some time, I suppose."

The doctor almost tripped over a box in the dim hallway.

"I am sorry about that, Doctor. I keep the lights too low. It's my vanity, really."

"What do you mean?"

"I find people stare less in subdued lighting. I asked Frederick to turn off most of the lights."

"He said something to the effect that the lights were low to decrease the secretion of melatonin so sleep experiments could be conducted."

"My face looks worse in the light, that's all. Frederick, you're sweet to protect me. I won't be the one in the tank for the next incursion into The Voice's domain. I hope my scars don't discourage the next volunteers."

"Who are they bringing in to go into the flotation tanks?" Kallaste asked.

"Some kind of psy warfare squad is on the way," Freddy said. "They better be tough to deal with what the Voice can do in the Mindscape."

"In the Psychonautic Sea, if you please!" Danzig said.

"Yeah, that's never going to catch on, Cora."

CHAPTER 26

Berkeley Campus
 Last Day

Under a bright white light, a skeleton lay face up on the conference table on a black plastic sheet. A blood-spattered green tie was still knotted around the blood-flecked neck bones. The tie was the sole article of clothing left on the meatless corpse.

Freddy took a chair far from the body, leaned back, put his feet up on the table and crossed them. "*That,*" he said, "is ridiculous."

Kallaste, Danzig and Cahill stood staring at the gleaming skeleton.

"The tie around the cervical spine draws the eye," Reddy said, "but look closer at the bones."

They all leaned closer. Whatever attacked the skeleton had picked the bones clean.

"There's not even much soft tissue left at the ligamentous insertions," Kallaste said. "There's so little connective tissue left, the joints have mostly fallen apart. It's as if the body was dropped in an acid bath, but those marks...."

"There are pits in the bone," Danzig said. "Even at the vault of the skull and the femur where the bone is thickest and hardest."

Kallaste pointed to the rib cage. "See there? It looks like the sternum was sawed in half. There are marks up and down the anterior of the spine...did they use a hacksaw, too?"

"Gross," Cahill said.

Reddy read from the notes on his phone. "This is the body of a late middle-aged man named Dennis Flanagan. His nickname was Desi. He was a Hollywood agent. He was killed three nights ago in the backyard of his home."

"Only three nights ago? That doesn't seem credible," Kallaste said.

"Like the French village wasn't credible," Cahill said. "You saw it with your own eyes."

"The way the world works is changing, Mik," Danzig said. "Adapt or look foolish playing by the old rules."

"I'll make a note to expect surprises."

"What is that green tie about?" Freddy asked. "And have they found the rest of him?"

"LAPD investigators have interviewed his maid, his gardener and several clients so far. The deceased always wore a green tie. It was his signature look in his business dealings. Several people of his acquaintance said they'd never seen him without a green tie."

"Whoever did this," Freddy said, "knew about the green tie thing. Why kill someone so thoroughly and leave the tie on? It's a message that this was a bad guy and that the killing was personal. A vendetta. Bet the guy deserved what he got."

"Dude!" Cahill said. "Harsh!"

"Agreed but solid reasoning on the personal vendetta," Reddy said.

Freddy pointed at his head. "Told you. Genius. I used to watch a lot of *Law & Order*, too."

"Anything else, Sherlock?" Cahill was used to being the smartest boy in any room and was feeling pressure to perform.

"Well, he was a Hollywood agent whose last name was Flanagan."

"So?"

"So what Irish guy named Dennis calls himself Desi? Sounds like a douchebag move."

"Frederick, please," Danzig said. "The man is dead. It's bad luck to try to bury a person's reputation deeper than the body."

"This guy was a Hollywood agent and Dufour was a director. They both died in weird, inexplicable ways." Kallaste said. "What's the connection? These guys obviously had an enemy in common. Find the connection and you've got whoever is behind this."

"We thought of that, of course," Reddy said. "The FBI has explored the commonalities and they believe that is a dead end. There are other factors I'm not permitted to disclose at this time which lead us to believe there is a larger force at work."

"Larger force? You mean a terrorist network instead of, like, lone wolves?" Freddy asked. "Are we talking homegrown terrorists? Or something embarrassing, like somebody we already let out of Gitmo?"

The agent said nothing.

"How can we help if you don't give us all the data?" Cahill asked.

"It's an issue of national security. Only those who need to know, need know. I'm sorry. If that aspect appears relevant, I will disclose it. For now, let's focus on using what we've got to track the culprits."

Kallaste's jaw was tense. "You said this man wasn't asleep at the time of his death. How can you tell that from a pile of bones? Looks to me as if the poor guy was devoured by piranhas."

"I have more than the body," Reddy said. "I have video." He used his cell to turn on a monitor and replay a surveillance recording.

The team sat at the table. No one looked at the skeleton. The screen showed a man beside a patio set in grainy black and white. There was no sound. The NSA agent fast forwarded through the recording until he got to the time stamp he was searching for.

The man poured himself a drink while a small dog disappeared among the bushes in the background. A moment passed without incident. Then a flock of savage birds struck. For a moment, they appeared to lift Dennis Flanagan off the ground.

The assembled gasped in horror and disbelief. Everyone but

Agent Reddy stood, their gaze riveted to the surveillance footage. The black shapes of the creatures appeared to take the form of the man. When they parted, the white skeleton collapsed to the concrete. The man was obliterated.

"Flayed, filleted and flushed," Cahill said.

"I know, right?" Freddy said.

"How do you know he was awake?" Kallaste asked.

"He looks awake," Reddy said.

"Everyone here appears to be awake," the doctor replied, "but without looking at your brainwaves, I couldn't really say for sure."

Before Reddy could reply, the agent's phone buzzed. He picked it up and frowned as he scrolled through a message. "Cahill? Have you got anything new and useful from your app yet?"

"I've been searching keywords like 'nightmare,' as you asked. The journals are lighting up. So far, scanning through, I've got 427 instances of fire imagery. That's the only common denominator I've noticed so far."

"Twenty-seven minus four equals twenty-three," Reddy said. He appeared to be speaking to himself.

"What's going on, Mr. Reddy?" Danzig asked.

"There's a new phenomenon." The agent turned his phone to the television and activated a news feed from CNN. The view, shot from a circling helicopter, was a live feed from Rio de Janeiro. The famous statue of Christ the Redeemer was on fire. As it burned, Reddy tapped at his phone screen. "*Hmph.* It's made of concrete and soapstone and yet it's burning like a house on fire. It defies logic."

"It defies physics," Kallaste said. "No doubt it's weird but what does it have to do with falling asleep and — "

"Wait for it," Reddy said.

The camera view switched to a long shot from down the mountain. Throngs of people marched toward the burning statue. It seemed everyone had a cell phone held high to record the miracle. Some laughed. Most cried. Many screamed. Fear and celebration and confusion sifted in equal parts through the mob.

Then the crowd all came to a halt and went silent. They bowed their heads. Some swayed for a moment. A woman in the crowd collapsed to the ground but no one moved to help her.

Ours is the army of the night. In Darkness Visible you will learn your plight. You will bow to us in dream's dark flight.

Danzig paled. "Did...did you hear that?"

The parade up the mountain continued, ignoring the fallen woman at first, then trampling her as people began to scream and shout and run.

"I don't think I heard that," Kallaste said. "Not with my ears."

"Telepathy," Cahill said.

"I heard it in English," Reddy said. "Others are receiving the same message but in their native tongues."

"'Ours is the army of the night. In Darkness Visible you will learn your plight. You will bow to us in dream's dark flight.'" Cahill recited. "What's it mean?"

"A cryptic warning?" Kallaste suggested.

"No," Danzig said. "Just before I was attacked in the Psychonautic Sea...I remember that phrase now. The army of the night. It's — "

"It's a declaration of war," Reddy said.

"How are you going to keep this a state secret, G-man?" Freddy asked.

"Despite our best efforts, we've lost containment. I can't connect with my section chief but this is out now. It appears our operational security might be in jeopardy."

He didn't mean to be funny but Cahill and Freddy burst out laughing.

The NSA agent closed his eyes, took a deep breath and held it a moment. As he exhaled, whispered to himself, "A collection of curiosities...a chain of mountains...a chain of events."

CHAPTER 27

Berkeley Campus
  Last Day

As the mob made its pilgrimage up the mountain, it halted again and the message was repeated. Reddy looked at the timer on his phone. "Twenty-three seconds." He did not look surprised.

"This is a disaster," Kallaste said.

"Oh, I don't know. It might not be all bad," Freddy said. "Maybe the world needs a burning statue to bring people to Jesus. It'll do wonders for Rio's tourist trade, if nothing else. Think of all the candles and Jesus bobbleheads they'll sell. I don't know what to make of that message but a little poetry — "

"No." Reddy muted the television. "This will go badly."

"I can think of several ways off the top of my head this will go *horrifically*," Kallaste said.

"Name one," Cahill said.

"Suicide cults who will act now because they believe burning stone is a symbol for the end of days, for one example."

"I'd predict an increase in the murder suicide rate when

psychopaths take this as a symbol that religion is over," Danzig suggested.

"This will precipitate hate crimes against people of non-Christian religions," Reddy said. "Riots will begin when people start looting and hoarding food in preparation for whatever apocalyptic scenario comes next. This will put quite a dent in the global economy."

"Really, Mr. Reddy?" Freddy asked. "You're worried about the *economy*?"

"One-fifth of the world's suicides are linked to unemployment, Mr. Chambers. More unemployment means more people die. Worrying about the economy means I'm trying to prevent bloodshed, too."

"Oh."

"Love, peace and hope doesn't motivate people as much as fear," Kallaste said. "We fear loss more than we aspire to gain. Every day I help people who are dealing with some kind of stress. Lost sleep isn't a problem. It's a symptom. We should be going to sleep when the sun goes down and getting up with the dawn. That's how our bodies are designed. Cave people stayed out of trouble because they didn't try to move around in the dark. We've become beings who understand and interact with the world through screens. It's not healthy and it's not going to stop. Our bodies are at war with our minds. We stay up longer and work longer hours while our lives are slipping away."

"Easy, Doc! What does all that have to do with Jesus burning in Rio?" Cahill asked.

"It matters because this is another confusion, a distraction. People are alienated from meaning and meaningful work. They aren't getting enough rest and security and play. We're already overstimulated. A statue on fire is more stress. You don't think that particular statue on fire for all to see will cause more problems? I guarantee you, there are a bunch of white guys watching the news right now who are going to get the same message from that image as they would from a burning cross. There will be a revival in the KKK today and hate parades tomorrow. Plus a threatening telepathic message for anyone who turns on the TV? End times talk will bloom."

The conference room went quiet as their gaze settled on the skeleton.

"I'm getting sleepy," Reddy said, more to himself than to the others. He looked deep in thought as he took a dose of dexamphetamine and washed it down with a drink from a water bottle.

"We're going to have to go public and tell everything we know, Reddy," Cahill said. "People are already having night terrors. If we can give them some sort of explanation — "

"We don't know enough to give them an explanation yet," Danzig said.

"We could explain away the burning statue," Freddy suggested. "Call it a magic trick and tell them the stone was soaked in kerosene or something."

"No," Kallaste said. "We have to find a way to stop these manifestations and bring the world back to its usual level of weirdness. Stop it and let this die after a news cycle or two. If we can stop this shit quick, it'll be a footnote on somebody's conspiracy blog."

"We can't go back to the status quo, Mik," Freddy said.

"I agree with Freddy," Cahill said. "Apparently, we have more faith in people."

"People believe what they want to believe," Kallaste said. "A few years ago a crowd believed the sun was rising in the West. They called it a miracle. No one turned around and spoiled the fun by saying, 'Hey, I think that way is East, actually.' Nobody checked a compass. They didn't look into solutions because they wanted a miracle, not another damn day where they have to get up and go to work and accept there is no magic in the world."

"There's magic now," Cahill said.

"You give one sad example — " Freddy said.

"I have others. Remember how so many pop icons died young in 2016? So many people died young and not so young. They dropped, one after another, because of drugs, illness and age. People talked as if there was some grand conspiracy. Unfortunately, people die young all the time. When something seems unusual, weird explanations start getting cooked up. A lot of people take Groundhog Day seriously, as if a rodent really can predict the weather by looking for its shadow. Mark my words, humans will kill each other because that statue is in flames. Somebody's toying with us."

"We need to interview witnesses to these manifestations," Reddy said. "Dr. Kallaste, please come with me. Dr. Danzig and Mr. Chambers, please continue your preparations for our guests. They should arrive shortly."

"What do you want me to do?" Cahill asked.

"Scan your app and watch the news. If you can make any connections between dreams and what happens on CNN, please let me know immediately."

"Why do I get the feeling I'm on the B Team, warming the bench?" Cahill asked.

"I assume that question is rhetorical, or is that an invitation to hurt your feelings? I'm unclear." The NSA agent left the table without another word to Cahill. He beckoned Kallaste to follow.

"Mik, I've got a living witness we need to talk to. I know you aren't a psychiatrist, but I want your impressions — "

"You want my medical opinion about whether she's crazy or not?"

"That would be fine. Whatever she claims to have run into, it wasn't the disembodied voice that cut up Dr. Danzig. This encounter happened in Wisconsin and she says she saw a face amid all these...shenanigans."

"You call all this, 'shenanigans?'"

"Until I can find a more appropriate word. Something more dire will present itself shortly," Reddy said. "Something apocalyptic, I'm sure."

"I'm not sure of anything anymore."

"I know what this is about now," Reddy said.

"What is it?"

"Like I said, it's war. It's a war that's been going on for some time now. I'd hoped it would stay cold. The opposition is heating things up."

"Then we're done, right? Can I go home?"

"Please stick around. Help is on the way. They'll be here any minute. In the meantime, we'll gather more intel and it's good to have another doctor around to manage the medications."

"And in case of emergency. You're expecting the worst. Are you going to tell me who we're fighting?"

"You wouldn't believe me."

"I'm getting more flexible about what I believe by the minute. Tell me."

"When I'm sure you need to know, I will."

CHAPTER 28

Berkeley Campus
   Last Day

Two guards stood on either side of the double doors to a large storage room. Much of the dim room was thick with dust. Shelving had been pushed aside. A line of bunk beds stood along one wall. A dozen people milled about, speaking to each other in hushed tones. Everyone turned to look as Reddy and Kallaste entered. The crowd fell silent.

"Jennifer Daimler?" Reddy announced. "I need to speak to Jennifer Daimler."

A young black woman in scrubs sat up and swung down from a top bunk. She stalked toward Reddy. "You better have a damn good excuse for flying me across the country with no notice. Me and a lot of people here."

"You want answers," Reddy said.

"I do."

"So do we. Please, come with us."

"Hey!" a large man rushed forward. "What about me?"

"I'll interview you in due course, Mr. Evans."

"Due course? When's that?"

"In the fullness of time."

For a large man, Evans moved with surprising speed. He grabbed Reddy by the collar and pulled him close as he raised his fist. The guards moved forward, snapping out their telescopic steel batons.

Reddy held up a palm, signaling the guards to stand down. "No need for violence. Mr. Evans will wait his turn like everyone else."

"I need to get back to my family. You people gave me something and now I can't sleep and the drugs make me shake. What the hell is going on?"

"None of us can sleep," Kallaste said. "It's for your own safety."

The guards raised their batons but Reddy waved them off again. "No. Mr. Evans will not hurt me."

"Why wouldn't I?" the big man snarled.

"Because you're an intelligent man who runs a garage repairing transmissions. You are on edge because of the injections we've given you. All these people have had the same injections and they haven't resorted to violence."

"I'm built different, maybe."

"If you lose your temper, these men will knock out your teeth and give you a concussion. Then I'll go back to my office, wash your spittle off my face and make a phone call to the IRS. By later today they'll be auditing your business for the last five years. If you're truly worried about your family, Mr. Evans — "

The man let go of Reddy and steamed back to his bunk.

Reddy smoothed his lapels flat. "Ms. Daimler, this is Dr. Mikola Kallaste. Would you both follow me, please?"

"Are you Miss or Mrs. Daimler?" Kallaste asked.

"Call me Jen. Jen's fine."

They shook hands.

Once they were outside of the big man's earshot, Jen couldn't contain her admiration for Reddy's tactics. "That was pretty smooth how you took the wind out of that guy's sails."

"I've played that card before. No one is particularly afraid of the NSA. They feign outrage at what we do but most people don't hear from us and we work in the background. People are reminded about the IRS every April and they're hated. Tax collectors make strong people weak in the knees and spine."

Daimler quirked an eyebrow at the doctor. "Can somebody tell me why I have to be here? The drugs keep us from sleeping but we're exhausted and irritable. People chattered at first but mostly they just yawn and wish they could sleep. I'd sleep but I'm too wound up."

Reddy stepped into an office that held nothing but a beat up filing cabinet, three chairs and a steel desk. "I'm sorry to inconvenience you. School attendance among elementary age children dropped sixty percent yesterday. It's as if a flu epidemic is sweeping across the States. Parents are calling the children in absent but they are not citing the flu."

"What are they blaming?" she asked.

"They aren't. I suspect most parents are too embarrassed to say their children are experiencing night terrors. Or, perhaps, they're too tired to go to school because they're too scared to sleep."

Kallaste nodded. "No way my mother or father would have excused me from school because I thought there were monsters under the bed. I was often tired, especially as a teenager when I was going through a growth spurt. Exhaustion never got me out of going to class, though."

"It's monsters I want to ask you about," Reddy said. "Have you seen one? Or more?"

"Yes," she said. "One is a woman who dresses in white. She's real. And the horses were real, too. The other is a big thing in black armor."

"Horses? What's that about?" Kallaste asked.

"Horses caused property damage in Fox Point, Wisconsin a few nights ago," Reddy said. "This woman...how old would you say the woman was?"

"No older than twenty-three, I think."

"Twenty-three. Of course."

"Excuse me?"

"Don't mind me. I find the number twenty-three reappears often.

It's an artifact. My late father used to call it my bad penny that keeps turning up. Some people ascribe the number special numerological significance. I suspect it is a symptom to the wary that reality is a holographic program running in the background. It's one of the seams with loose stitches that we can find if we look for it. Reality is coming apart at the seams, you might say."

"Sure," Kallaste said. "That's not a crazy idea at all."

"That was sarcasm, I think. Amusing." The agent attempted a grin and failed. "The black thing in armor. Did it have any distinguishing features around the head?"

"You mean the horns?"

"I do."

"How did you know?"

"Apparently, this is an old enemy," Kallaste said.

"Old enemy, new tactics," the agent replied.

"What I've learned from hanging out with Agent Reddy," Kallaste said, "is everything I think I know is wrong."

"There's the world we see and there's what's really going on," Reddy said. "Twas always thus."

CHAPTER 29

Berkeley Campus
   Last Day

Reddy opened a file drawer and pulled a cell phone from a plastic evidence bag. He fiddled with the device and turned it on. "I would have called you in earlier, Ms. Daimler, but this phone had to travel through several back channels to arrive here. Bureaucracy is one of our enemies, too. Getting this piece of evidence released to us took more time than cracking the owner's passcode."

The agent selected an app and a video played. They heard anguished screaming. Reddy hit pause and turned the phone so they could see the screen. "Do you recognize this person?"

The video was blurred and shaky but, for a moment, the camera captured a woman in a long flowing white dress. She floated in a starlit sky.

Jen did not hesitate. "Yes. That's her."

"You're sure?"

"Yes."

"Thank you."

"Do you know who she is?"

"We've run her through facial recognition programs, both photometric and geometric. No luck yet."

"Good luck with that. Can I go home now?" Jen asked. "How about I call you if I see the Woman in White when I take a nap?"

"I think it would be best if you stayed with us in case she contacts you again."

"I don't know why she would."

"We don't understand why she contacted you the first time, so she might."

"I think she was lonely. She was quite a talker. You brought me all the way out here to identify the Woman in White, right?"

Reddy nodded. "I'm relieved there appears to be only one Woman in White."

"I hadn't considered that there would be more than one," Kallaste admitted.

"Mik, why don't you take Ms. Daimler down to the cafeteria for coffee and breakfast? I'll move you to more comfortable accommodations as soon as I can arrange it. You'll be working with Dr. Danzig. Please stay with Dr. Kallaste until we can work out those logistics. How do you feel about not taking any more drugs to keep you awake?"

"I'd love it. They make me feel like crap."

"Good. And just decaf for you. Sleep when you can."

"Wait. You *want* her to fall asleep? Why?"

"I know why," Jen said. "You want me to talk to the Woman in White again."

"And the being with horns, if possible, but I think we have more to fear from the monster in armor than the mystery woman."

Kallaste began to object but Jen waved him off. "It's fine. The Woman in White is a nightmare bitch but we're not going to solve this by doing nothing."

"I have something else I should show you," Reddy said. He backed up the recording and showed the entire video. It began with a man mutilating himself with his bare hands.

"This surveillance footage was downloaded and edited together from two of the Border Patrol cars' dashboard cameras. Presumably, they had planned to erase the recording before they returned to base. This is pretty grainy but we picked up some new data points that are relevant. Watch what happens."

The deaths of the three Border Patrol officers they could see made Jen and Kallaste cringe. The demise that was clearest was that of the man who turned to glass. He stood in front of the vehicle, lit by headlights and directly in front of the dash cam. At the edge of the camera's view, a man burst into flames and ran past the group of Mexicans. The burning man disappeared behind the group. The glow of his immolation outlined the people on their knees. Most of the border runners were face down in the dirt. Their pitiful screams were muffled but no less harrowing.

"They're terrified," Reddy said, "but it's not the Border Patrol that scares them anymore. The man on fire is somewhat distracting as he runs through the shot." He rewound the recording. "This time, watch the baby."

As the human torch ran past, the flames briefly lit the baby as it shuddered in its mother's arms.

"The kid looks like it might be convulsing," Kallaste said.

"Yes," Reddy said, "or having a nightmare. This next bit I didn't put together until I saw the entire recording."

"Don't be coy," Jen said.

Reddy stopped the recording and pointed to the glow of firelight behind the Mexicans.

"I've seen that before," Jen said.

The doctor squinted at the screen. "What?"

Reddy pulled out a stylus and pointed to the screen. "As the child convulses, see what rises into the light for a moment. See that silhouette?"

"A deer?" Kallaste ventured.

"A monster with horns," Jen said. "He calls himself Cord."

"There's another reason I've singled you out among those who have witnessed manifestations, Ms. Daimler. We managed to pick up the parents and child from this group in Black Canyon City, Arizona. They brought the child to a clinic."

Reddy showed them a picture from his phone. The image showed a baby with a white symbol that took up most of its back.

"Is that a burn or a tattoo?" Kallaste asked. "I've never seen a symbol like that."

"It's the same as mine," Jen said.

"What?"

"I've got that symbol on my back. I didn't know it until I came here. Agent Reddy insisted on blood tests and a full physical. I didn't know it was between my shoulder blades until a nurse took a picture of it and showed me." A single tear slipped down her cheek before she could wipe it away. "I got it from Cord."

"You didn't even feel it?"

"Nope."

"How long could it have been there without you knowing?"

"Since I met the monster, I suppose. Looks like Cord is looming behind the baby. I saw that symbol on the thing's gauntlet in my dream...nightmare, I mean."

"Our top semiotics team is in New York. They specialize in understanding such images. They think it's a representation of a lock and key."

"The monster said it was the symbol of his house. I'm to be his slave. I told him that wasn't going to happen. Until I found out about this mark he tagged me with, I thought I'd gotten out of the nightmare without being branded."

Kallaste yawned and rubbed his eyes with both hands. "This is too sick. There has to be a way this makes sense — "

"Mik," Jen said, "when I turned twenty, I got a summer job delivering flowers. The only hitch was the flower shop's delivery van was a stick shift. I couldn't drive stick. When I said to my father that I was nervous about it, his answer was, 'Hardly anybody drives a stick shift, anymore.'"

"Yeah, I'm not being helpful. Sorry. It's reflexive. This is so crazy."

He turned to Reddy. "Why don't you have real experts on this instead of turning to us?"

"Because the best people for the job are already recruited. That task force is in New York working on this."

"Who are they?"

"They're the ones who have been fighting the war against the monsters, until now. They've met Cord and his kind before. He's already killed a lot of people. Given the chance, he'll kill again."

Kallaste looked from the agent to Jen and back again. "A guy in black armor with horns who attacks people in their sleep — "

"Not a guy," Jen interrupted. "Never think of it as human. It isn't." She trembled with fear and anger. "It was a monster. I haven't believed in monsters since I slept in onesies and worried about them in the closet or under the bed. This is the real shit, man. Serial killers, ISIS and Rush Limbaugh's got nothing on this thing."

CHAPTER 30

Berkeley Campus
Last Day

"Please, go next door to the cafeteria," Reddy told them. "I hope to have more news for you soon. All your questions will be answered when I get clearance."

The agent watched Kallaste and Daimler leave. He rose, shut the door behind them and turned the lock. Back at his desk, he fast forwarded through the Border Patrol footage.

From the incident report, Reddy had a diagram of how the cars were parked and where the bodies were found. The directions were marked with a compass and, though Reddy found such details extraneous, measurements between the remaining bodies had been taken at the crime scene. Several Border Patrol officers were missing and Reddy expected they would remain so. The video had not shown all their fates.

On the screen, Reddy watched the part of the video he had not shown Kallaste and Daimler. The Mexican man who'd been hit with a flashlight drove off to the South in one of the Border Patrol's Jeeps. The rest of the group scattered to the North.

For a few moments, only one man was left in view of the dash cam: the blind and castrated man in the sand. He was still alive and bleeding profusely. Perhaps he'd heard his Jeep's engine still running. He crawled toward the camera, each movement an agony. In his last moments, he must have thought he could call for help or use the shotgun in the Jeep to kill himself. He was denied that privilege.

Halfway to the car, a dark figure rose out of the firelight and smoke from the burning gully. Reddy slowed the progress of the recording until the display was in slow motion. The thing that emerged from the half-light was the monster as Jen had described. Until she saw the picture of the brand between her shoulder blades, she'd told no one about the thing that looked like a demon. The armored monster had antlers, much like a deer. On its right hand, the thing wore a clawed gauntlet. Some kind of metal skirt hung from its waist. Cord's belt was an ornate chain with heavy links and silver medallions — war medals, perhaps. In one giant hand, the monster held a long sword that gleamed in the headlights.

Reddy had read reports from New York. He knew of the previous attempts at cross-dimensional invasion. Most of the top secret reportage had been vague and couched in euphemisms, jargon and abbreviations. Reddy had seen the messages from Brooklyn, increasingly intrigued. He'd seen footage of flying blue demons under fire from chain guns. Surveillance video showed red demons running through what looked like a church courtyard. He'd even monitored satellite coverage as a small town in Iowa exploded. However, Reddy had never seen a monster drive a sword through a man's torso so hard that he was pinned to the ground where he lay.

Like a butterfly pinned to a cork board, he thought.

The Woman in White disappeared from the Laredo video footage. Reddy could find no further trace of her. It seemed it was she who had stopped the Border Patrol's bad deeds from continuing. He watched with growing trepidation as he observed the monster from two angles.

Jeep headlights illuminated the carnage as the horned monster fed on the Border Patrolman. The blind man did not stop screaming immediately. The monster's head jerked forward and back as it hurriedly gulped down long strips of flesh. Like grizzly bears, apparently the enemy had no scruples about eating its prey before death. It just began to feed, dead or not.

Reddy ticked off the crimes he'd witnessed on his fingers, as if he could count the cost of immeasurable suffering. Multiple inventive murders, exoculation, castration, flaying, vivisection...mercilessness.

And those very evocative horns. Abomination on top of abomination.

Thomas Reddy was not a religious man. However, he didn't wonder why the Choir Invisible called them demons. Cord looked like the devil himself.

An untruth of summoners...a damning of jurors...a tissue of lies...a host of angels...a baptism of fire.

CHAPTER 31

Berkeley Campus
> **Last Day**

The small room that served as a cafeteria was nothing more than a makeshift kitchen. Someone had stacked flats of water bottles five feet high on either side of the door. A kettle sat in the corner beside two huge coffee urns. A tray of instant meals and assorted pull tab cans of fruit sat beside the sink.

"MREs," Kallaste said. "I hate them, except for the peach cobbler."

"You've had this stuff before?"

"Oh, yeah. Lots of calories. Half of one bag is too much unless you're exercising really hard. What can I offer you, Jen? Oatmeal? From what I see here, a can of peaches is the best choice."

"Peaches it is. Who do you think the Woman in White is?"

"I don't know."

"She looked like she was saving those people."

"In the most terrible way possible. She's no hero."

"But she's not the mastermind, either. She defers to the monster. Calls him Big Daddy."

"From that video, she doesn't look like a terrorist. A lot of useful idiots get sucked into terrorism, though."

Jen stopped eating, her plastic spoon halfway to her mouth. "What do you think a terrorist looks like, Mik?"

He paused. "Um. I don't know. You know...."

"Brown? Is that what you meant? Because she's a pretty young redhead in a happening prom dress?"

"No, that's not what I meant. Are you enjoying making me squirm?"

"Yes, but I'm also concerned your first reaction was that a nice-looking white girl couldn't be a terrorist."

"I think I'll let you talk for a while and wait for you to screw up and offend me in some way," Kallaste said.

"Can't wait."

"What did the Woman in White tell you?"

She related every detail of riding the horse through her neighborhood. Then she related everything between the time she blacked out and woke up in her hospital's ER.

"Sounds like a power move," the doctor said. "Petty intimidation. Do you have any enemies, Jen?"

"Nope. Everybody loves me except an ex-boyfriend, but that's no thing. And I'm not sure it was a power move. She might be lonely. She definitely wanted to show off."

"Really?"

"There was something weird about the encounter...besides it already being off the charts weird, I mean."

"Well, at least she didn't set you on fire. With the Woman in White, dreams cross over into our world and become reality."

"Next time I see her, I'll know I'm in a dream. That will put us on more equal ground. Since I woke up, I've been reading about lucid dreaming. Recognizing that you're dreaming is half the battle."

"Can you do it?"

"Not yet. Haven't been able to sleep much. Then a couple of FBI agents showed up at my work and they wouldn't let me sleep."

"All dreams seem so real, it takes a lot of practice to dream lucidly.

Not everyone can do it."

The doctor's cell pinged and Reddy's voice came over the speaker. "Please go to Dr. Danzig's lab. The tank team has arrived. If they're successful, we won't need Ms. Daimler to be a sacrificial lamb."

"I thought I was a stalking horse," she said. "And how did he know we're together?"

"He gave me the phone so he could eavesdrop and know where we are at all times," he said.

Reddy sounded irritated. "I told you, Mik, it's about efficiency. Finish your breakfast."

"When this is all over," Kallaste said, "I'm moving into a Faraday cage in Colorado. I'll dispense weed, nap anytime I want and I'll never touch a phone again. I'll go off the grid, sleep in a hammock under the stars and forget all this stuff. The world is already complicated. We don't need secret wars and conspiracy theories turning out to be true."

"Really?" Jen asked. "You think you can stuff the cat back in the bag?"

"Nah. That's probably the Ritalin talking. It gives me lots of good ideas but I don't act on them when the stuff wears off."

"You should write the good ideas down."

He made a face that told her he wouldn't be acting on that suggestion, either. "Let's go meet the cavalry."

"Yes," she said. "A heavy dose of helpful deus ex machina would be great right about now."

Kallaste gave her a warm smile. "Since nothing has worked so far, things are bound to turn around, right?"

"That theory is disproven by the millions of gamblers who go broke and have to hitchhike home from Vegas, but sure. Tell yourself that. Bound to turn around."

"Sure, I'm a laugh-in-the-face-of-Death kind of guy."

"Are you?"

"No. More of a chuckler. I chuckle in the face of certain Doom."

In awkward silence and growing dread, they finished their peaches.

CHAPTER 32

Berkeley Campus
   Last Day

Captain Harrison Frist stood in Dr. Danzig's lab with the air of a general surveying the battlefield. He was a craggy man in his late fifties, tall and rigid. His buzzcut was silver. Frist wore fatigues but he would have looked like a military man in yellow plaid on a golf course. Two of his men stood at ease behind him. They did not look relaxed. The only patches on their fatigues were the American flags on their shoulders and their last names stitched to their chests: Rodriguez and Huff.

Dr. Danzig limped around the tanks, checking the temperature of the water, testing the saline content and confirming that the intercoms worked correctly.

In the observation booth, Freddy lazed in his chair. His stretched out his long legs with his bright red sneakers up on the desk. He wore headphones and occasionally said, "Check one, two. Check one, two, three," as Danzig lurched from one flotation tank to the next. Freddy smiled wide at Frist. The captain glared back.

"She's on crutches. Shouldn't you be in there and let her fly the desk?" Frist asked.

"Dr. Danzig doesn't trust me with the water chemical checks. I'm color blind."

Reddy strode in. "Captain Frist? We spoke on the phone."

Frist did not smile as he shook the agent's hand. "You're Reddy. I know. I wish I was."

"You wish you were what?"

"Ready."

"Ah. I see."

"You must have heard that one before."

"Forty-six times, yes. Why do you feel unprepared?"

"We'll make do. We lost two people getting here."

"I was not informed."

"I didn't want to advertise it. Two of my best remote viewers, one man and one woman. They must have fallen asleep on the plane."

"Lots of people fall asleep on planes," Freddy said. "How were they — "

"My people are trained to plug into the *Unus Mundus*, Agent. The enemy found them there. My man tried to open the door and go for a walk at 30,000 feet. The other stormed the cockpit and tried to crash the plane. We almost went down in Iowa. We had to restrain them."

"How are they now?" Reddy asked.

"Private Duncan is catatonic at a hospital in Frisco. The other tried to go AWOL as soon as we got back on the ground. He's out of my unit and on his way to the stockade." Frist rubbed his jaw. "The man had a good right hook but the woman damn near broke my ribs with a spinning heel kick."

"Did they say what they saw?"

"No, but the woman said a word you should know."

"Tell me."

"Ba'al. Does that give you a feel for the dreamland we're navigating?"

Reddy took a deep breath and let it out slowly. "I've had other clues that pointed me in that direction."

"Makes the *Unus Mundus* a hellscape."

Each man's phone buzzed. Frist and Reddy turned their backs as they read their messages. When they turned back, both looked grim.

"New York?" Reddy asked.

"The Brooklyn base," Frist said. "I trained most of the people in that Remote Joe unit. All dead. Six of them, all good people. They were targeted. No one else on the base was hit."

"Who died?" Kallaste asked. Jen peered around his shoulder as they stood in the doorway.

"A group of remote viewers," Reddy replied.

"These people have clearance?" Frist asked.

"The way things are going, clearance won't matter soon. I need everyone to know what I know in this regard."

"It's aliens, isn't it?" Freddy stood. "Lemme guess! It's the Elohim as described by the ancient Sumerians! Giant superior beings came to Earth from a distant planet, sowed their seed with our DNA when we weren't much more than monkeys. Then, *whammo!* Now they're back and looking to take over. Changing the laws of physics and taking no prisoners for the New World Order that's going to shake out our shit! To quote Al Pacino, *Hoo-ah!*"

Reddy and Frist stared at Freddy, nonplussed.

Undeterred, Freddy clapped his hands and gave a double thumbs up. "The Illuminati lizard people who really run the world are about to lose their power. Am I right? I bet I'm right!"

Kallaste sighed. "Freddy, if you're going to be a pioneer for stoners, you're really hurting the cause. Agent Reddy, what is really happening?"

Reddy looked around the room. "Aliens."

"*Ha!* Called it!" Freddy crowed.

"Aliens, sort of," Frist added.

"We have been aware of these beings for a long time," Reddy said. "They are not from outer space. They're from another dimension."

"Inter-dimensional travel, like in that bad Indiana Jones movie!" Freddy scowled. "As if galactic overlords invading from outer space wouldn't be bad and badass enough!"

"The aliens have attempted numerous incursions into our dimension. They have an army. It is called the Darkness Visible. Until recently, they could only break through in ones and twos and small groups."

"They came through with several platoons in Iowa once," Frist said.

"Twenty minutes ago, our base in Brooklyn was hit. I believe the aliens are taking a new tac to influence events in our dimension."

"It's like Pearl Harbor and 9/11 only we're the sleeping giant and we're *still* asleep. They're getting at us from inside our skulls," Freddy enthused. "Digging through the ole brainpan. Skullduggery, is what it is! Skullduggery!"

"Freddy," Kallaste said. "You've had too much caffeine. Shut up."

"I would, Skipper, but around here, I'm the Gilligan. Can't stop the alien invaders from coming for us in our sleep!"

"Given what's happening in Rio and Micronesia, they don't just kill us in our sleep, anymore," Reddy said.

"But in our sleep is where we'll launch our counterattack," Captain Frist said. "That's where we can find them and get at them. Doors to the *Unus Mundus* swing both ways. We have to take the fight to them."

CHAPTER 33

Berkeley Campus
   Last Day

Kallaste turned to Reddy and Frist. "How do you plan to counterattack exactly?"

"I'm not a physicist, but I've scanned the summaries," Reddy said. "To attack us, the aliens create a rift in the energetic walls between dimensions."

"The way it's been explained to me," Captain Frist said, "it's like each plane of existence is on a different frequency, like on a clock radio. We share the same time on the clock but their plane of existence is on a different frequency from ours. If you tune to the spot on the dial between stations and the frequencies mix a little, you can hear two radio signals at the same time through the static. That's when they cross the rift. It's difficult, it's not stable and it doesn't last long. That's the *Inter-dimensional Physics for Morons* version."

"Freddy is high on Greek coffee and exhaustion," Kallaste said, "but essentially, you're saying aliens are out to get us and you've dealt with them before."

"Not us personally," Frist said, "but some of my people were assigned to play recon as part of the New York task force. The aliens have changed tactics. This is turning out to be more successful than their battles with the Choir Invisible."

Jen elbowed the doctor to make room in the doorway and peered into the small control room. "What the hell is the Choir Impossible?"

"Choir *Invisible*, Ms. Daimler," Frist said.

"You know me?"

"I know things," Frist said cryptically. "I understand you're on Agent Reddy's team. Once we nip this in the bud, I'll expect you to forget everything we discuss here."

"I have a non-disclosure agreement for you to sign," Reddy said. "Let's skip the formalities and get to it, shall we, Captain? Given that Ms. Daimler is the only one who has seen the enemy's avatar and reality as we know it is falling down, I see no further advantage to keeping anyone here in the dark. We're all on the same team."

"Yeah!" Freddy stood and cheered. *"Go Team Human!"* When he took in their stony faces, Freddy sat back down in his chair and pretended to fiddle with dials.

"Very well," Frist said. "Choir Invisible is the code name for the international strike force tasked to repel inter-dimensional incursions. Its members have unique talents and abilities for this type of warfare. Conventional means won't do the job."

"The Choir is assigned to keep said invasion attempts quiet so we don't stagger into a new normal," Reddy added. "The old normal has glitches and problems, but it works better than an enemy from another dimension conquering us. We definitely don't want a new normal."

"You sure?" Freddy asked.

Reddy gave him a forbidding look. "Quite sure, Mr. Chambers."

Freddy grinned. "But if everyone knew we were under attack, I'd stress less about my credit card bill. Humanity would come together and — "

"Those in charge are not so optimistic, Mr. Chambers. The aliens will invade and take all our resources given the chance."

"Ooh," Freddy said, "I wish you'd said the monsters are coming for our women. That would have been retro-cool and funny."

"Why isn't the Choir Invisible here?" Jen asked.

"They're working the problem from their end," Frist said. "We'll do what we can from here. Their focus is on kinetic action plans."

Kallaste gave Jen a wink and spoke in a stage whisper. "The captain means we're the nerd squad and the Choir Invisible kicks ass."

"You said Jen has seen the enemy's avatar," Kallaste said. "That's the Woman in White. Why does the alien need an avatar to attack us?"

Frist cleared his throat. "The physics wiz in New York has a theory. We know it's difficult for the aliens to crawl into our plane of existence. When they try to come through the rifts, the passages between us and them are quite temporary. The rifts are difficult to establish. Otherwise, they'd just send one or two aliens through at a time until their army filled the Midwest. We think the aliens have found a susceptible person and given them unusual abilities."

"Superpowers, you mean," Freddy said. "Agent Reddy show me and Cahill a clip of her ripping through some Border Patrol fascists. The Woman in White is like, Dr. Doom, or something."

"We prefer the term KBFO, for Kinetic Brainwave Fusion Operative," Frist replied. "For that they need a useful idiot. They've found an idiot and made her a traitor."

"To do what?" Jen asked.

"To keep the channel open," Frist said, "to keep the rift stable. Instead of getting an alien army through an inter-dimensional tunnel for an invasion, they're wreaking havoc by attacking us through the *Unus Mundus*. They're softening us up. The avatar would act like an anchor — "

"Or a hand on the radio dial," Reddy added, "keeping the clock radio tuned to the channel between dimensions."

"*Mm.* Cool. Entering dreams and performing telepathy and telekinesis sure sound like superpowers to me," Freddy said.

Frist sighed. "To put the problem in layman's terms, thoughts are things. Thoughts precede our greatest accomplishments. Thought creates our most formidable weapons. When remote viewers get to work, we tap into an altered state we call SABA, the See All, Be All. We access this specialized brain state by entering what we call the *Unus Mundus*. That is our destination. There we can interact with the alien forces, interdict and repel."

"*Unus Mundus* is too weird," Freddy said. "Sounds like the Latin term for, 'guy with one ball.'"

At this, Huff and Rodriguez smirked. Still, they said nothing and stared, eyes forward.

"I call it the Mindscape." Freddy said.

"That's a bunch of jargon," Jen said, "but you're talking about harnessing the power of the collective unconscious, meditating your way into it, I suppose."

Everyone looked surprised.

Jen frowned. "What? I've read a few pop psych books. 'Thoughts are things,' sounds like it could be lifted right out of a dozen self-help books. That's Deepak Chopra, isn't it?"

"I was thinking that bit was from *Nemo*," Freddy said.

"Why didn't you tell us about the aliens before?" Jen asked. "I thought I was crazy seeing that...thing."

"We weren't sure all these events were even related," Reddy said. "It was possible this was a different enemy. There are multiple dimensions. We don't know how many."

"*Whoa*," Freddy said. "Mind blown! Are we enemies with everybody? Well...why should it be different anywhere else?"

"We've got multiple tactical issues to work out," Frist said. "One of my remote viewers who was attacked while in the dream state named the enemy specifically. I have a soldier in a catatonic state who only repeats one word."

Freddy sat up straight in his chair. "Hodor? Tell me it's Hodor!"

"Ba'al."

"So...I'm not clear here," Kallaste said. "Is that the name of the alien race, like saying the alien leader is Klingon? Or is that like one monster leader's name or — "

"Ba'al is the leader of the Ra," Frist said. "They're...well, all you really need to know is, if they can find a way to eat us and take over, they will."

Cahill pushed his head between Jennifer and the doctor. His skin was shiny with sweat. "Reddy! You better come to the conference room. I have...news."

"Very well," Reddy said. "Captain Frist. You have preparations to make, I presume?"

Frist nodded. "We'll get hooked up and set up with Dr. Danzig's Lilly tanks after we go through our hypnotic induction sequence."

"Good. Mr. Chambers will assist you and Dr. Danzig. Mik? Ms. Daimler, please join me in the conference room."

Freddy called after the agent, "Sure you don't need me?"

The NSA agent looked over his glasses at the young man. "I don't think we should be in the same room together, Mr. Chambers. People may confuse our names. We wouldn't want that. People don't pay attention, you know."

"Oh. Okay, dude."

"Also, if I stay in the same room with you much longer, I might ask Captain Frist to shoot you."

"Oh...okay."

"That was a joke."

"I know."

"But with serious underlying intent that you calm down."

"I get it."

"Good. I just wanted to be sure...."

"Sweet Baby Jesus Christmas! You're an alien, too, aren't you? Earth humor!"

As Reddy left, Dr. Danzig finished the preparation of her equipment. She opened the door from the tank room. "Okay, what did I miss?"

"Hm. Where to start?" Freddy said. "Nah...it's too much. To sum up, aliens from another dimension are invading our dreams and making bad shit happen, Cora! Is that hella cool or what?"

"You want me to shoot your assistant, ma'am?" Captain Frist asked. "It *did* come up in the meeting just now. From what I've seen, it may be the only way to shut the bastard up."

CHAPTER 34

Berkeley Campus
    Last Day

Reddy pulled out a chair at the conference table for Jen. "Please, Ms. Daimler."

"What about the people in the storage room?"

"You're the only one carrying the alien's brand. I'll interview them when I need to but right now, you're our most likely conduit to the collaborator if Captain Frist and his team miss the mark."

"I don't know how else I can help unless the Woman in White contacts me again. Maybe I should just go have a nap and hope for a meet up. Not that I can really sleep with all that's going on."

"Please stay awake a little longer. I want to hold you in reserve," the agent said. "I'm hoping the Remote Joes will lead the charge so you won't have to make contact."

"Make contact? Is that a euphemism for tearing me apart with weird birds?"

"With the attacks on the remote viewers, it's apparent the enemy knows what we're up to. We're all in danger now, awake or asleep."

"That doesn't make me feel better at all," Cahill said.

"No, it shouldn't. Intelligent people are more prone to anxiety. To remain mentally healthy and optimistic requires some degree of delusion."

"There might be a depressing compliment buried in there somewhere," Cahill said. "Let's hope Captain Frist's people can locate the Woman in White. This could all be over soon."

"Are you being dumb and optimistic?" Jen asked.

Cahill smiled. "If I'm being dumb, I probably wouldn't know it, would I? Now...can we get back to me and my news? Having a nervous breakdown here!"

"Please proceed, Mr. Cahill," Reddy said.

"Here's the deal. Something big is coming and it will happen tonight." He pushed a button several times on his laptop to increase the volume. "Here's a piece of the recording I picked up."

Cahill hit the space bar. The computer's little speaker made the words tinny and harsh but the message was clear enough. A man's deep bass said, "You have twenty-four hours before we come for you. If you believe in gods, bid them farewell for none can save you. Soon you will pay for your defiance and selfishness. We come to feast."

Reddy crossed his arms and chewed his lower lip. "That's all?"

"Isn't that enough?" Cahill asked.

"That does sound discouraging," Kallaste said.

"Wait till you hear this." Cahill clicked the laptop's mouse and the same message was repeated by a woman with a high voice. He clicked again and the message was delivered by what sounded like a young girl. The next voice had the crack of a teenaged boy entering puberty.

Reddy interrupted Cahill's demonstration. "Stop. Are there are any different messages?"

"It's the same, except for a detail at the top — "

"How do we know when the twenty-four hours starts?" Kallaste asked.

"All these voices were recorded at the same time in Los Angeles. Midnight last night! That means midnight tonight is zero hour! We're talking doom in *this* time zone. *As in the one we're in!* Shit! Why couldn't it have been Nebraska? Who'd notice?" Cahill typed rapidly on the keyboard and clicked the mouse once more. "Listen. It's the whole message."

This time, it was a choir of voices speaking as one: "We are Ba'al of the Ra, Commander of the Darkness Visible. You have twenty-four hours before we come for you. If you believe in gods, bid them farewell for none can save you. Soon you will pay for your defiance and selfishness. We come to feast."

"How was this recorded?" Kallaste asked.

"Well...that's the thing. You know how I said I had a sleep journal app?"

"He doesn't just have a sleep journal app," Reddy said. "He has a sleep monitoring app where you place the phone by the bedside. The microphone records your movement to gauge your sleep quality through the night. These recordings are from the app."

"Wait," Jen said. "The recordings are *stored*?"

Cahill reddened and gave a slight nod. "Um. Not all of it exactly. With data compression, I — "

"Do people know their recordings go beyond their phone?" Jen asked. "My god, how much sex do you record each night? You're bugging people's bedrooms — "

"I'm not doing anything illegal," Cahill said.

"How can that be legal?"

"It's all in the terms of service when they buy the app."

"How many pages is your TOS?" the doctor asked.

"Look, if people don't read and just click agree, that's not my problem."

"Nobody reads those things," Kallaste said.

"They clicked 'agree!' Look, you guys are getting all judgy but this is the way the world works. Ever use Google Earth? The National Geospatial-Intelligence Agency is Google Earth's largest customer. The US military and various intelligence units use the same maps you use to navigate to the grocery store and back."

The doctor turned to Agent Reddy. "Now I understand why he's here."

"Not just because I'm a funny guy who looks remarkably like a fat George Clooney?"

Reddy shrugged. "I could have scooped the information but time was of the essence. It was easier to bring Mr. Cahill into the fold. Time seems even more important now. We have a hard deadline. At midnight, I expect either a full scale invasion or...who knows what? Mass mind invasion, perhaps."

"If they can burn Christ the Redeemer in Rio, they could set fire to anything or anyone," Kallaste said.

CHAPTER 35

Berkeley Campus
    Last Day

"Maybe they'll set fire to us and then eat us," Cahill said. "I don't want to die as some alien monster's barbecue."

"Do all the aliens have horns?" Jen asked.

"There are several varieties that we know of," Reddy replied. "Have you ever seen classic illustrations for *Paradise Lost*? Think demons and monsters. They are carnivorous."

Cahill appeared more pale and even sweatier. He whispered, "Demons! Monsters! *Cannibals*," to himself. "God!"

"I don't think you could properly call them cannibals," Reddy said. "They aren't of our species. Predatory would be more accurate —"

"Demons?" Kallaste said. "Really? C'mon."

"Well, I'm sure they don't think of themselves that way but they do have horns. My contact within the Choir Invisible tells me that if Ba'al's army breaks through a stable dimensional rift, we won't be at the top of the food chain anymore."

"And now they've given us an ETA for their invasion," Jen said. "They must feel pretty confident."

"The truly fascinating thing about these beings is that they may have walked among us for a long time," Reddy said. "We believe they are responsible for some of our legends. Minotaurs, monster sightings, demon possession...it's all a rich historical and mythological stew."

"Demon possession?" Kallaste glared at the agent. "You can't be serious."

"Yeah, we're deep in *X-Files* territory now," Cahill said. "Agent Reddy? You play Mulder. Looks like Mik has dibs on Scully's skeptical role."

"Sorry, but a demon taking over a person's body for nefarious purposes is a bridge too far for me."

"Casting out demons is biblical," Cahill said.

"Lots of crazy stuff is biblical," Kallaste replied. "We've learned about the workings of the brain and figured out seers have schizophrenia. Most people with social problems, like killing others, have neurochemical imbalances."

"There are antecedents in religion and folklore that proved relevant in our covert war with the aliens," Reddy said.

"I put my faith in neurology, the DSM V, psychiatry and...I'm sorry. I'm getting whiplash from all the cognitive dissonance. I'm a subscriber to *The Scathing Atheist* podcast, for God's sake!"

Jen let out a burst of laughter. "For *God's* sake?"

Reddy cleared his throat. "I've seen recordings of the aliens in battle. Regular bullets don't work. According to the Choir invisible, our ammunition must be blessed three times before it's effective. Consecrated earth and holy water burns them."

"Holy shit!" Cahill said.

"I don't know if the task force set up to stop the aliens has experimented with sacred excrement, Mr. Cahill," Reddy deadpanned. "I do know the Choir Invisible uses blessed swords in combat to kill the alien invaders. Some kind of paranormal component is at work that we don't understand."

Cahill looked shaken. "If we survive this, I might go back to church."

"From the research, it appears any church will do," Reddy said. "The alien physiology is burned and repelled by holy objects, holy water and consecrated dirt, but it doesn't seem to matter what denomination of spiritual person does the blessing."

"This could explain a lot of really bad horror movies," Jen said.

The NSA agent nodded. "Historical antecedents could be the root of modern fiction, yes."

"I love horror movies, especially the cheesy ones," Jen said. "Maybe I'll look at them a little differently now. *The Exorcist* just got scary on a whole new level. Imagine something evil taking over your body for real and making you do things."

"Are there werewolves, too?" Cahill asked Reddy. "Should we stock up on silver bullets?"

"No, Mr. Cahill. To my knowledge, there is no such thing as werewolves."

Kallaste's mouth was a thin hard line. "But if the aliens — "

"Demons!" Cahill said.

"Fine. If the demons have been around that long, why are they a problem now?"

"Perhaps their earlier forays were reconnaissance for a later invasion," Reddy said. "They might have been curious about us for ages but mass migration across dimensions wasn't a possibility for them. They seem to be expanding their efforts."

Kallaste threw up his hands. "But why now? We're obviously so different, why do they want to come here at all?"

"The Choir Invisible reports that the stability of their environment is askew. Ba'al sees expansion of his empire to our dimension as a reasonable solution."

"Stability of their environment?"

"Floods, fires, natural havoc."

The doctor stared at the agent for a beat. "You're saying we're being invaded because monsters from another dimension aren't dealing with climate change well?"

"In fairness, neither are we," Reddy replied. "I take it the aliens are a little farther down the road with their disaster. In any case, an invasion and expansion of Ba'al's forces here would be sub-optimal."

"We're at war and almost nobody knows it," Cahill said, "Out there, students are finishing exams, walking around campus, moving back home, wondering if their first love in college will still love them in September. Somebody's falling in love today. Someone's shoveling shit to get to pay day and someone else is sweating over a bad quarterly report, worried about making deadlines and getting fired. How much of all that will matter tomorrow? God, I need a drink. There are so many liqueurs I haven't tried because I worried they'd make me fatter. Screw Weight Watchers!"

Reddy checked the clock on his phone. "It appears we have about sixteen hours left, if Ba'al is to be believed. Let's hope the remote viewers can track down the Woman in White. We might be able to shut down the invasion from this end of the dimensional rift. If the Remote Joes are successful, Mr. Cahill will avoid the downfalls of alcoholism and can continue to worry about his diet."

"When you put it that way," Cahill said, "saving the world hardly seems worth it."

"Thank you, Mr. Cahill," Reddy said. "We cherish your ability to keep the situation in hand and in perspective."

"You're a funny guy when you try, Mr. Reddy."

"I sensed an opportunity to lighten the mood and it seemed like an appropriate time to be jovial, given our grim circumstances."

"And now you've killed the moment."

"If Mr. Zuckerberg had invasive sleep monitoring apps, I would have chosen him for my team. Sadly, he's still focused on data collection through social media scraping."

Cahill smiled. "Too bad you need me so bad."

"Mr. Zuckerberg was not available, in any case. He knows about the coming invasion and is hiding with his family and entourage in an underground bunker in Iceland. Our operational security is quite lax, it seems."

"Word is spreading?" Kallaste asked.

"There was a small leak from the Pentagon. Rumors are rife throughout Washington. I fear that no matter how many whistle-blowers we shut down, the panic will soon spread everywhere. The Nikkei Index has taken a hit and I shudder to think what the Dow Jones will do today."

"The message said to say goodbye to our gods," Cahill said. "I haven't prayed for a long time but maybe this is a good time to get reacquainted."

Jen gave a wan smile. "My mother said that if you don't pray when things are going well, don't bother when you're hanging by your toes over an alligator pit."

"I say, go for it," Kallaste said. "People have relied on deathbed confessions to save them from the pit for centuries. God doesn't mind coercing hypocrites, apparently."

"But you won't be praying with me?" Cahill asked.

"I'm a doctor. That's my only religion. In weak moments I play the lottery. I have a rabbit's foot hanging from my rearview mirror. It wasn't very lucky for the rabbit, though, was it? You be superstitious. I'll hope for the best. I think it's all the same in the end."

"Never thought I'd have to go to war. But we're all drafted, aren't we?" Jen sat forward in her chair, her head in her hands.

"The Remote Joes are the pros," Kallaste said. "Let's let them do their stuff."

CHAPTER 36

Berkeley Campus
   Last Day

Kallaste sat beside Freddy at his monitoring station in the booth outside the flotation tank room. Captain Frist, Huff and Rodriguez had stripped down to their underwear. ECG and EEG sensors glowed blue on their chests and heads. The hatches to the tanks stood open and ready.

"I remember when sensor leads were all wires, suction cups and adhesive clay," the doctor said.

Freddy slid the doctor a sideways glance. "Gee, Grandpa. What was the world like before wi-fi?"

"I'm only thirty-six," Kallaste said.

"Li-fi is going to blow you away."

"What's that?"

"It's what comes next after wi-fi. Connection at the speed of light. When those aliens come through, I don't think the war will last long. They're gonna dig our fish tacos and tech. Peace will be made when we show them how to make alien porn. Our tech is evolving so fast, it's a revolution that will short-circuit the war. No way our world falls apart now. Things are about to change all at once. To guys like Reddy, change is the enemy. I can't wait! Everything is going to work out. You'll see."

"You've heard everything?"

"Man, I'm the original know-it-all."

"Then read the room, Freddy. The general mood is that if the Remote Joes don't come through, we're screwed."

"That's why I want you to remember this conversation. When the moment comes, you'll call me a genius. I'll say I told you so and Agent Reddy will finally understand how silly and paranoid he is."

"Until then, we're at war."

"Maybe Frist will meet the aliens in the Mindscape and work out a peace agreement right now. We give them some resources so they can live and we learn more about the way the universe works. What do they use for power? How are they crossing into our dimension exactly? I'm sure there is plenty of valuable information to exchange."

"From what Agent Reddy said, we're dealing with monsters, inside and out."

The grad student let out a derisive chuckle. "Reddy's with the NSA and Frist is deep Psy Ops. What do you expect them to think? In every war, we demonize the other side."

"Freddy, the other side actually *do* look like demons."

"Yeah, well...maybe we'll learn so much about quantum physics, we'll soon be making trans-dimensional phone calls. By combining the diversity of cultures, we'll get stronger. Soon, what we'll be able to do, between their knowledge and our science, will look like magic. Think it through. We could learn how to explore the possibilities of life in many more dimensions. That's worth a little war, if you ask me."

"How many lives would you exchange for new facts? Who gets to die to satisfy your curiosity?"

"Easy, man. For one thing, don't pretend all lives are worth the same. Secondly, cross-dimensional travel could solve a lot of our problems and save generations of lives into the future. Suppose we find an empty dimension to throw our trash into, for instance? Or vent our pollutants somewhere it won't hurt? What if we step into another dimension to escape our sun when it explodes? All you see is war. I see immense potential. Everyone resists progress until it's the new normal."

"Our mission is to keep the old normal."

Freddy didn't appear to hear the doctor at all. "Maybe we'll even be able to export Kanye, the Kardashians, Nickelback and Congress to another dimension. You're a smart guy, Mik. Open yourself to more possibilities."

The doctor sat back in his chair and crossed his arms. He stared through the booth's glass at the remote viewers. Eager to change the subject, he said, "I didn't realize Captain Frist was going into a tank, too."

"They are two Remote Joes down so Frist said he had to enter the breach. When they're set, they'll climb into the tanks and I'll check their signal one more time before we go to radio silence. I'm not supposed to talk to them when I go back in. Just close the hatches and shut up. I don't think Captain Frist likes me very much. Too bad. I kind of like him. When they make a movie about this, he should be played by Sam Elliott."

"What are they doing now?"

"Prepping. They're taking so long, I've had to boost the heaters a bit to maintain the temp. Frist wanted to leave the tanks open so Huff and Rodriguez can go straight into the tank when they're done the voodoo they do."

"What is their prep exactly?"

"Let's eavesdrop." Freddy leaned forward and flipped three switches. "The tank microphones are hot."

Though the tank hatches stood open, Captain Frist's instructions to his men were fuzzy whispers in the control room's sound system. The words were unclear but Frist's speech had a compelling cadence, as if his induction was not just about the words but the way he said them.

Kallaste leaned close to the sound system's speaker, straining to hear more. "Almost sounds like he's singing to them."

"You ever hear throat singing or get high listening to a didgeri-doo?" Freddy asked. "Reminds me of a beat like that. It's cool but I can't dance to it."

Rodriguez looked glassy-eyed, as if he was staring into distant nebulae. Huff's eyes were closed.

"I heard them chanting something at the beginning, just to get into an astral plane sort of mood, I guess," Freddy said. "When I want to visit an astral plane, I eat some weed and put on some James Taylor."

"What was it like? The Captain, I mean, not James Taylor."

"Frist started off his speech louder, like an old-time preacher. As his orders went on, his voice got softer."

"I feel way out of my element here. I'm a sleep specialist. Reddy should have recruited a pharmacist and a shaman."

"Once we perfect Dr. Danzig's studies and go deeper into my work, all this mumbo-jumbo won't be needed to get to higher states of consciousness. We'll just suck on a lollipop with the right mix of psychedelics. If the government hadn't panicked and shut down the LSD experiments way back, it would be us invading the alien dimension instead of the other way around."

"I think it would be better if everybody just stayed in their own dimensions and tended to their business," Kallaste said. "You sound pretty happy about all this chaos. I feel like I'm witnessing Hitler getting ready to invade Poland."

"Dude! Everybody loves chaos. If we didn't love it, we wouldn't have it. We watch the news to get upset. We invite drama into our lives. Bad boyfriends and evil exes mean better cocktail chatter. Fear means more adrenaline pumping through our veins. Writing mean *Yelp* reviews translates to sweet dopamine hits! Life is all neuro-glandular stimulation and artificial outrage."

"You've got a strange take on peace and progress."

"We hate peace. Screw peace. Peace is boring. And progress? The road to progress is littered with evil geniuses, so-called lunatics and the bodies of innocents. Madame Curie glowed in the dark but gave us X-ray tech. Edison cheated Tesla but the electric march played on.

Whoever figured out how to run a car engine on salt water got murdered by the oil and gas industry to keep it a secret. And here we are, drama and import imminent. Do you really want to be home prescribing CPAP machines to fat guys with fat necks at this — "

"Historical moment bound for tragedy?"

"Tragedies are opportunities. Little Finger has it right. 'Chaos is a ladder.'"

"I get the reference but I don't watch *Game of Thrones*."

"No wonder we don't understand each other," Freddy replied. "Stability is boring. Boring circumstances make boring, passive people. Give the couch potatoes a useful tragedy and they'll be moved to change the world."

CHAPTER 37

Houston, Texas
   Lady Bird High School
   Last Day

The city streets stood eerily quiet when Crystal Perry arrived at school. At fifteen, she was a slight, pretty girl with a button nose. Her bright green spiky mop of hair was shaved short on one side. She'd been up most of the night working on algebra but her homework was not finished. Over the last couple of days, fewer and fewer kids showed up to class. Everyone who did make it to school acted logy or irritable. Every eye was red and heavy-lidded. Some students complained of vivid dreams that left them feeling like they'd run marathons in their sleep. Mostly, widespread absences were attributed to a bad case of the flu.

Weighed down by a backpack full of textbooks, Crystal waited and watched from the bleachers beside the football field. School was not officially cancelled but very few students had wandered into the building before the bell rang. Even the teachers' parking lot was mostly empty. Lady Bird High looked like it had been abandoned to an early summer vacation. Crystal could go home unnoticed but that option was much worse than staying at school and completing her algebra assignment.

The margins of her textbooks were full of doodled dragons, two-headed and drawn in neon green ink. Each body had six legs and bat wings which wrapped the body like a cocoon. Crystal loved her dragons. She especially liked combining attributes of dragons from several cultures. Her sketches pulled from Indian, Slavic, Japanese, Chinese, Jewish and Persian dragon art. To the girl, these mythological creatures symbolized luck and power, two attributes Crystal felt she lacked.

She was a good student but she preferred her art to the demands of teachers. She simply did not — could not — take notes in class. Though her drawings were precise and admirable, handwriting stymied her. Her writing was painfully slow and nearly illegible. A school psychologist had recommended she use a keyboard but, so far, no money had been found in the budget to get her that help. Her parents could not afford to buy her a laptop.

After several useless attempts to take better notes, Crystal found her solution: she listened without taking notes. She read the books, highlighted the important parts and she remembered. Sometimes Crystal thought her memory was a little too good.

Her mother, Sherry, had been laid off from her job as a truck dispatcher the day before. Few trucks were running and deliveries fell further and further behind schedule. Many shops in Houston were closed. Businesses that remained open were understaffed. Grocery stores ran out of staples. Long lines had become the norm. No sleep aids were left on drugstore shelves.

Hoarders and preppers milled together in line-ups outside of retail stores exchanging rumors. "This is it," they said. "It's not what the government is saying that's suspicious. It's what they're not saying. Where's the CDC with vaccines for this so-called flu? And how come nobody we know is sick? How come the media isn't talking about it? What the hell is going on when I try to grab some shut-eye?"

Some were driven to unrelenting insomnia. For most, the nightmares made them afraid to sleep. Those who could sleep sometimes woke screaming, their bedsheets twisted and soaked with sweat. Many had experienced terrifying visions of fire. No one could rest even if they could sleep.

Then came the incident in Rio de Janeiro. Flipping channels, Crystal's mother watched the news networks, agitated and constantly commenting on whatever was on the screen. News anchors and reporters jabbered on about a statue of Jesus on fire. The news coverage was relentless even though there didn't seem to be any real news to report. Everyone was short of facts but they were long on opinion. Camera crews hurried around frenetically as reporters pulled random crying people from crowds to ask what they thought the burning statue might mean. Mid-sentence, Sherry Perry would flip back and forth, climbing through rounds of channels to watch religious programs before trying the news again.

The fundamentalist evangelists either preached fear or optimism (although even the optimistic ones doled out a helping of scary predictions for non-believers). Panels of religious leaders argued about the redemptive and purging properties of fire and what the burning statue might symbolize. Most seemed sure the events in Rio boded ill for all those who had sinned in the past.

"Idiots," Crystal's mother said. "Idiots, all. This is a come-to-Jesus moment if I ever saw one."

Not a few politicians made pronouncements that implied they were not really surprised by the event. Some thought the burning statue meant something big and beautiful was about to happen. Only one commentator on FOX — a comedian named Mike Schmidt, suggested the burning statue was a hoax. After much badgering, the comedian conceded that the spectacle could be the work of clever, but fairly harmless, terrorists. Outraged and sweating, Bill O'Reilly shouted Schmidt down before insisting his guest's microphone should be cut off.

"What do you think, Crystal?" her mother asked.

"Makes for good TV."

"Oh, this is much more important than that. O'Reilly's super Catholic. He has it right. The Rapture is close."

Talking louder doesn't make you right. Crystal was too smart to share that thought with her mother.

Before Crystal slipped out of the house, Sherry looked up from the television screen. "This is a good thing, baby girl. A terrible justice is coming."

"A *terrible* justice?"

"Signs and wonders, right there. Look at it. It started up in the night and Rio's Jesus is still burning for all the world to see. It's impossible and all these folks can't explain it, but I know what it means."

"What's it mean, Mom?"

"Clear as day. Jesus is burning. It means no more Mr. Nice Guy. God sent his only begotten son to help us out. Jesus knocked on the door before. Now he's coming to knock it down."

"Huh?"

"Don't be slow, Crystal. Open your heart door to Jesus. He's trying to save us."

"Save us from what?"

"Save us from what he's gonna do if you don't open your heart door. I thank God I got you upright and baptized."

"Um — "

"But your daddy's gonna *burn!*" Sherry Perry's face split into a wide jack o'lantern grin.

Her mother's delighted laughter chilled her. Crystal couldn't remember her mother laughing quite like that before.

"Just like in the Bible, girl. The righteous will be able to look down from heaven and watch the sinners suffer in eternal torment. I hope they have popcorn in heaven because watching your daddy scream is all I'm gonna do for the first few centuries, just to get back mine. I hope Jesus pipes all that gnashing of teeth in Hell over the intercom to heaven, too. It's going to be you and me and sweet tea in a hammock between palm trees and a cool breeze while we watch your father twist and shout, burn and learn. That's biblical. It's gotta happen. It's gonna happen. Justice will be done."

As Crystal looked up at the empty sky over Houston, she yawned and stretched. She wondered what it would be like to be someone else. Did other people have nasty thoughts as often as she did? Did they swear as much in their heads? Did they worry any less? Did anyone know what they were doing?

She thought about the comedian on TV, how decent, thoughtful and funny he was. She thought about her mother and how mean she could be. Crystal looked to Lady Bird High and considered all the calculus she had to learn after she figured out algebra.

Why do I have to know any of that shit? I can't fill out a job application. I'll just end up working at Walmart. "Maybe this is hell and Jesus is coming to let us out. Maybe we've suffered enough."

At the corner of her eye, she caught a slight movement, like a flutter of wings. She looked at her notebook and found doodled dragons where algebraic equations should be.

One of the dragon heads peered up at her from the page. Another dragon face seemed to smile at her, then gave a quick wink.

The girl gasped. "Something *is* coming!"

The doodles of dragons were silent. Their mouths did not move. However, in her head, Crystal heard the twin dragons answer as one, "Soon."

CHAPTER 38

Berkeley Campus
Last Day

The Remote Joes appeared to be wrapping up their preparations to enter the tanks.

"What did Frist say, when they began their induction?" Kallaste asked.

Freddy shrugged. "I could barely catch a few words here and there. *Kononomai, nonamaji,* something something. Might as well have been chanting the spell to open the Necronomicon. After that, it got into some pretty standard hypnotic induction."

"A bunch of my colleagues still don't believe in hypnosis," the doctor said. "They sure won't believe a word of this."

"Don't believe? Anybody who's been to a Vegas show knows hypnosis is solid. That's just dumb denial of what we don't fully understand. I don't get people like that."

"The known is comfortable, Freddy. For instance, I wish I didn't know any of this was happening."

"No, man. This is the shit! This is ground zero for a new era and you get to witness it." He pointed at the Remote Joes through the glass. "I'd love to do a bunch of studies on these guys. I have a thousand questions. Dr. Danzig doesn't like making our research about the woo-woo stuff, but after all we've seen, she'll change her mind."

"What's their hypnotic induction process? What did you hear?"

Freddy shrugged. "Remote Joe stuff. I haven't met remote viewers before but it is a little like the *Men Who Stare at Goats* movie. They seem to have an individual approach to getting into a receptive state. Standard new age hippie military human potential mind focus tricks."

"*Hippie* military?"

"Well, that is what they are. Regular military thinks they're nuts, I'm sure. You know how it is."

"I don't. Tell me how they get receptive."

"Frist did a guided meditation with Huff that sounded like the end of a hot yoga class."

"And the other one?"

"Rodriguez chanted. It was pretty cool. I didn't recognize it from any of the Asian or Native American chants I've studied."

"You've studied chants?"

"Sure. Before I got into flotation tanks, I did sweat lodges while I worked on a double major in psychology and pharmacology. My goal is to have three PhDs before I'm forty. No offense, but one medical degree to get to the title of doctor is the easy way."

"You're obviously a busy guy," Kallaste said. "So busy I guess you don't notice how offensive you are."

"I am a busy guy so I'll just say sorry once and we'll move on. I should be running the lab and Cora should be at home changing her bandages. She doesn't value me like she should."

"I'm sure Dr. Danzig and Agent Reddy consider you a valuable asset, Freddy."

"Thank you, Mik. People think I joke around too much but I often find myself sublimating my rage and impatience with humor. Ambitious people often have strong personalities. The school system and the current university structure are not set up for precocious people. I did peyote and went on a spirit quest when I was thirteen."

"*Thirteen?*"

"My parents weren't geniuses but my mom was a hippie libertine who believed in astrology. I taught myself oneironautics when I was nine — "

"Oneironautics?"

"Lucid dreamers are hobbyists. For people who are serious about the practice, it's called oneironautics."

"Oh. I guess I should have known that," Kallaste said. "It's not something that comes up much in my practice. Most people I treat can't sleep."

"Oneironautics is entry-level psychonautics, Mik. These things should be taught in elementary school along with hypnosis. The ability to focus the mind is so important but it's hardly ever spoken of. I can think of a thousand ways to change the world for the better starting with getting all of Congress high before they pass any bill. I'd pull the compassion out of them."

"I had no idea you were so passionate, Freddy."

"I'm frustrated with the way things are. The system is trying to slow me down. The average age of PhD candidates has risen more than a decade since the seventies as student debt skyrocketed."

"You're saying the establishment holds PhD students back to get more money out of them?"

"That and cheap labor, making us teaching assistants. I should already have surpassed Cora. She has some old-fashioned ideas about her field that have more to do with PR than advancing theory and practice. The field needs a new Timothy Leary to popularize our exploration of consciousness. We have so much potential tied up and gagged in department committees."

"And Dr. Danzig is not a good spokesperson?"

"Capable but too conservative and not imaginative enough by half. She only sees blood studies. I see the big picture. She resents me for it, too."

"I'm sorry to hear that." Kallaste hoped for a way out of this conversation but Freddy seemed determined to plunge on.

"Cora should be teaching Stats 101, not opening the envelope of the human experience. New fields of study need missionaries with zeal, not research papers no one will ever read. Cora can't tell a knock-knock joke without making the punchline sound like a eulogy."

"Maybe you're too ahead of your time."

"Then I'll make this my time. I'm most interested in how our consciousness will expand in the next ten years. There's many ways up the mountain. People will always find a way to achieve altered states, whether they use sex, chocolate croissants, coffee, weed, Jack Daniels, driving too fast, running until the endorphins kick in, roller coasters, reading a book, spinning round and round like little kids until they fall down dizzy...you name it."

"That summary sounds pretty all encompassing of human behavior."

"Yeah. I've just paraphrased the introduction to what's going to be my first PhD thesis."

"If you're right, what *isn't* about achieving an altered state?"

"Nothing," Freddy said.

"That can't be true. We've got a baseline of reality we need to acknowledge, right?"

"It's that base reality that drives us to altered states. We don't even stop that search while we sleep. The brain is always reaching out and keeping busy. *Everything* is about achieving an altered state. Life is too hard. Everybody needs a way to blow off steam or escape. Facebook is a trance. Every book is a holodeck. From every social interaction to every little hobby meant to pass the time until death, it's all about escaping the horror."

"The horror? Which horror?"

"The banal," Freddy replied. "Everything we do is meant to activate the drugs that are already in our systems, to escape that slippery thing you think is Truth. If we can't do it naturally, we'll use artificial means. We're bound for the ground. We can't face that so we distract ourselves as long as we can."

"Sounds like you think we're all truth deniers and drug addicts."

"Absolutely, we are. You ever been to a chiropractor? When they get that cracking sound from popping a nitrogen bubble in your joints, the chiro-cracker gets a little boost of dopamine just like anybody popping bubble wrap. The surgeon transplanting a kidney is in a trance of his own. And don't get me started on the horse tranquilizer that is the internet."

"You think that constant pursuit of the next high is a good thing?"

"Good or bad doesn't matter. You can't deny biology. We all do it. We're all just keeping our minds busy, pretending we aren't going to end up dead. Nobody wants to think the body they were born with will soon be filled with hungry worms."

"Don't take this the wrong way, Freddy, but I think I prefer your jokes."

"I thought Captain Frist might hit me so I took a downer to even me out. Too much caffeine in my system was making me jittery."

"You aren't jittery now?"

"I talk a lot unless I'm on weed. My mom gave me my first hit on a joint. It was the only thing that shut me up. Mom's solution is not recommended for children but her options were calm me down or kill me. She wasn't a good mom."

"Uh, okay. Just don't fall asleep. Where's Dr. Danzig?"

"Interviewing the people in the storeroom. She's looking for commonalities, trying to track the Woman in White. So far the only thing those people have in common is they saw some really weird shit that came true and they're afraid to go back to sleep."

"What sort of things did they experience?"

"One dreamt of a whirlwind and when he woke up in the morning everything in their house but the bedroom was destroyed. Shades of *Poltergeist*. Another dreamt she was lost and naked in the woods. She woke up in the forest five miles from home."

"Weird, but explainable by sleepwalking."

"That wasn't her whole story. She killed a vole and was chewing on its raw guts when she woke up. For a few hours after the police found her, she could speak fluent Mandarin. One of the EMTs was Chinese. He says she was saying one thing over and over. 'The end is nigh,' basically."

"That sounds similar to the message Dr. Danzig got and what Cahill has picked up."

"Yeah. I don't know which I'd prefer: to be cut up with water that turns to glass or the memory of vole guts in my mouth for the rest of my life."

The remote viewers moved to the tanks and Captain Frist nodded at Freddy through the glass.

"Showtime, Mik. Strap in! This is going to be so cool!"

Kallaste sighed. He couldn't share the young grad student's excitement. He was tired and he wanted to sleep. But now he was afraid to close his eyes.

CHAPTER 39

Houston, Texas
Lady Bird High School
Last Day

Crystal bent her head to her notebook, so close her nose almost touched the page. She felt herself slipping into a doze and struggled to keep her eyes open. Crystal stared into the dragon's eyes.

Twin dragon heads.
One body.
Dragon brothers.
Two sets of deep dragon eyes.
Solemnity.
Dignity.
Knowledge.
Fearlessness.
Strength.

One dragon head's eyes were as red as blood. The other's were black. Crystal could feel herself melting and melding with the spirit of the dragon as she peered into the white shine she'd sketched at the edge of one black iris.

In the dragon's eye, she saw her mother toast the television with a mug again. A shiver vibrated up Crystal's spine as Sherry Perry giggled. Her mother spilled some coffee on the carpet. She did not worry about the stain. Sherry slurped her drink and continued flipping channels back and forth so fast that the screen bathed her face in a slow pale strobe. That vacant smile reminded Crystal of scary clowns.

Crystal's perfect memory of that cruel smile tired her. Exhaustion soaked into her bones. She suspected that one day, when she spoke at her mother's funeral, she'd carry the image of that smile, heavy as a weight on her heart. Whatever nice thing she could say about her mother would be made a lie when Crystal thought about how she toasted a burning statue, how she prayed for eternal torment for the man she'd married.

When she was little, Crystal assumed all laughter must equate to happiness. Her mother soon taught her laughter's darker hues: smug, grudging, ironic, fake, derisive and cruel.

Crystal's laugh was of the nervous variety more often than not.

She yawned uncontrollably and decided to curl up under the bleachers. The public address system told her an assembly was being held in the gymnasium and Phys. Ed was cancelled. Relieved, Crystal knew she could stay in the cool shadows under the bleachers. She wanted to be left alone with her dreams of dragons. If she had her druthers, Crystal would be home in bed, asleep and blowing off any worries about math homework. Her plan had been to grab a nap before going in to tackle the last of her algebra assignment. She needed to get good marks if she was to earn a scholarship and get away.

She hoped for a generous grant to go to an art school. One day, she might move to California and get a job with a graphic design studio. Maybe even create amazing CGI for the entertainment industry. The girl had contemplated running away many times since her father left. However, the smarter course would be to escape to school. Once she got away, she promised herself she would never return, even if all her high hopes went to hell and she ended up mopping floors forever.

In her most hopeful moments, Crystal stared at her reflection in the bathroom mirror. Sometimes her mother hovered outside the bathroom door, listening intently. Equal parts defiant and under Sherry Perry's thumb, Crystal whispered low so she could be sure her mother would not hear. She promised herself, "Someday, I'll create my own graphic novels. They'll be so good, I'll burn everybody's brain meats and melt their faces. I'm going to get far away from here. From Mom. No matter what it takes."

Her parents' marriage had ended not in divorce but in mystery. One day, her father, Ted Perry, came into her room early in the morning, eyes bloodshot, cheeks wet. He gave Crystal a hug and a kiss and whispered, "I gotta go, baby. I'm sorry, I can't afford to take you with me. I got a line on a job on an oil rig. As soon as I save some cash, you can come visit, maybe even stay. You'd like that, wouldn't you?"

"What about Mom?"

"Your mom and me need a break. I can't stay with that woman no more. She used to be so sweet, sweet as you. Now, it seems I can't do anything right. I look at her the wrong way and she gets mean. It doesn't take nothin' to set her off."

"She's the same with me."

"I know."

"Two of us are okay," Crystal said. "She's the wrong one — "

"There's nothing wrong with you, Crystal. Just, please, stay sweet."

"Why isn't she the one who has to leave?"

"That can't work. I can't pay the rent here."

"Don't leave me alone with her."

"I got to. I can't take it no more."

"Then don't leave without me."

"She's the one with the job, baby. How'm I gonna feed you? Time to face facts."

That was nine months ago. Every week, a new one-page letter in Ted Perry's loopy scrawl arrived. Each note held promises of finding the right job or making a bit more money. It seemed the more Ted Perry chased money, the faster it ran from his grasp. He'd send for her, but not now. Never now.

Crystal's mother asked the same question with each new letter: "What's your father got to say about me?"

"Nothing."

That wasn't true but she didn't want to listen to her mother unleash a tantrum. The tantrums came often enough on their own. It would begin with banging a pot or dropping a dish in the sink. The harangue would progress. Sherry would shout louder. She'd stomp up the stairs and slam a bedroom door.

Later, her mother sometimes apologized. "When I'm yelling at you, I'm really yelling at him."

"It sure feels like you're yelling at me."

"That's only because he's not here and you are."

Not for much longer, Crystal thought. She was too smart to say so aloud.

Under the bleachers, Crystal lay curled up and seemingly safe. But someone had noticed her. As the stranger drew closer, her gaze settled on the girl with green spiky hair.

Crystal Perry was too smart to share dangerous thoughts with scary people. However, private thoughts and deadly dreams were not safe from the Woman in White.

She smiled down at the sleeping girl, waiting for Crystal to enter the most susceptible and suggestible stage of sleep: REM. As the girl's eyes began to search for input, shifting back and forth beneath her closed lids, a door to the *Unus Mundus* unlocked. In a stage whisper, the Woman in White said, "I am Deathless. You could be Deathless, too."

CHAPTER 40

Berkeley Campus
   Last Day

Huff and Rodriguez lay quiet in their flotation tanks. The green screens on the EEG and ECG monitors came alive as the bluetooth signals came in.

Their low heart rates surprised Kallaste. Rodriguez's pulse was 45. Huff's heart pumped at a steady 38. They looked fit but both men were in their thirties and didn't strike the doctor as runners. What was more interesting was that their EEG readouts seemed to match, almost perfectly. Their brainwaves were both deep in theta. They'd used different approaches to change the frequencies of their brainwaves but somehow they had synchronized.

Captain Frist had not achieved an altered state. Nothing unusual appeared on his EEG readout. Kallaste began to wonder if Frist's move to join his men was a symbolic tactic, showing leadership after the enemy had nearly crashed their plane on the way to Berkeley. Then, as soon as Freddy closed the tank hatch, Frist began in sharp, shallow breaths.

Freddy returned to the control room. As soon as he heard the output from Frist's speaker, he smiled.

"Is he panicking?" Kallaste asked.

"He's not."

"But he's hyperventilating. He'll pass out in a minute."

"I don't think so. The inductions for Huff and Rodriguez took a lot of time. Captain Frist is taking the express elevator to where he wants to go."

"What do you mean?"

"That's some form of breathwork. Sounds like a lot of work but still easier than a sweat lodge, if you ask me. I'd prefer psychedelic cactus or psilocybin mushrooms, personally."

Frist's quick, shallow breathing continued. The doctor found just listening to it made him want to take a deep breath.

"We slip in and out of non-ordinary states of consciousness all the time," Freddy said. "Ever drive somewhere and at some point you think, gee, I hope those last three stoplights were green because I was daydreaming while my body worked on automatic."

"I think everyone has probably had that experience. But this — "

"Captain Frist is going to a non-ordinary state of consciousness. Don't be alarmed if the journey sounds taxing."

"His heart rate is up to 148. He may as well be running."

"Wait. Watch."

"Have you seen this before?"

"Yes."

"It's weird."

"When weird starts to look normal, you know you're doing some interesting shit."

Captain Frist went quiet as his pulse steadily sank to fifty-eight beats per minute.

Kallaste watched the screens. Huff and Rodriguez had a couple of blips up of alpha waves and then their readouts synchronized again. "There they go," the doctor said. "Delta waves. Huff and Rodriguez are in deep slow-wave sleep. These guys would be the envy of insomniacs everywhere."

Soon, their commander joined them.

"Non-REM," Freddy said. "Give them time. The alien made contact with Cora when she was in a dream state. The way Captain Frist talked about the *Unus Mundus*, I guess that's the intersection they're looking for."

"The intersection?"

"Between our world and other dimensions. If the Woman in White is wreaking havoc with people's dreams, she'll do it from there."

Jen appeared at the door to the outer office and knocked softly. "I'm sleepy but I don't want to sleep yet. Can I watch?"

"Watching these guys nap in the middle of the day isn't exactly exciting, but we're glad to have your company," Freddy said. He pulled over a chair and gestured for Jen to sit.

"Where's Reddy?" Kallaste asked.

"He's got his eyeballs on his phone, like always," Jen said. "Talking to the FBI again, I think. It's hard to gauge his mood but I don't think he's happy with them. I figured I'd see how these guys find the bitch."

"Easy," Freddy said. "Didn't you say in your debriefing that the Woman in White didn't start this? I thought I read that in Reddy's memo."

"Yeah. She said she was just test driving her abilities. Something like that. So?"

"Maybe the lady in white is like...uh, pawn of the aliens. We need to focus on finding a way to shut down the real enemy."

"Yeah, right." Jen peered through the glass. "You weren't there when I met her. I'll call her a bitch if I want to. How much do those flotation tanks cost, anyway?"

"Forty-thou a pop for the three most recent ones. We got 'em through exploration grants from Google and Onnit."

Kallaste let out a low whistle. "How come so much? I mean, what would a full-sized pool cost?"

"These are all custom jobs," Freddy explained. "Underwater sound system. We aren't using it right now, but there's a TV screen in each tank for advanced learning experiments. That's something I want to explore when I have the time. Aldous Huxley was sure sleep learning was the way into the future. We need to look into that."

"Still sounds like a lot of cash to me," Jen said.

"The instrumentation is precise. The water is heated to skin temperature so it's hard to tell where your body ends and the water begins. Add a couple tons of salt for buoyancy and it really feels like you're floating in space."

"Does anybody get claustrophobic?"

"I got scared once when I hit the edibles a little too hard," Freddy admitted. "Usually, floating in the dark, disembodied and without a care in this world is beyond relaxing. When you're doing it right, it can be a psychedelic experience that lets you figure things out. Imagine your brain is a computer. A float can clear out the cache and reboot the neocortex. I've come up with my most brilliant ideas in there."

"Is it really like being out of gravity?" Jen asked.

"We've had a couple of old astronauts come through here to relive their glory days. When we're not using the tanks, the education department rents some time from us, too. I think the people who get the most out of the tanks besides Cora and me are those who come in with arthritis."

"I wouldn't mind one of those in my Physio department back home," Jen said.

"Three of these tanks are cream of the crop," Freddy said. "The one we're not using was here in the mid-seventies, back when psycho-nauts were trying to find a way to get to the Mindscape. After LSD was banned, they were desperate to find easy ways back. A bunch took mescaline and all they got was fear and loathing in Las Vegas."

"Everything old is new again," Kallaste said.

"Some refugees from the Esalen Institute came to Berkeley, too. They tried to get academics to take their work seriously. The human potential movement was sidelined when the hippies sold out. We're finally on the brink of a new revolution in human psychology after a detour through rampant consumerism."

"If we live past tonight," Jen said.

Kallaste gazed at the EEG readings. "All three are sleeping and have entered Rapid Eye Movement. Pulses steady. Respiration steady."

"And they've all reached atonia," Freddy added. "Paralyzed in Dreamland. Sounds a little like paradise, doesn't it?"

CHAPTER 41

The Unus Mundus
 Out of Time

Captain Frist smiled as he opened his eyes. He found himself in the White Space. Depthless and blank, he considered this the foyer to the *Unus Mundus*. As he looked around, all trepidation left him. He wished he could stay here forever but his mission awaited. He stepped out of the White Space and into a field adrift in cherry blossoms. He'd first seen cherry blossoms fall like snow in the Akira Kurosawa film, *Ran*. That was 1985. Since seeing that movie, every time he entered the *Unus Mundus*, he recreated that scene.

With a thought, Mount Fuji appeared in the distance. Frist looked down at himself. He wore Samurai armor.

He pulled the short and long swords from his belt and lay them to the side. "I hope I won't need you."

The ground was covered in white snow and cherry blossoms of pink, white and yellow. With another thought, a log cabin made of cedar appeared. The captain began gathering brush for a fire. He could have just imagined the campfire and it would have appeared. However, there was little satisfaction in that.

"Huff? Rodriguez? I'm here. Come find me." His words echoed across the landscape. They would find him and there was no rush. The cherry blossoms continued to fall. It was the most peaceful scene Frist could imagine. He most enjoyed the silence of this place, quiet as a grave. He puttered back and forth to gather fallen branches. It was a calming exercise to ground him in the unreality in which he found himself. If remote viewers stayed in the White Space, they got disoriented and anxious. Then they fell out of the correct mind state, never graduating to the place where they became small *g* gods.

Frist knew men who had entered the Mindscape and lost their minds. They stayed in the *Unus Mundus* until their bodies died. When they died back home, they died here, too. And vice versa. That's why he thought of himself as a small *g* god in the *Unus Mundus*. (Back in Peoria, he was a Presbyterian.)

"I like your armor, Captain Frist." That was neither Huff nor Rodriguez. The voice was disembodied, deep and rumbling.

Frist stood erect and showed his hands were empty. "Hello."

"Hello."

"Who's speaking?"

"An emissary of Ba'al."

"Good. I'm an emissary, too. Show yourself."

The bright day turned to night. The campfire Frist had been building burst into orange flame, lighting the night and igniting the cherry blossoms that fell into its teeth. A tall figure in shining black armor stepped forward.

"You are?"

"I am Cord of the House of Cord, Emissary of Ba'al, Commander of the Dead Fifth Arm of the Darkness Visible, citizen of Ra."

"That's a mouthful."

"I have two mouths."

"Convenient. Nice horns."

"Thank you."

"I am Captain Frist. I've been sent here to negotiate peace. Are you empowered to make decisions in the hopes of a diplomatic solution?"

"I have power."

"Er...okay. Let's start from there."

"Who do you represent?" Cord asked.

"I'm here under the authority of the President of the United States."

"The President is sleeping."

"Yeah, well, we had to make prearrangements after our last clash in New York."

"Clash?"

"The detonation."

"Yes. The detonation. I was there. One of the few who survived. The explosion is why I am now an emissary. I command no one."

"But — "

"My command was the Fifth Arm of the Darkness Visible. Now there are none."

"So your title is a ceremonial honor?"

"It is an anchor around my neck. A source of shame. I have many sources of shame, thanks to your kind." The alien pulled off a gauntlet to reveal a clawed hand. Then he pulled off one shoulder guard and his chest plate.

Captain Frist winced. In the flickering light of the campfire, the monster's skin was wrinkled and twisted into an array of horrific black scars.

"I believe you call these kinds of scars keloids," Cord said. "Pretty things aren't they? Like worms trapped just beneath my skin. I was not close to the blast but the superheated air still boiled me in my armor. The flash blinded one of my wives. The force of the blast killed the rest of my family."

"In fairness," Frist said, "I'm told you were going to use that nuke on us."

Cord growled. "When the losses are so gargantuan and so personal, it is foolish of you to speak of fairness. I'm trying to save my race. To deny us is genocide."

"Please," Frist said. "Let's sit and talk."

"They sent a warrior to negotiations peace with another warrior?"

"Our politicians are cowards. Back home, we call them chicken-hawks. What do you call your politicians?"

"We have only one leader: Ba'al. He is a god."

"Ah." After an uncomfortable silence, Frist sat in the circle of firelight and gestured for Cord to do the same. The captain's swords lay nearby, covered in cherry blossoms.

CHAPTER 42

Houston, Texas
   Last Day

Crystal blinked and lazily rubbed sleep out of her eyes, sure she'd only dozed a moment in the cool shadows. At the end of the bleachers, a stunning woman dressed entirely in white peered in at her. Startled, Crystal snapped wide awake.

"Hello, Crystal."

"How do you know my name? I don't know you."

"I know lots of things about you, Crystal Perry."

The girl scrambled to her feet. "What?"

"You heard me."

"I don't — wait. Who are you?"

The Woman in White laughed. "I'm your fairy godmother." It was a pleasant laugh, filled with joy and music.

"Who put you up to this? Did someone from the school — "

"A friend pointed me your way."

"Who?"

"Big fellow. Armor. Horns. Calls himself Cord. I don't know much about him. I like to think I know a false note when I hear it, but of course, everyone is so full of shit it's hard to tell what's the truth and what's not, am I right?"

Crystal allowed a small smile. "Yeah."

"That's your experience with your father, right? Does he love you?"

Crystal stiffened in surprise but she answered without hesitation, "Yes. My dad is full of shit."

"Where is he? At least with your mother you know where you stand. She's a crazy lady. Crazy is simple. No complex motivations there."

Crystal's smile disappeared. "Look, I don't know what you think you know but — "

"Your father left you with the crazy lady. That's what I know. That can't be love, can it?"

Crystal picked up her bag and bent to make her way out from under the bleachers.

"I don't blame him entirely," the woman called. "Not like your mother. Perhaps your father isn't clear on his intentions, either. I'm sure he's really looking for a job but maybe he's not in a hurry. Maybe he's enjoying a much-needed rest. We used to call women like that hags and harridans. The language isn't so rich anymore. These days if a woman is unliked, she's labeled a bitch and that's it. Not fair to your mother, really. Mental illness is just a bad brain. A bad brain should be its own punishment. But kids shouldn't have to suffer, should they? That's not fair. You've got a good brain and your parents are hurting you, Crystal."

"I don't want to talk about this." The girl turned to exit at the far end of the bleachers but the woman's voice seemed to follow her as if she was at Crystal's side.

"I've been thinking a lot about what's real and what's not," the woman continued. "I've been given this world and I want to make it better. Strange things are happening but if I'm going to live here, there has to be a purge. That's what my companion thinks. He's very persuasive. I bet I could persuade you, too. Push anybody hard and long enough, it doesn't take much to make them push back. That's what happened to me. Life pushed me around too long and too hard. You should join the winning team, Crystal. I'd like a daughter to share the fun with."

Crystal emerged into the slanted sunshine and stopped dead. The woman appeared before her in a blink. In her flowing white gown, she appeared to glow.

As if the mystery woman could read Crystal's mind, she said, "Texas sunshine is so bright, it bleaches everything white. You've never been to Marfa. You haven't seen the lights at night. Cord says that's where Ba'al will descend."

"Who?"

"Ba'al. The leader of the Ra. Cord says that when peace comes to Earth, the walls between dimensions will fall. Peace and prosperity... the whole bit. The dream of a perfect world is achievable. Cord assures me Justice rides with Ba'al. I think Justice might be one of the four horsemen of the apocalypse...the one that carries the scales."

"You sound as crazy as my mother. Crazier."

"Don't you want peace and prosperity?"

"I — "

"Rhetorical question, dear. Your fairy godmother already knows the answers to all your questions. I think Cord sent me your way so *you* would discover the answers."

"Like what are you — "

"All you think about is how you can escape and be happy."

"Everybody wonders that."

"Do they? You do, certainly, but you have ambition. Intelligence and ambition is such a curse. The people with small dreams are spared so much. They can laze away their lives. They can never go anywhere or do anything and never yearn for more. You'll never be content living small, Crystal."

"What do you suggest? Get a lobotomy so nothing bothers me?"

The Woman in White laughed again and Crystal's nerves stopped jangling. Her jaw relaxed and her shoulders loosened. Somewhere, far off, a song began to play. Crystal recognized the slow beat. Her father used to sing along to it endlessly as he did the dishes. It calmed her father so much that it soothed her, too. It was a song from *The Thomas Crown Affair*. Crystal had never seen the movie but she knew it was a cover sung by Sting. *The Windmills of Your Mind*. Her father loved that version of the Dusty Springfield song. She loved it, too. As the song grew louder, Crystal searched for its source but could not find where it emanated from. The air shimmered with the music.

"It's in your head, dear."

Before Crystal could voice the thought, the Woman in White said, "Yes, it is like we're in a movie, isn't it?"

The dazzling sun burned ever brighter. Crystal felt hot and dizzy, sure she was about to lose consciousness. "What's happening?"

"I'm going to make everything perfect. To kick out the old shit, this world needs an enema, don't you agree?"

Crystal began to sway to the slow, hypnotic rhythm. She could feel the music's beat in her chest. She turned in a circle, put her arms out and began to spin faster.

"This is how Cord convinced me things needed to change. With me, it was Nina Simone singing, *Feeling Good*. God, I love that song. Nina Simone and a big fella that looks like the devil freed me."

"I don't understand."

"I didn't, either. Not until I felt the power. Never you mind. Just open yourself to possibility. I can remove all the obstacles to your peace and prosperity. I can get rid of every little thing that ever bothered you. All you have to do is say yes and I'll take care of the rest."

"I...I don't know."

"You do. I know you know. All I want to hear is that you're on board so, when the walls fall and Ba'al comes, you'll be on the winning team."

"This is...this is not real."

"I think this is as real as anything is. This is like a movie, as real as you want to make it. Let's make a more perfect world, here and now. Small people try to tell us not to play God. Playing God is what we're here for. That's what Cord taught me. The greatest worship, the finest emulation of God, is to be what God is. You know what God does, don't you, Crystal?"

Between the silky violins, an answer came. But Crystal did not simply hear the words. She felt them in her chest, as if someone was spelling the words on her heart with cool fingers. "God destroys and creates."

"You are so right. Get the head out of the way and listen to your heart. Show me, Crystal. Step into my movie and let yourself sink into the plot. We all tell ourselves stories about how the world works. I'm giving you the chance to play God. Feel the rush of power? Like nothing you've ever felt. Like a drug that's been denied you too long."

"Yes."

"Who is standing in your way, Crystal? Who are the people who have failed you? Who bullied you? You're a lion pretending to be a mouse, girl. Picture everyone who ever tried to make you less than what you really are. Picture everyone who taught you to shut up and take abuse. Let's start with the woman who makes your every laugh a nervous laugh."

Thus, the gates of destruction opened in the sunny skies over Houston, Texas.

CHAPTER 43

The Unus Mundus
   Out of Time

"You wish to discuss terms of surrender?" Cord asked.

Captain Frist took a deep breath, centering himself. *I am the mountain, he thought.*

"Captain Frist?"

"Give me a minute."

"You aren't channeling your spirit animal, are you? I spoke with a human here once before. He did that. It was annoying."

"Someone from the Pentagon? A Remote Joe?"

"No. A civilian. His name was Ted."

"Who was he?"

"No idea. All he could say was, 'Bad trip, man! This is just one bad trip!' I cut his head off and sent him home. I would guess Ted's spirit animal was a sheep. Too bad none of your chickenhawk politicians could come visit me in The Place Where We All Meet. I could dispatch them all for you."

"Tempting but that's not how a negotiation works."

"I didn't say I was here to negotiate."

"I can offer you things you might like and we could save a lot of lives."

"Ba'al is not interested in saving your lives, Captain. Los Angeles. San Francisco. New York. Boston. These will be the first cities to fall."

"You do that and we'll fight back with everything we have. Not just the United States. Everyone. We have more nuclear weapons."

"So what is your proposal?"

"I can give you the Choir Invisible."

"You would sacrifice the battle group dedicated to fighting us?"

"We know there is a girl among the Choir who is closely tied to a powerful advisor to Ba'al."

"Ba'al is a god. He needs no counsel from advisors. It is a courtesy he extends to certain of our people."

"I meant no offense."

Cord nodded and gave a dismissive wave. "Your intent offends me."

"You want the girl spared?"

"You speak of Tamara Smythe. We've met. I wasn't impressed. She'll be dead soon enough without your help."

"Iowa, Castrator of Demons, they call her."

"*That* title is offensive. To my knowledge, she only slew one of us in such a way. And she betrayed her blood. The halfling is of no consequence. I do find it disturbing that your government would serve up your warriors so casually."

"The Choir Invisible is sworn to defend Earth and defeat you. The ultimate goal is to keep the peace and save lives. If their sacrifice achieves that, they die for the greater good. That's glory."

"What you call glory, I call betrayal. All of my company died in service. I lost them all to the blast. That is my shame but to be killed in service is no disgrace. To send your army to us as a sacrifice? I can think of no greater dishonor or cowardice. Ba'al has no interest in making peace with cowards."

"Okay. Plan B. How about we just give you South Africa?"

"No."

"Okay. Too hot. How about Greenland?"

"No."

"You're killing me here. Last ditch: Canada?"

"No."

"You sure? It's big. Lots of resources and places to move around."

"We don't want Canada."

"Got it. Too cold. Okay, what can we give you so you don't destroy everything? Work with me here. Help me help you."

"Your resources and your obedience. All of it. Only that will satisfy Ba'al."

Frist took a deep breath. "All of it? Well, is that all?"

"Your lives whenever we choose to take them. We are conquerors now, not explorers."

Captain Frist closed his eyes and checked his heart rate. Yes, steady. He was in no danger of falling out of the *Unus Mundus*. Better, he could feel Huff and Rodriguez moving through the dark, closer, into position. Frist opened his eyes. "You aren't coming at this in the right spirit, Cord."

"You don't understand us at all."

As he stared earnestly into the alien's black eyes, Frist shifted his weight and slipped closer to his swords. "Help me understand."

"The Ra were once a peaceful people. We discovered a way to move between dimensions. We were scientists, philosophers and explorers once."

"You're right. I didn't know that."

"Did you know that a few of us have walked among you for centuries? Some helped humans. Some even took their impersonations so far they forgot they were of the Ra."

"What happened?"

"We entered a dimension where we found enemies. They are called the Beriod. We made the mistake of teaching its inhabitants how to cross into our realm. They started taking over our society and muddying our bloodlines with genetic manipulation and contamination. They ruined us."

"The Beriod invaded you and won?"

"Not precisely. We rose up and transformed our society to crush them. The explorer class became the military. We killed thousands of them before the bulk of them fled back to their home dimension. That realm is forbidden and sealed, never to be opened again, by order of Ba'al. Now we are as your conquistadors were. We must expand our empire for god and for gold."

"I don't see — "

"We did unspeakable things. Torture. Murder. Some want to return to the old ways but we fear that we will be made fools again. We worship strength now. Ba'al is our strongest leader. He will never allow another incursion into our realm. Our world is dying. We must come to your dimension to save our race."

"Does your race have a little concept we like to call irony?"

"Don't condescend to me, Captain Frist. I was a scout for years. I've lived among you. I know your world. I know my enemy far better than you know yours, obviously. In the '90s, I watched *Friends* every Thursday night."

Captain Frist tried to stifle a smile and failed.

"The irony, Captain, is that we allowed the interlopers to return to their dimension. We were arguably more compassionate than your kind. Humans don't want us on Earth. Your leaders, many of your world leaders, are dedicated to keeping us out. It's genocide."

"Why don't you go to another dimension instead of ours?"

"The atmospheric conditions in your dimension are the most hospitable to our physiology. We don't have time to keep on exploring and hoping. We must move our population to Earth to survive. Every day we delay means more dead children of Ra. Sulphur poisoning. Lead poisoning. The air is thick and hot in Ra, much thicker than when I was a child. We must end this."

Captain Frist leaned forward but his right hand found the hilt of his katana buried under a fall of sweet smelling cherry blossoms. He took a deep breath. Cherry blossoms smelled more like roses than cherries. He found it calming and he needed to be calm. Frist regretted what he had to do next. "You don't see that we could help you if we both compromised?"

"We tried cooperating with the Beriod. It failed. Our cultures are incompatible. You must bend your knees to us. We will not be diluted again. This is an all or nothing situation. Ba'al demands all."

Frist gripped his sword and swung it up from the ground. As he did, Huff and Rodriguez descended out of the darkness. If they couldn't negotiate with the Ra, they'd send a message back to Ba'al. They'd send his emissary's head.

The tip of Frist's katana swept through the alien's neck. There was no resistance. The captain fell to the ground in a puff of cherry blossoms. As Huff's and Rodriguez's swords clanged together, the armored monster disappeared in smoke.

"Projection," Frist warned.

Too late. Cord appeared behind Rodriguez. The monster struck Huff in the side of the head as he pushed Rodriguez into the fire. Cord held him to the flame. Rodriguez screamed as the flames lapped at him and spread.

"Rodriguez! Drop out! Drop out!"

Still screaming, the Remote Joe disappeared from the monster's grip.

Cord straightened. "It seems our negotiations are at an end. Very well. For Ba'al. For vengeance. For blood and glory!"

"Stop!" Frist screamed. The night was replaced with the White Space. Mount Fuji, the cabin and the cheery blossoms were gone in a blink.

Cord looked to Huff at his feet. The alien picked him up by the back of the neck. "I wonder, Captain Frist, if you have idolized this place too long. You vacation in the *Unus Mundus* and make pretty flowers fall through the air. But this is not the battlefield."

"Put that man down," Frist said.

"You know how to give orders. You take orders. You don't understand true subjugation yet. You don't know sacrifice. When we destroy your cities with your own weapons, you will understand shame. You will know defeat."

"Leave my man alone. You want a fight? Blessed swords, you and me, right now."

Cord laughed. "I told you, wrong battlefield. I wonder, will you drown in your little tube? Or will you die screaming in agony? Let's find out. Whatever happens to you in your tank of water, this man will experience it, too."

Cord laughed.

Frist screamed.

In panic and agony, Huff joined his superior officer.

As the Remote Joes disappeared from the White Space, Cord said, "The screams of the defeated. I never tire of that song."

CHAPTER 44

Berkeley Campus
Last Day

The microphone from Captain Frisk's flotation tank came to life. His voice did not sound like his own. It was high and panicked. "Help!"

The hatch to Captain Frist's tank caved inward, as if a giant fist had punched a dent in the metal.

"Get me out of here!"

Rodriguez was already screaming incoherently. Within seconds, Huff was banging on the walls of his isolation tank, as well.

Jen was closest to the door to the tank room. She reacted first, rushing straight to the closest tank. It was Frist's. She grabbed the handle, intent on ripping it open. It should have yielded easily. The hatch would not budge. "Jammed!"

Dr. Kallaste and Freddy were right behind her. They both grabbed the bar handle and yanked. Still nothing.

Jen opened the next closest tank. Huff crawled out. His eyes were so big and wild she could see the whites all the way around his pupils. The Remote Joe seemed physically unharmed. He lay on the cold wet floor. Trembling, he tore off the pulsing sensors attached to his head and chest.

The top of Frist's tank crushed down. The metal creaked and ground. The captain continued to pound on the walls of his tank, screaming to be let out.

"We need leverage!" The doctor cast about for something to wedge under the hatch handle but saw nothing of use.

"We need a cutting torch," Freddy said.

"Got a fire ax?" Jen shouted.

"I don't think there is one down here," Freddy said.

The tank collapsed further and the shell breached. Salt water rushed across the floor from the leak.

Jen ran to Rodriguez's flotation tank. She gave the hatch a vicious yank. It opened so easily she fell on her back. In a flash she was up again, pulling the remote viewer out of the tank. She got her arms under the man's armpits. The Remote Joe was covered in black burns and bubbling blisters.

"Hey!" Jen called to Huff. "Help me with him!"

Huff crossed his arms and rolled over to his side. Then he curled up, pulling his knees to his chest, shaking as if naked in a snowbank.

Jen crouched and braced her feet on the tank casing to pull Rodriquez free. She could feel the intense heat radiating from his burnt body. She yelled to Kallaste, "I don't think he's breathing! Somebody help me!"

Rodriguez began to slip. She adjusted her grip to catch him under the arms. His blistered skin shed from his arms like long gloves. Jen fell, cushioning Rodriguez's fall so he would not hit his head on the floor. She wound up cradling his head in her lap, crying and fighting the urge to vomit. His burnt skin clung to her fingers, his fingertips to hers.

"Mik!" Jen shouted.

Her voice was swallowed by the sound of shrieking metal. Frist's tank collapsed another two feet at once and more salt water gushed across the floor. Frist had screamed in panic before. Now he screamed in pain.

Freddy and the doctor pulled on the hatch handle. It creaked open a couple of inches but that was all.

"Freddy! Call the fire department and EMS!" Kallaste yelled. "Get the guards down here! We need help!"

Captain Frist's flotation tank squashed flat like a soda can under a heavy boot. Kallaste and Freddy fell. Huff threw up blood and his eyes rolled up as he lost consciousness.

Water gushed from the side of the crumpled tank. Then the water ran red.

CHAPTER 45

Berkeley Campus
  Last Day

Captain Frist was crushed in his flotation tank. Rodriguez died from his burns. Kallaste tried to revive Huff. Even with an onsite defibrillator and the quick arrival of the EMTs, the last Remote Joe was gone.

Jen was still shaky as the EMTs took the bodies away. "What did Huff die of, do you think?"

Freddy shrugged. "Maybe he saw what Captain Frist went through. Maybe it was a direct attack on his brain. Our perception of dream time is distorted so maybe what was just a couple of minutes to us felt like hours or days to him. Maybe Ba'al showed Huff the depths of the hell dimension he comes from. Maybe he was driven mad by visions of babies cooking in ovens and his heart gave out."

"A little less horrific speculation and hyperbole and more facts would be useful, Mr. Chambers," Reddy said.

"Any luck finding a connection between the Woman in White and the dead men in Hollywood and France?" Kallaste asked.

"No," Reddy said. "There was a connection but the person of interest was too unlikely. That was our best hope."

"Why was the person unlikely?" the doctor asked.

"The only connection between the director and the agent is very old and ill. She doesn't fit the description of the avatar. The Woman in White remains a mystery."

Jen had been resting her head on her crossed arms on the conference table. She raised her head and stared at Freddy for a moment. "Hold on. Maybe Freddy's got something there."

"What? What did I say? I didn't say anything!"

"About Ba'al being able to show whatever he wants, do whatever he wants."

Agent Reddy looked up from his phone. "Proceed, Ms. Daimler."

"You can do whatever you want if you're in a lucid dream, right?"

Kallaste nodded. "Most people fly or have guilt-free sex if they're really good at lucid dreaming."

Everyone looked at him, surprised.

The doctor blushed. "What? I'm speaking statistically. There have been studies."

"Ahem. Okay," Jen said. "Remember how I told you the Woman in White looked familiar?"

"Yes," Reddy said. "It was an avenue we explored exhaustively. We can connect no one fitting that description to the Hollywood agent or the director who died in France."

"That trail is cold," Freddy said.

"What if the Woman in White doesn't look like that anymore?" Jen asked.

"What are you suggesting, precisely?" Reddy asked.

"I was sure I'd seen her before. Maybe I would have known who she was if I'd had a name to work with. How old were those guys from Hollywood?" she asked.

"The agent was late middle-aged," Reddy said. "The dead man in France was quite elderly."

"What if the Woman in White is presenting her idealized self? Maybe she's pulling the Facebook con, showing only the good stuff. The way I saw her might be the avatar at the height of her beauty.

What if she's the old lady you ruled out because she didn't fit the description?"

"If she can change her look in a dream," Freddy said, "she could choose to look like anyone. Why not dance around Dreamland as Scarlett Johansson in her Black Widow uniform?"

"I'd definitely be ScarJo," Cahill said, "though she hates that nickname."

"Or be Barack Obama," Freddy suggested. "That would really throw you off."

"Actually, people don't tend to do that in lucid dreams," Kallaste said. "They rarely pretend to be people they are not."

"Why not?" Freddy asked. "Lucid dreaming is like having your own personal holodeck every night. When I'm lucid in the dream state, I'm a combination of Superman and Batman, but surrounded by more babes."

"We're usually ourselves," the doctor replied. "Even for the practiced lucid dreamer, it's difficult to exit your identity. You're you all the time. Lucid dreamers enact their fantasies as an idealized version of themselves."

Freddy laughed derisively. "So you're saying this old woman can't exit her identity but she managed to edit it so Jen wouldn't know who she is in a line up?"

"People get old and brains do age," Jen said, "but minds stay young. I've worked with elderly men who still make a pass at me. They couldn't get up from their wheelchairs but they like to think they're much younger than they are."

"Sounds like you're on to something," Cahill said. "What do you suggest we do? How about it, Agent Reddy? Got a super duper biomarker facial recognition app that identifies the Woman in White off Jen's description? Maybe age the composite photo until you've got a new suspect? Better hurry. We're on a tight schedule to the end of the world."

Reddy pursed his lips. "We do have that technology but I don't think we'll need to resort to it. When the FBI conducted their interviews, they took a picture." He snatched up his phone. "She was once a client of the Hollywood agent and she was the dead director's second wife."

The agent flipped through files until he found the image he wanted. He turned the phone to show Jen the picture. The screen showed a haggard woman with IV tubes in her arm. She was asleep. Most of her hair had fallen out and she looked small in her hospital bed. "Meet Mrs. Edith Gray. Could this be the Woman in White?"

Jen squinted. "I couldn't say. I need to see her eyes. Aging and gravity are brutal but the eyes stay the same."

"This just doesn't sound likely at all. Not to me, anyway," Freddy said. "She's a poor old woman. What would a powerful being like Ba'al want with her as his avatar?"

"According to our physics experts, they need someone on our side of the walls between dimensions to keep the channel to the *Unus Mundus* open," Reddy said. "Imagine a simple telephone: two tin cans strung together. The vibration and the signal doesn't get through unless the pair holding both ends of the line keep the string taut."

"I don't get the physics of it," Freddy said. "Sounds like a crackpot hypothesis hanging by a string."

"I'm told the high end math can only be understood by three or four physicists and they all work for the Choir Invisible at the moment," Reddy replied.

"That's a convenient way to shut down anyone who disagrees with you," Freddy grumbled.

Dr. Danzig cleared her throat and spoke for the first time since the beginning of the meeting. "Suppose Ba'al needs an avatar in our dimension who is a stable anchor. We have been looking for a lucid dreamer who is a young woman. If Miss Daimler is correct, we have found the avatar."

"That's a big if," Freddy said. "I say we leave the old lady alone, pack up and head for the hills. Let the US Army and the Choir Invisible deal with Ba'al and the Ra when they invade. When that Lilly tank went down, that was a sure sign it's time to leave this to the dudes with tanks and guns and Blackhawk helicopters."

"If Ba'al's army breaches the dimensions, Mr. Chambers, they will do so in populated areas. Our intelligence says Brooklyn is the most likely site of the first wave. The Ra have been very active there in the recent past. The United States hasn't gone to war on its own soil in a very long time. A high rate of collateral damage is certain. We have to prevent Ba'al's forces from coming through. This one old woman could be the key to that lock."

Freddy shrugged. "It's a lot of woo-woo and speculation."

"Man, I liked you more when you didn't sound like a YouTube commenter," Cahill said. "Ditch the negativity. We're all about to die, after all."

"We'll die of exhaustion before the demons get us," Freddy said. He yawned. "When's the last time anybody here slept? I feel like crap."

"We all do," Kallaste said. "I suspect we're already falling into micro-sleeps. You think you're awake but you're not for seconds at a time. We're trying to save the world but we shouldn't be operating heavy machinery. I'll review our dex dosages and see if I can stave off the crash. It won't be much longer before we all fall asleep. The body and mind can't go on like this indefinitely."

Danzig looked for a long moment at her assistant. "There's another bit of data that strikes me as relevant. These manifestations have been happening all over the world, day and night. Most people don't and can't sleep nearly that much, yet the manifestations have happened in multiple time zones. If I were to choose an avatar for my entry to another dimension, I'd choose one that was unconscious as much as possible."

Agent Reddy showed Jen his phone again. "Here's the same woman when she was young."

Jen stared at the screen. "She has an IMDB page?"

"Sure! Hollywood, baby!" Cahill said. "How about it, Jen? That her?"

"The photo is in black and white. I'm not sure. It could be her."

"What if the Woman in White is an idealized version of this person?" Cahill said.

"This actress was pretty when she was young but the hair is different. I'm not sure. Have you got any more pics of her?"

"No. Look at that face. Take your time," Reddy said.

"I'm sorry. A lot of old starlets had the same look. The hair could be throwing me off."

"Are you saying white people all look alike?" Freddy asked.

"No! I'm asking, what if I'm wrong? I have to see her eyes to be sure, that's all. Live and in color."

Reddy stood. "Then let's go. This woman is our only shred of a lead." He checked the time. "Let's go check her out ourselves."

"Where?" Jen asked.

"A nursing home in Bandon, Oregon," Reddy said.

"Bandon?" Freddy looked sour. "That's more than eight hours away! Too late!"

"By jet helicopter," Reddy said, "we can get there in two hours."

"Cutting it close. It's already past four. We lost a lot of time with the Remote Joes' attempt...and the aftermath."

"Sounds like we should try — " Cahill began.

"Sounds like a wild goose chase," Freddy said. "Isn't it obvious? The Woman in White is the alien, Ba'al or Cord or whatever. It crossed over to our dimension and — "

Jen slammed her fist on the table. "I've spoken to the Woman in White. The way she talked, I don't think that was an alien. She spoke like a human. I'm almost sure she is. The monster in armor talked differently, like he was in an old movie where the gladiator makes speeches before cutting everybody up with a spear. I can't believe those two are from the same planet. Let's go wake up the old lady and chat."

"Sounds like you want to give her a stern talking to," Cahill said.

"Fine," Freddy said. "Nobody's getting back in a flotation tank for a while so give me a minute to grab my bag and pee. I'll come with you. I've never been on a jet copter."

"I'll stay," Danzig said. "With my crutches, I'll only slow you down. If I have a nap and the voice gives me any new information — "

"You have my number, Dr. Danzig," Reddy said. "Thank you."

"I'll stay and monitor the app, in case Ba'al has anything new and creepy to say," Cahill said.

Everyone got up from the conference table to leave but Cahill caught up to Kallaste before he got to the door. "In case things get worse, remember that thing I told you about doing something heroic?"

"And me dying, yes."

"No matter what happens, save Jen. I think she likes me."

"You kidding?"

"Yes, I am," Cahill said. "They're coming to feast, Mik. It looks bad. Good luck, whatever happens. Don't do anything heroic."

To the doctor's surprise, Cahill stepped close, hugged him and kissed him on the cheek. "In case we don't see each other again, I wanted you to know I think you're cute."

"You're joking around again, right?"

Cahill sighed. "Why are all the pretty ones so dumb?"

CHAPTER 46

Houston, Texas
Last Day

Sunlight dulled as gigantic dark clouds rolled in. Thunder echoed across the city. Crystal looked up in wonder. "It feels like tornado weather."

"Oh, no," the Woman in White said. "The danger will arrive in a form that is much more personal. You want those purged to know who did the deed."

"Wait. I don't know what you mean."

"Patience, sugar plum."

"What are you doing?"

The Woman in White smiled. "Doing what fairy godmothers do."

Black clouds turned the day to twilight. "I'm going inside," Crystal said.

"No, stay. You're going to want to see this. This is what you have dreamed of with every casual insult. I'm drawing on every moment of shame, every humiliation. You have a remarkable memory, Crystal. It's time to harness it and make the offenders pay. This is the culmination of your dreams. This is your salvation."

"Salvation? Why?"

"I'm saving your life. Ba'al will spare you if you carry his mark. When the apocalypse comes, you're definitely going to want his mark on you."

A grinding, metallic sound shattered the sky, startling the girl. She dropped her backpack and covered her ears with her palms. "What is that?"

"Skyquake. They've been happening forever but no one on Earth guessed it was power piping through from beyond the wall."

"What wall?"

"The walls between dimensions, of course."

"Of course."

"Don't take a tone with your fairy godmother, kid." Crystal gasped as the Woman in White rose off the ground and hung in the air before her. Hot wind whipped and pulled at the hem of her dress. The woman's gown flowed out behind her, stretching and reaching so far that Crystal could not see the end of the train. The sight would have inspired awe on a sunny day. In the sudden twilight, Crystal came close to peeing her pants.

"You're going to love this, dear. I'm only acting on your heart's desire. Your wishes are granted."

"What wishes?"

"Your *secret* wishes. Everyone has them."

No rain fell but the thunder rose, rumbling and clapping in almost constant applause. As the grinding metallic sounds of the skyquake crashed on, the rising wind pushed Crystal to her knees. She stared up, searching for the source of the sound.

Far off, she could still make out the violin strains of *The Windmills of Your Mind*. The song was no longer soothing. The lyrics were drawn out as if Time itself bent and strained under a great weight. The music turned sour and tinny, as if played from a far carnival carousel. The beat fell like a hammer, out of rhythm. Crystal tried to stand but the sad yearning in the notes of her father's favorite song, now ruined, pulled her down. Her knees were as melting wax. The ground itself turned to warm molasses, holding her fast. All Crystal could do was stare at the sky. She ground her teeth. As bolt lightning split the sky, she saw a crack in the darkness widen.

"Is it Ba'al? Is he...is it coming?"

"Soon. When that happens, everyone will know. This spectacle is just for you. This is your coming out party, my dear."

Crystal's backpack, forgotten on the ground beside her, fell on its side. Out of an open pocket, half a dozen notebooks spilled across the dirt and spread open. All but one blew beneath the bleachers and clung to the dark underside of the seats. Crystal watched them go and thought of frightened spiders fleeing the light.

The girl's gaze fell on the remaining notebook. The fluttering pages riffled and shook before being pinned flat. She spied the green dragons she had doodled idly in class while she listened to a lecture on Martin Luther's Protestant Reformation of 1517. She screamed as the twin dragon heads turned to look her in the eye. Her stomach turned as each beast gave her a slow smile, baring rows of jagged teeth.

Her art came alive. Her texturing of the scales seemed to ripple off the page, from 2D and into the third dimension. The beast's serrated teeth looked long and lethal. Every muscle was defined and coiled. Her sketches, equally fantastic and startlingly realistic, rose off the page and grew in size, rising into the suddenly cooling air.

The crackling storm stuttered and strobed bright white light, leaving the girl, small and terrified in the lightning shadows of her creation.

CHAPTER 47

En route to Oregon
Last Twilight

The helicopter was bigger this time, a V-22 Osprey. Jen, Dr. Kallaste, Agent Reddy and Freddy weren't settled into their seats before the helo lifted off and turned north.

The NSA agent dug into a bag and took out a metal box. He spun the dials on the combination lock. Reddy pulled out a handgun from the black felt, loaded it and stuffed it in his jacket pocket.

"What you got there, Agent?" Freddy asked.

"A Glock 23."

"You think you'll need that?" Kallaste wondered aloud. "I thought your phone was your weapon of choice."

"My weapon of choice is a mainframe in Virginia. However, if I'm right, this will be the closest we get to solving our sleep problems."

"Dial down the crazy, Mr. Reddy."

"Something wrong, Mr. Chambers?"

"Wrong? Yeah. If the old lady is the alien's human anchor in this dimension, what are you gonna do? Shoot her dead in her bed?"

"I certainly hope it won't come to that."

"You ever shoot an old lady before?" Freddy asked through gritted teeth. "I don't imagine it's like plinking away at paper targets on a gun range with your buddies."

"I have no buddies. And I've never had occasion to shoot an old lady personally, no."

"How many people have you killed, huh?"

"That's classified."

"None, then?"

"No, I mean that's classified. I've never had to pull the trigger personally. My intelligence work has led to the deaths of a number of terrorists, however."

"I imagine it will be different up close, shooting an innocent old lady in a hospital bed."

"If she's innocent, I won't shoot her."

"You know what I think?" Freddy asked. "We should just keep going up to Canada. If the Ra really are coming through tonight —"

Reddy silenced him with a hard look. "This is our last stab at finding the truth before the deadline, Mr. Chambers. If it comes to nothing, our pilot will carry us all to an aircraft carrier off of San Diego. You'll all be evacuated to the USS George Washington or the Ronald Reagan. Maybe we can continue our investigations from there, unless you'd prefer to take your chances on land, of course. If we fail, the war will proceed apace shortly."

Kallaste thought of his ex in New York. If the military thought New York was a focal point of the Ra's invasion, they would surely evacuate civilians. He'd asked Reddy, but the agent could only say, "Strategies and options are being discussed higher up."

Freddy fidgeted in his seat and was quiet for a time. Then he pulled his mic down so the others could hear him over their headphones. "You ever think how weird it is that the battle seems to be with one guy?"

Kallaste looked up, glad of the distraction. "What do you mean?"

"When we go to war, it's not like the bad guy leader himself plans to come kick our ass, right? Leaders have lessers, minions and underlings. Cora heard a voice. Jen saw a Woman in White. What if this is all some kind of hoax?"

"Your own boss got cut up. I blacked out and woke up in an emergency room," Jen said. "You saw how Captain Frist died. Did that look like a hoax to you?"

Freddy paled. "No, I don't mean that was a hoax exactly. I just mean that...I don't know. Maybe when we got into the *Unus Mundus*, we opened up a can of demons. We went deep into another dimension and something bad followed us home."

"As I've explained, Mr. Chambers," Reddy said, "we've encountered the Ra before. They have opened another front in the battle for our dimension."

"Okay, but what do we really know about this alien race?"

"We don't know much about how their society is organized," Reddy said. "It bothers me that we have so little recon or intelligence on their home dimension. That does not bode well. We are all tasked with reading the *Art of War* but no one truly seems to learn its lessons. Even if this goes well, which I don't expect it will, it's going to hurt."

When Jen touched the agent's arm, he pulled back. Flustered, Reddy muttered, "A sleuth of bears. A string of camels."

Freddy rolled his eyes. "Our best and brightest, on the case."

Jen gave Reddy a crooked smile she meant to be reassuring. "Maybe Ba'al is like a tribal chieftain who has to be the strongman to keep his lieutenants in line. The thing I met after the Woman in White.... I got the feeling Cord was like some sort of royal messenger— "

"Ha! The guy at the other end of the cosmic telephone line is named Cord. I just got that!" Freddy said. "After we solve all our cross-dimensional ecological problems, I wonder how long it'll take before they have Starbucks in their dimension? That's how we'll know we won the war, no matter who wins the short-term battles."

Jen glowered at Freddy. "We'll know more about our enemies when monsters pour through a dimensional rift. I have a better question. Mr. Reddy, you seem to suggest this is a new kind of attack. What was the old kind of attack?"

"They're responsible for a lot of death and destruction that we ordinarily attribute to other means."

"Other means?" Freddy asked.

"I can't say more about that, Mr. Chambers."

"Can you tell us, when they aren't attacking us in our sleep, what weapons do they use?" Jen asked.

Reddy took longer to answer than before. "Their weapons are often primitive. I told you, they are not vulnerable to our usual ordnance, not without blessing it first. They're fairly bulletproof, otherwise."

"Primitive? Like slingshots?" Kallaste asked.

"Swords, spears, shields."

"Oh, man! I do *not* want to get hacked to death," Freddy said. "That's like in my top ten bottom ten, best worst deaths."

"The Choir Invisible is very good with swords and such," Reddy said, "though we've also been utilizing magic against the aliens, as well."

"Whatever our problems, the real answer is never magic." Kallaste's jaw looked tight.

Freddy smiled. "Call it the new physics, then. We're surrounded by wonders that would look like magic to anyone who hadn't seen the development of technology. Think of it this way. Plenty of ships are at the bottom of the ocean. They're all there even if you don't know about them. What happens when we discover those secrets? Our worldview opens. Knowledge flowers. This could be the greatest opportunity for advancement of human consciousness — no, we could elevate the consciousness of the collective mind, alien and human!"

"That speculation is pretty generous considering what we've seen they're capable of doing," Kallaste said. "You're forgetting what happened to Captain Frist too easily."

"He didn't like me," Freddy said. "I didn't want that for him, but hey."

Agent Reddy received a notification on his phone accompanied by an alarm. He studied the text. "Bad news," I'm afraid. "There's been an explosion in Washington. The Capitol Building is gone. Early reports indicate that a hundred people sleepwalked to their deaths. They all wore suicide vests. Congress was in session. They don't have a body count yet."

"Was the President — "

"He's in a secure location but he's asleep. The Speaker of the House is missing and presumed dead. The Vice President is on Air Force One but...he's sleeping. No one can wake them. They appear to be in some kind of coma."

"They're trapped in the *Unus Mundus*," Freddy said. "Brilliant strategy. The aliens blocked our way into the Mindscape when they shut down our Remote Joes. Now they've got our high commanders locked up. Sleep paralysis would be my bet. If I were the aliens, I'd keep the President asleep until I was ready to wake him in the real world to establish terms of surrender and sign the peace treaty."

Agent Reddy shrugged. "Call it magic."

"Anybody else want to skip Bandon and keep going to Canada?" Freddy asked. "Who's with me?"

Reddy's phone rang. It was Cahill. The agent put him on speaker so they could all hear him. Dr. Danzig was yelling in the background, urging someone to wake up.

Cahill was breathless. "The people in the storage room are all asleep! The ones you held at Berkeley for questioning! They're all talking in their sleep, saying the same thing."

"Let's hear it," Reddy said.

The sleepers all spoke with one voice. In a low growl, they chanted, "Los Angeles! San Francisco! New York! Boston!" They repeated the names of the cities without deviation.

"What's it mean?" Kallaste asked.

Reddy looked grim. "Those cities will fall first."

"This can't be happening," the doctor said.

"I've worked with terminal cancer patients," Jen said. "That's what they all say." She looked out at the dying light. She wondered if tomorrow's dawn would find cities in rubble as it pushed back the curtain of night.

Freddy fished a pill bottle from his bag and swallowed three pills with a can of Coke. "There have always been multiple realities at work at the same time: life on the French Riviera, life and death in refugee camps, life in Date Your Sister, Tennessee. What will happen when all our Earthly realities come together against a common enemy? I'll tell you what. This will reboot our whole system."

"The system we've got works pretty well," Kallaste said.

Freddy had another long drag on his Coke can. "Sure," he said. "Works for you. Does it really surprise you that most of the planet would welcome a complete overhaul of the system that's treated you so well?"

Kallaste shook his head. "Whose side are you on, Freddy?"

"Humans, of course. I'm just looking for the silver lining. When everything is stuck in mental stagnation and entitled inertia, we *need* chaos to change the future."

"You're an anarchist, Mr. Chambers?"

"Labels are so easy for guys like you. I don't see things in black and white. In the *Unus Mundus*, there is no death and the world never ends. I want to escape to the Mindscape. I want to live to go check out other dimensions. Screw Canada. Take me to a dreamy heaven and let me live there forever."

CHAPTER 48

Houston, Texas
Lady Bird High
Last Day

The roiling clouds looked like an angry gray sea. Lightning flashed as the two-headed dragon coiled through a rip in the clouds. Green and glowing, it was the same color as Crystal's hair. She stared up, transfixed by the impossible.

"It's not impossible," the Woman in White said. "Nothing is impossible here. That's what makes it heaven."

The fabric of the woman's dress was a sail in the rising wind, unfolding and expanding, stretching toward the horizon. The dress stopped billowing and turned into ribbons of white snakes shooting away to the east. The fabric soon tightened and coiled back, like a line that had hooked a fish.

It's sentient, Crystal thought. *Her dress is a snake.*

"No dear," the woman replied. "I'm sentient. I feel like I've been asleep for a long time and now I'm finally awake. Awake and free and in control. You have no idea how foreign that feeling is to me."

Above them, the green dragons coiled and roared. Another

skyquake shook the ground with eerie metallic echoes. As the gown's long train pulled back, dress material fell around Crystal like piling drifts of snow. The Woman in White let out a joyful laugh which made Crystal yearn for silence.

Finally, Crystal could see the end of the train. The bands of fabric had wrapped her mother tightly. Sherry Perry looked as if she was trapped and pulled through the air in a giant fist. Her mother screamed on and on. As she arrived before Crystal and the Woman in White, she was suspended twenty feet in the air. Her face was cut and bloody. Shattered glass glinted in her hair.

Crystal had often thought her mother insane. Kids at school often called their parents crazy but they weren't talking about a genuine psychological disorder. They complained of early curfews, unfair punishments and unreasonable expectations. Sherry Perry was truly crazy. Crystal was sure now because, upon being pulled from her seat in her living room through a plate glass window and carried by — what, exactly? A dress that acted like a giant arm and hand? Crystal couldn't explain what she saw. She only knew she saw it.

And her mother cackled and shrieked in delight. In Sherry Perry's dark eyes, there was only madness. "Take me to heaven! Take me to heaven! I'm ready, Lord!"

I'm dreaming, Crystal thought. *I'm dreaming and I can't wake up. It happens sometimes. Maybe it's some kind of stroke. Maybe I'm dying. Maybe I'm dead.*

Amid neon dragons spiraling down upon them, the noise and the utter senselessness of all that occurred, Sherry Perry did not look afraid. She was angry. That's how the girl knew for sure her mother was crazy. She was furious with Crystal. Sherry kicked and cursed. She tried to wriggle free even though she was high enough in the air to seriously hurt herself if she somehow escaped the grip of her bonds.

"Mom?"

"Enough," the Woman in White said. "A fairy godmother can do much more for you than this bitch ever did." Her mother shot up into the sky. The dress unfurled, releasing her high up.

One of the dragons caught Crystal's mother in its jaws. Teeth as long as swords impaled her. Sherry Perry was still alive when the flames came. Finally, her mother found fear and understood it. Her screams were no longer angry. Then her screams stopped abruptly.

Crystal bent forward and threw up. She might have forgiven herself if that had been the end of this bizarre scene. The Woman in White ignored her mother's anguish. More folds of the dress shot out, weaving their way among buildings and stretching out of sight. In a moment, the Woman in White found more victims.

Before the casualties were sent to their fiery death in the sky, each one was pulled forward terrified and bewildered. The Woman in White showed Crystal each victim before she cast them away. Crystal knew them all.

Webster Dillion had teased her about being poor and needing food stamps in Grade 6.

Karen Storey had invited everyone but Crystal to a birthday party years ago.

A teacher named Block had given the girl a bad time because her notebooks were blank except for her drawings.

Three boys whose names Crystal didn't even know had made fun of her green spiky hair on the first day of school, embarrassing her in front of a whole cafeteria full of kids.

A music teacher in fifth grade had berated Crystal in front of a bunch of band kids because she didn't practice trumpet enough.

Each of them, one by one, no matter how great or small their offense, was sent to their death as Crystal cried and screamed and begged for the merciless carnage to stop.

"We *can't* stop, dear," the Woman in White said. "Once we get rid of these people, you're safe. There will be no one left alive to remember any lack, fault or embarrassment. This is what a purge looks like. Ba'al wants peace in order for him to enter our dimension. This is how we'll achieve it. Cord taught me the joy that comes with revenge. It is addictive."

The next victim was Crystal's father. Ted Perry was unconscious and lay slack in the grip of the wrap.

"No, please!"

"But he's a failure, dear. Worse, he makes you weak."

"Knowing that he got away was the only thing that kept me from killing myself," Crystal said.

"But that's not part of the rules of the game."

"This is no game."

"Of course, it is. You can only do whatever you really want — "

"No!" Crystal screamed. "No! No! No!"

"This is what you really want. You're holding back because you still think you're not supposed to be honest."

The twin dragon heads turned their burning eyes to her. Their fierce roar was deafening. The molasses in which Crystal had seemed to be stuck became packed dirt again. The piles of crinoline and snake-like tendrils fell asunder. The Woman in White disappeared.

Under the bleachers at the edge of Lady Bird High's football field in Houston, Texas, Crystal Perry awoke with a start. Her cheeks were wet. She was sure she'd been crying and crying out in her sleep. Her throat felt raw. A puddle of vomit lay inches away from her face. Repulsed, she recoiled, relieved the nightmare was over.

Above her, a man moaned in pain. Crystal scrambled to her feet, grabbed her pack and ran for the sunshine. The sky was no longer black and a flying two-headed dragon did not coil in the sky ready to strike. The otherworldly noises had halted. Crystal chuckled at her mistake. The nightmare had seemed real but it was just a nightmare. Or so she thought for a moment.

Far off, screams driven by fear rose. She heard distant sirens and shouts she couldn't quite make out. Car alarms blared on, ignored.

But it was the moan that kept Crystal moving. Somehow she guessed who it must be. She found her father crumpled atop the bleachers. "Dad! Dad!"

His eyes fluttered when she shook him but he was not fully conscious. She looked at his legs. Both appeared to be broken and bowed at odd angles, as if he had fallen from a great height.

"Somebody help! Somebody help me!"

The disembodied voice of the Woman in White returned. "I did try to help, dear. You see, it's my job to make peace. Wherever I find that I am not in heaven, I'm supposed to make it so."

Crystal shook her father's shoulder harder. "Dad! Wake up!"

"Dreams seem real because, somewhere, they *are* real," the Woman in White said. "Like reading a book — "

"Shut up! Shut up! Shut up!" Crystal straightened. "Somebody! Help! My dad — "

Her eyes widened in shock. The school grounds behind the bleachers were a scene of war. From where she stood to the forty yard line, the dismembered remains of charred bodies lay twisted, broken, half-eaten and discarded.

The voice of the Woman in White seemed to be retreating and trailing away on the dying wind, "I was like you once. I was weak. And now I am Deathless. Shame. You could have been, too."

Her words echoed off Lady Bird High's gymnasium which, somehow amid the chaos, had caught fire. Thick gray smoke rose from the gym's roof.

Crystal wept. "Whatever they did to me, they didn't deserve this!"

The girl pinched herself. Then she slapped her own cheeks. The blow stung but, to Crystal's great disappointment, she really was awake. The murders had happened. The Woman in White had used Crystal's memories and anger to select her victims and kill them. There was no going back to being ordinary after that.

Smoke billowed high into the clear blue sky followed by the school's fire alarm and Crystal Perry's anguished cries.

CHAPTER 49

Bandon, Oregon
Last Dusk

The sickly sweet odor of industrial cleaners greeted the group as they entered the small hospital. "Why do all these places have to smell like this?" Freddy asked.

"All hospitals have this same odor," Kallaste said. "The cleaning fluids have to be strong to cover up what goes on here."

"I thought Edith Gray was in a nursing home," Jen said.

"After the FBI visit, she showed some signs of distress. She was transferred here for better monitoring."

Freddy scowled. "What did they do to her?"

Reddy looked surprised. "The FBI? Nothing, Mr. Chambers. I read the transcript of the interview. It was brief. The subject came in and out of consciousness and seemed confused."

"The drugs often make nursing home patients hazy," Kallaste said. "They get overprescribed a lot."

"The FBI should be leaving little old ladies alone," Freddy said. "Hasn't she suffered enough by this age?"

"Agent Shin conducted the interview and she was nothing but respectful. Intimidating elderly women is a task Homeland Security leaves to TSA Agents in airports."

"Nothing good will come of this," Freddy warned. "The clock is ticking. Just get us to an aircraft carrier. This is a dead end. Literally."

Reddy yawned and fished a pill bottle from his jacket pocket. His phone interrupted him, buzzing an alarm signal the others had not heard before. The NSA agent turned away so they could not see his screen. When he turned back, he looked grim.

"Anything wrong?" Jen asked. "I mean, what else is wrong now?"

"Houston experienced an extreme weather disturbance today. To quote Agent Shin, 'Thunderstorms with a chance of dragons.'"

"What does that mean?"

"Shin is investigating."

"Are your pills wearing off, Agent Reddy?" Freddy asked. "I could give you something stronger, if Dr. Kallaste can't."

The agent paused to swallow two pills and took a long drink from his water bottle. "Thank you, Mr. Chambers, but one can only go without sleep for so long. I might end up sleeping through the apocalypse. That might be preferable."

"The only drug I can think of that's stronger than what you've already got is cocaine," Kallaste said.

Freddy bobbed his head. "I know my pharmaceuticals, Doc. Cocaine was what I was offering."

"Let's put a pin in that," Reddy said. The agent held out his credentials as he approached the nurse at the admitting desk. "I need to speak to Mrs. Edith Gray. She is under your care, yes?"

"Her doctor is having a nap but I can wake her," the nurse replied.

"No need. Where can I find the patient?"

"Room 23."

"Auspicious."

"Excuse me?"

"I should have guessed." Reddy strode forward and the others followed.

Jen grabbed Reddy's arm before he could enter Gray's room. "Hey. Let me talk to her alone. This is my theory and if I'm wrong, I don't want to terrify a little old lady on what may be my last night on Earth."

Reddy bobbed his head and opened the door for Jen. "We'll be right here."

In the evening light, it was a cheerless room. To Jen's left, a bed with rumpled sheets lay empty. To her right, the small figure of Edith Gray lay in the fetal position. She appeared to be in the midst of a fitful sleep. Her eyes were screwed shut and her jaw was a hard line. The monitor behind the old woman showed her heart rate was sixty-eight. Her respiration came fast and shallow.

Jen pulled a chair to the patient's bedside. Something from Jen's training came back to her. She slipped one hand beneath the old woman's hand rather than covering it. Bedridden patients liked to feel in control of something. By keeping her hand under Gray's hand, she could choose to pull away whenever she liked.

Jen studied Edith Gray's face. She looked like an apple doll, wizened by time and too much sun. Her skin was pale and thin as paper. Blue veins wound up her thin arms like garden snakes. Tears slipped down the old woman's cheeks.

This can't be the Woman in White, Jen thought. *Freddy was right. This trip was a waste. The apocalypse is almost here.*

"Hello?" the woman said. "Who's there? What's happening?" Gray did not open her eyes. Her voice was strained and weak, as if she was speaking on a poor telephone connection.

"Hello. Um...everything's okay. I think you had a bad dream."

"I thought I was dead," the old woman croaked. "I was worried about it. Then I wasn't worried. Then I was again."

"You're okay."

"The drugs," the woman said. "They helped, I think, but they make me fuzzy. Where are we? This feels different."

"I'm told your doctors moved you from your nursing home to a hospital, just to make sure you're okay," Jen said.

"If I'm okay, why am I in a hospital? Nothing's okay anymore." Her eyes were still closed. The old woman touched her own cheek. She did not wipe her tears away. Instead, she brought her fingers to her mouth. "Salt. This feels...real. But all of it feels real. I've been having strange dreams."

"This is real,'" Jen said. "A lot of people have been having strange dreams lately. You're not alone."

"No. I suppose I'm never alone."

"Can I get you some water, Mrs. Gray?"

"*Hmph.* Mrs. Gray. Gray was my maiden name. Once I was a Dufour. It sounded so fancy...."

"Gray and Dufour are nice names."

"Oh, I have had even better." Still, the woman did not open her eyes. She appeared to be on the edge of drifting off again.

"Mrs. Gray?"

"Mm? Edith, please. But do what you must, nurse. Then let me sleep some more. I'm so tired, I feel like a lazy house cat stretching out in a warm spot of sunshine by a big bay window. I had a cat like that once. Lazy shit. Always envied him. And now here I am...."

"I need to speak with you just for a little more, Edith."

"Which nurse are you? Is that Trudy?"

"I'm not a nurse. My name is Jennifer. Everyone calls me Jen."

The old woman sighed. "Did my grandson send you? I haven't seen him lately, except sometimes when I sleep. He talks to me in my dreams. He always tells interesting stories. He's very imaginative."

"No, ma'am. I'm here with...I need...can you open your eyes, Edith? Please?"

Be blue, be blue, she thought. *Blue like the edge of flames.*

Finding the alien's connection to Earth's dimension frightened Jen. Failing to find the avatar frighted her only slightly more.

The alien had murdered the Remote Joes easily. She feared Reddy would demand she try to make contact with the monster in the white room again. She doubted she could even make the attempt without anesthesia now. The idea of seeing Cord again frightened her. And what could she do that the Remote Joes could not?

With effort, the old woman opened her left eye. It was not flame blue. It was cataract white. She was helpless and harmless. Agent Reddy's last desperate move was a useless gesture. The demons were coming to feast. There was nothing anyone could do to stop the invasion now.

CHAPTER 50

Bandon, Oregon
 Last Day

The old woman made a sour face as she tried to shift to a comfortable position. "Do I know you, dear? Your voice is familiar but I suppose I've known several Jennifers."

"My last name is Daimler." Jen looked over her shoulder. Kallaste and Agent Reddy peered through a small window in the door. She shook her head and mouthed, "Not her."

"You have a lovely voice. We're always worrying about the wrong thing. My voice went with my lungs. I used to be able to project to the back of the theater. Too many young actors today can't project. Without a microphone, they all look like they're screaming. Have you ever acted? Some commercial voice over work, maybe? I'm sure I know your voice."

"I thought I knew you from somewhere, too," Jen admitted, "but I was wrong."

"Oh, you know me from the movies, dear. You know...it is a sad thing when you begin to feel your best years are behind you. I felt that way too early in my life. I was a cheerleader in high school. Did you know that? If I'd known how things were going to work out, I would have cherished that time more. Instead, I was always in such a hurry to get on to my brilliant career. I had real promise but things don't always go as planned, do they?"

"I'm sorry. I don't watch a lot of movies. What did you do?"

"A few B movies, mostly. Not much you should know — not now, anyway. Not at this late date. Young people don't even know old Oscar winners, anymore. Still, much ado was made of me for a short while. Everyone enjoys that, I suppose. That's why brides make such a big deal about the big day. We have so few big days...."

"I should let you sleep." Jen began to get up to leave but the old woman gripped her hand.

"I made three movies in one year about biker gangs taking over a small town. Can you believe it?"

"Sounds like fun."

"It was, mostly. Then I got my big break. Do you remember *Iron Eyes*? Kirk Douglas was the leading man. I was the love interest. Not much for girls to do in movies in those days besides run and scream and kiss and be protected. Still, it was a big break. Then I made the mistake of sleeping with the director. Well, that wasn't the big mistake. Marrying him was."

"That was Mr. Dufour?" Jen wondered if the old woman knew Francois Dufour was dead, surrounded by a town full of corpses that looked like zombies. Surely, if they knew about the massacre of Tour-tour, the people who took care of Edith Gray would spare her that image.

Edith coughed from deep in her lungs. In trying to catch her breath, she wheezed. The wind in her lungs was a light breeze through thick cobwebs. When she caught her breath, she said, "I don't know why I thought a man who slept with one young starlet wouldn't sleep with another. I got pregnant, never got back on the screen. I managed some theater work later. I don't think I was all that good when I was on screen. In the screen test, they wanted to see what I looked like in a bathing suit. With casting directors, it's boobs, face and legs, in that order. I was the whole package then but I was lazy and didn't rehearse enough. Once I practiced more and learned the lines, I figured out how to live the lines."

"Sounds like you've had an interesting life." Jen glanced toward the door again, wondering how she could exit without being rude.

"When I got some time in the theater walking the boards, that's when I turned into a decent actress. I got my body back soon after I gave birth but Francois was old-fashioned. He didn't want me to work. I waited too long to divorce. The best work I could get on television was as an extra, filling in the background of an Arby's commercial. How far we fall from the promises we make to ourselves. Francois ruined my chances at being a real star. I never got a chance to graduate from B movies."

Jen wanted to bolt, but as a fresh tear slipped down the old woman's cheek, she had to stay a moment more. "How many children did you have, Edith?"

"One girl, one boy. I loved them so much."

"That's more important, right?"

"The boy had a heart attack at his desk at fifty-seven. Worked himself to death trying to make a living. The girl, Mary, married, divorced and died alone. Breast cancer, two Christmases ago. Like me, she married too young. I tried to warn her but all I got was condemned for it."

"I'm so sorry."

"My daughter was never ready for the rigors of motherhood, poor thing. My grandson was hard on her but she was hard on him first. All water under the bridge and over the dam now. It's cruel, you know. I thought so much mattered when I was a child so I had an unhappy childhood. Then I got older and I realized how great it could have been if someone had taught me how to relax and enjoy the moment. Same as now, I suppose. No matter where people are, they are always thinking of being somewhere else. No one is in the moment. I don't even know if anyone really enjoys anything, anymore. They rush to eat their food without tasting it. And the movies are so vulgar now. It's as if they think cynicism is the same as wit. And the way everyone treats old people? Ha! If only they knew our true thoughts. We just don't tell everything, that's all. Hiding our lights under bushels. If I were young again, I'd change all that. I should have been a director."

"I should be going, Edith. I'm sorry I can't stay longer."

"You wait, young lady. One day, maybe around age forty or so, you'll see a picture and think yourself ugly and fat. By fifty or sixty? You'll wish you were forty again and realize how thin and pretty you really were."

The way things are going, we'll be eaten by monsters from another dimension before the end of the week, Jen thought.

She gently extricated herself from the old woman's grasp. "Thank you for the advice. I'll remember that. Thank you for your time. Do you have someone coming to visit you? Family?"

"My grandson visits sometimes. He'll do better than any of us. After my heart is done," she tapped her chest, "people won't remember me but he'll have a name to last. You'll all end up working for him someday. Genius, he is...though I suppose all grandmothers think that, even when the kids are plain idiots."

Jen laughed politely.

"Look up my movies."

"Um, okay. Sure."

"Look for me by my stage name. I was born a Gray and it looks like I'll die Gray. Heh." She touched her sparse hair. "And gray. You don't remember *Iron Eyes*, do you?"

"Sorry, no. But I'll be sure to check it out. I really should be going, Ma'am."

"No reason you should know me. It wasn't *Citizen Kane*, or anything. *Iron Eyes* was my *Citizen Kane*, though." She coughed some more before the rattle in her chest settled. "Next time you have a chance, look up *Iron Eyes*. I saw it on that channel that plays old movies on Saturday afternoons once. If Kirk Douglas dies before I do maybe I'll have a little resurgence. People will see me in my prime and wonder, whatever happened to that pretty young girl? Sorry to say," she gestured weakly at her bed, "here we are."

Jen stood by the door. "I'll definitely look for it. I want to see it. Maybe you should get some more rest."

"*Iron Eyes.*"

"I won't forget." Jen grabbed the door handle. "I hope you feel better soon. Thank you!"

"In the credits, you'll find my stage name. Edie Chambers. After her divorce, my daughter actually preferred it so much she took it back for her own. She said she loved me best on screen. My daughter said she never liked me as a Gray. Wasn't that a tad mean?"

Jen froze, turned and stared. "Your name was Chambers? Your daughter's name was Chambers?"

The old woman stared back. Both of her eyes were open now. Her left eye was a snow white cataract. Her right eye burned flame blue.

CHAPTER 51

Bandon, Oregon
Last Night

Agent Reddy opened the door and Freddy called from behind him. "Nana? Are you talking my friend's ear off? How are you feeling? Are they treating you well?"

Jen turned back to find Kallaste and Reddy standing in front of Freddy. They both had their hands in the air. Annoyed, Freddy told them to put their arms at their sides.

"Freddy! I'm so glad to see you," Edith said. "I'd like you to meet... I'm sorry, dear. I've forgotten your name."

"Jen."

"I know her, Nana. We all came on the same helicopter."

"I know your grandson, Edith," Jen said.

"I thought I did," Kallaste said.

A gleeful grin spread across Freddy's face. "I did warn you, Mik, I'm the original know-it-all."

The alarm notification on Reddy's phone sounded. Reddy looked at it, reflexively. Freddy slapped him on the ear. "Put your phone down, Thomas."

Reddy thumbed a button on the screen and the speakerphone came on. It was Agent Shin. "Sir? Are you there?"

"He's here," Freddy said. "He can't answer you right now."

"Report," Reddy said.

"We've lost contact with four nuclear missile silos. They've gone to Defcon 2 and will not stand down. They won't answer our calls to call off the countdown. POTUS is still in a coma. We don't — "

"Enough." Freddy took the phone from Reddy's hand and threw it into a far corner of the room.

"The people manning those silos are dreaming of the apocalypse, aren't they?" Kallaste asked.

"Oh, yes," Freddy said. "The President is giving them direct orders, as far as they know. The men in the silos think Washington is already in flames. They'll be sleepwalking through the protocol they've practiced. At midnight, they will turn their keys together." Freddy looked this watch.

"Los Angeles. San Francisco. New York. Boston," Reddy said. "Those are the targets, correct?"

"Freddy?" Edith looked bewildered. "What..what's happening? Who are these men?"

"I'm Mik Kallaste."

"Hello, Mrs. Gray. I'm Agent Reddy — "

"Reddy and Freddy," the old woman said. "Isn't that confusing?"

"We're very different people," the agent replied.

Freddy reached up from behind and flicked the agent's ear hard. "This is *Thomas*, Nana. Have you finished the pills I gave you already?"

"Oh, thank you, Freddy. The doctors said I was having nightmares and crying in my sleep. I don't think I'm very well. I seem to be in and out of sleep. Mostly konked out, it seems."

"Do you know what's been happening?" Jennifer said. "With people sleeping, I mean?"

Edith shrugged. "The nurses said a lot of people are having a hard time sleeping. I've had the strangest dreams. I dreamt a woman —

Korean or Japanese, I think — asked me questions. She said she was from the FBI. Can you believe it?"

"That wasn't a dream, Mrs. Gray," Reddy said. "Agent Shin did try to interview you."

"I'm sorry." She pointed to her head. "I'm very fuzzy, lately. Fuzzy on the inside and outside." She touched her sparse hair self-consciously. "I used to wear wigs but the damn things made my head too hot."

"Have you finished all the meds I gave you, Nana?" Freddy asked again.

The old woman struggled to sit up and reached for her night-stand. "The medicine? I'm sorry. It must be in my drawer back at Foxgrove. When they transferred me from the nursing home, I-I didn't take the bottle. I'm sorry. They moved me when I was asleep. The doctors said they couldn't wake me up."

"That's okay, Nana. I have more medicine for you. It will help you sleep and rest. You're going to feel much better soon."

"I don't know. I have such strange dreams when I take those pills." She looked down at her rumpled bedsheets. "It feels like I've been running in my sleep."

Freddy stepped back cautiously and slipped his pack from his shoulder. He stretched out one arm to hand it to Mik by the strap. "Give the bag to Jen. Jen? Could you please look in the side pocket? Nana needs her medicine."

When the doctor leaned forward to hand her the bag, Jen spotted Reddy's Glock 23 in Freddy's hand. It was pointed at the agent's back. She'd known he had to be armed but the sight of the pistol in his fist kicked up her pulse. "What does the medicine do, exactly, Freddy? Maybe you shouldn't take it, Mrs. Gray. Your doctors don't know about it, do they?"

"Nana knows I wouldn't do anything to hurt her."

"But you *are* hurting her," Kallaste said. "Back in the lab, you talked about how someday we wouldn't need hypnotic induction to achieve altered states. You weren't speaking theoretically, were you?"

Freddy could not resist beaming a smug smile. "Someday is

already here, Mik. It's my own mix of shrooms, diazepam, melatonin and l-tryptophan. Add a little Ayahuasca and a dose of demon weed ground up in a pestle and here we are, at the dawn of a new age, plugging into a new world."

The doctor frowned. "You used diazepam? That's Valium, Freddy. Don't you think that's too dangerous to give to a frail, elderly woman? It's a respiratory suppressant. It might have mixed very badly with her prescribed meds."

"Experimenting with psychedelics on your grandmother does seem unwise, Mr. Chambers," Reddy said.

"That's why he chose his grandmother to be the aliens' link instead of doing it himself," Jen said. "Isn't that right, Freddy? You risked Edith's life because you figured she was old and on the brink of dying, anyway."

"Shut up, bitch!"

Edith struggled to sit up. "Freddy! What's going on here? You explain it — "

"He's a traitor, Edith," Jen said. "Don't take the medicine."

"The drugs are just a way to transport you to the Mindscape, Nana."

"I don't...I don't understand — "

"When you're plugged into the Mindscape, the aliens can help you and you can help them."

"Aliens. You mean the big demon guy? I remember him from the bad dreams. Big Daddy. He called himself Cord."

"Nana, the aliens need your help now. I need your help. Won't you help me? All you need to do is take my pills and sleep."

"I think we need to sit down and talk," Edith said.

"No time for that. The wheels are already in motion. Just one more sleep and you'll wake up in a world that will be better."

"No, Freddy. Why did you do this without telling me — "

"You weren't supposed to wake up before everything was done. We're running out of time. This move is going to be really good for me...and everyone, in the long run."

"She said no," Jen said.

He brought the gun into view, losing any pretense of hiding it. He pointed it at Jen's head. "I am very disappointed that you are not helping."

"Your arguments are usually more interesting and cogent, Freddy," Kallaste said.

Freddy turned the weapon on the doctor. "Maybe you'll find me more persuasive now. I'm not here to argue. I'm in control and everybody is going to do as they're told. I've got a lot of shit to do. Omelettes need eggs. Let's get crackin'."

CHAPTER 52

Bandon, Oregon
  Last Night

"You people have got me all wrong," Freddy whined.

"You said you used demon weed?" Reddy asked. "Seems appropriate."

"I tested it on myself. I was already in the Mindscape when the aliens contacted me with the formula for a better psychonaut mix. That's what opened up the connection so they could act in our world. I went back to the lab and combined the compounds."

"You built the aliens a gate to our world," Kallaste said.

"And Nana's the key."

Edith tried to sit up. "I don't really understand — "

"This is going to sound crazy," Jen said, "but your grandson is using you as a sort of channel for aliens from another dimension. They're doing bad things."

Edith lay her head back on her pillow. "That doesn't sound so crazy. It would explain a lot. Freddy has talked to me about lucid dreaming from when he was a little kid. I should have learned it. From what I remember...wait. Is that big island really on fire? And that, that dragon thing? Did that happen? Cord...he walked around the world with me, doing things. Those were the bad dreams."

Agent Reddy cleared his throat. "Mrs. Gray? You attacked the Border Patrol, didn't you?"

"That was real? There were bad men, about to hurt a Mexican family.... *Hmph. That* dream, I remember. That was a good one." She smiled. "You should have seen those men scream."

"It wasn't just a dream, Nana. You were a superhero. My drugs made that happen. You could save more people from bad men. All you need is to take my prescription."

"Edith? It wasn't all good. You unleashed terrible revenge fantasies on your old agent and your husband," Jen said.

The old woman's hand went to her mouth, "Francois is really dead?"

"I'm afraid so. He was found dead, surrounded by a town full of dead people. I don't think you just killed Francois, Edith."

"They...they looked like zombies at the end, didn't they? Like from a silly movie?"

Jen moved back to Edith's bedside and patted her hand gently. "I'm sorry, but yes. A whole village, gone. Whole *families*, Edith."

Tears welled in the old woman's eyes. "I thought that was just a... just something dredged up from the movies."

"You thought it was a figment of your sleeping brain," Kallaste said. "It's not your fault, Mrs. Gray. It's Freddy's."

"It's so much like a dream," the old woman said. "I can barely remember it."

"Do you remember your agent...er...Mr. Flanagan?" Reddy asked. "Picked apart by birds in his backyard?"

"Desi? *Hmph.* I remember the birds," she said. "Hard to forget that. Served him right. One dead Hollywood agent is a like a hundred lawyers at the bottom of the ocean. A good start. Still...I thought I'd put the bad business with Francois behind me. I do feel terrible about that."

"There were children among the dead in France, Edith," Jen said.

Sweat beaded down the old woman's forehead. She fanned her flushed face weakly. "I didn't know it was real. I swear it. I'm so sorry."

"You thought it was all a dream," Jen said. "You were in an altered state. You're not responsible. Your grandson is."

"Everybody stop talking about me like I'm not here!" Freddy insisted. "*Yoo-hoo!* Guy with a gun, here! What's it take to get some respect?"

"Do you imagine the world will thank and respect you when the aliens detonate our nuclear weapons on US soil?" Reddy asked.

"Oh, Freddy!" Edith said. "What have you gotten yourself into?"

"Take the medicine, Nana. The aliens will do the rest. Everything will be fine."

"Your grandson has a fantasy that he is the hero," Agent Reddy said.

"I'm among the few psychonauts to make contact with aliens from another dimension," Freddy said. "How many other seekers can claim that? Graham Hancock? Timothy Leary? Joe Rogan? If I was an astronaut, you'd be saluting me and asking for my autograph."

"Edith? The aliens have been using you as an anchor in our dimension," Agent Reddy persisted. "When their plans come to fruition, our intelligence is that the nukes, when placed correctly, will open two rips in the energetic walls between our dimension and that of the enemy."

"Pawn sacrifice, Thomas," Freddy said. "You're right. At the edge of the blast radii, precisely calculated, two rifts will open. The walls between dimensions will fall. I'll save an entire race of aliens. Humans will die but we can make more. We always do. Historians will see that I changed the course of history for the better. The opportunities — "

"The Ra will come pouring in," Reddy said. "Los Angeles. San Francisco. New York. Boston. Ba'al will have his revenge, times four."

"Revenge?" Kallaste asked. "What did we ever do to them?"

Agent Reddy sighed. "The Choir Invisible. They managed to set off a nuclear weapon in the alien dimension. We crippled their forces but, alas, not forever."

"We *nuked* somebody?" Kallaste looked pale.

"The first such attack since Nagasaki, yes," Reddy admitted. "In retrospect, it might have been a tactical error. The Choir Invisible has some personnel who are...questionable."

Freddy ignored the others and looked to his grandmother. "Don't listen to them, Nana. Remember what you told me when kids gave me a hard time for carrying a briefcase to school? A jealous bully broke my glasses and I came home crying. Remember? You told me, 'Genius always looks like crazy foolish at first.' I believed you. Trust me now. My drugs are perfectly safe."

"No," Reddy said. The agent fell silent when the young man pointed the gun his way.

"The aliens don't want you dead, Nana. They want you alive and well and sleeping peacefully."

"But I haven't been sleeping peacefully," she replied. "And I killed Francois. And the zombie people — "

"Please, Nana, just do this for me a little bit longer and everything will be fine. The aliens know things. They live much longer than we do. That's why there are so many of them. That's one of the reasons we have to help them come here. They need our help but they can teach us so much, too. This is going to change our understanding of physics. When we learn more about the alien physiology, we can live a lot longer, too. Humans and the aliens are going to rescue each other! Think of it, Nana. No more nursing homes. Maybe they can even make you young again."

"Did they promise you that you'd live forever, Freddy?" Jen asked. "You're hoping for immortality. That's what this is really all about, isn't it?"

"You people are whining about losing a few cities. I'm talking about stopping a genocide and extending the lives of every human for the rest of time. The aliens have already managed to combine races through genetic manipulation — "

"Eugenics," Kallaste said. "You're talking eugenics."

"Just another path to perfection, Mik. The human race got out of the eugenics business too early. Just because the Nazis did it — "

"Just because the Nazis did it?" Jen balled her fists, furious. "No good argument can come from the start of that sentence."

Freddy Chambers was undeterred. "You know why a goldfish is worth a buck and a dog is so expensive? When a goldfish dies, you flush it and get a new one. You don't even have to bother naming a goldfish. Dogs last longer. They're worth more. When I save the alien race and we figure out how to live forever, trust me, everyone will forgive."

"So the ends justify the means," Jen said. "It's the argument every selfish dictator, pathological megalomaniac and scared little prick makes."

"I think I just figured out why nobody's listening to me. I talk too much."

Freddy shot Reddy in the right knee.

CHAPTER 53

Bandon, Oregon
Last Night

The agent dropped his bottle of water and it rolled away. Reddy screamed in pain as he crashed to the floor.

"Shut up, Thomas, or I'll shoot you again, somewhere vital."

Reddy bit into his hand, moaning, but quieter.

An alarm sounded in the hallway.

"Someone heard that shot," Kallaste said. "They'll be coming,"

"In a few minutes, that won't matter."

Reddy pulled himself against the wall, leaving a trail of blood behind him. He winced as he reached for his bottle of water. Jen bent to open it for him as the doctor pulled off his belt. He stepped forward to tend to the agent's wound.

"I didn't say you could move, Mik," Freddy said.

"You've proved your point. You're the asshole with the gun. I wasn't sure you'd use it. I thought you were better than this. I thought you were smarter. You aren't just misguided, though, are you?"

Kallaste tightened the belt around Reddy's thigh as Jen held the

NSA agent still. "I'm going to need something, part of an IV pole, maybe, to twist this into a proper tourniquet."

"I'll be fine," Reddy muttered. "We're in a hospital and you're a doctor. It is as it was foretold in the prophecy."

Everyone stared at the agent. "Prophecy?" Jen asked. "What the hell are you talking about?"

"The Choir Invisible has an oracle. Sometimes the seers are not dependable but, when we ran the war game scenaria, this was the only way that gave us a chance. I didn't carry a gun before because we assumed Freddy would take mine. When I found no weapon in his bag, I had to make mine available for him. The pills I took earlier were not to keep me awake. They were pain killers. Those pills are not as effective as I'd hoped."

"Oh, for God's sake," Freddy said. "Did the oracle see me kill you all?"

"No," Reddy said. "Killing three innocent people in cold blood with a handgun would not fit your conception of yourself. Like you said, murder is not like plinking away at paper targets."

Freddy pointed his weapon at Reddy's head. "You are annoying."

"I am aware," Reddy replied.

"Sit back and watch. We're about to make inter-dimensional history. And Nana? You don't really have a choice. The alien is in you, waiting to go to work."

Edith's eyes went wide. "*In me?*"

Freddy opened the backpack himself. "Take the meds, Nana. You are linked to Cord. That's why he's called Cord. It's not a name. It's a rank and a job title with them. He's an advanced scout, tied to you. All the aliens named Cord are scouts. One of the ways they come here is through their connection with a host. You are the host, Nana. You were since the first dose."

"You really mean demon possession, don't you, Freddy?" Jen asked.

"If you like."

"He calls them aliens, Edith, but they look like demons. They act like demons. This is starting to make more sense in a crazy-assed way."

"Freddy, I've got to stop this bleeding," Kallaste said. "Let us leave so I can help Agent Reddy properly."

"Just as soon as Nana takes the meds. It's that or we watch Thomas bleed out. Wars end, Nana, but they always bring new innovation and change with them."

Edith looked to Agent Reddy. "What should I do?"

"Don't take the drug, Edith. If you do, Cord will finish what he started while you slept."

The old woman looked to her grandson. "Freddy? I hurt people. I don't regret killing my old agent. He was a prick but there were others. I'm worried that the things I did in the dreams, when I thought there were no real consequences...like it was just a play —

"Nana, take the pills. Two little pills! Take them! Now! Do I have to shoot all three stooges here?"

Edith stared at her grandson a moment more. "Do you think we're defined by the best things we do? Or our worst? I'm proud of what I did to the Border Patrol but...I went too far trying to help the girl with green hair. Way too far." Tears slipped down the old woman's face.

"It — the alien — it's *inside* you, Nana." Freddy shook two red pills out of the bottle. "You carry the mark on your back don't you?"

Edith nodded. "Yes. The nurses at Foxglove were checking me for bedsores when they found it."

"I've got it, too. You're like me. We belong to Cord. We're safe." He looked to Jen. "Like her. The aliens won't hurt us. We are the chosen ones. Anyone who carries the mark can be a host. We will be spared. The aliens can't kill everyone if they come through my way. To come to Earth and act here, they need us. If they find another way to come through the dimensional rift, we'll have no such guarantee. It's simple math. We cooperate, we live. We don't, everybody dies. Just two more pills for a new world, Nana. Please."

The old woman took a pill and put it in her mouth. Freddy gestured to Jen with the gun. "Give her Reddy's bottle of water to wash down the goodness. Let's get this new future started!"

"No," Jen said.

"The mark makes you safe from the aliens," Freddy said. He pointed the weapon at her head again. "Not from me. Like I said, it's simple math. Do as I say or I'll erase you. Cooperate or I'll do it myself after I empty this gun into all of you."

"Give her the damn water bottle, Jen," Kallaste said.

Jen sighed. "Simple math, huh?"

"Go ahead," Agent Reddy said.

Surprised, Jen looked back at the agent bleeding on the floor. "Are you sure? There's nothing else we can do?"

"Go ahead," Freddy said. "All of you, rush me. I'll shoot you dead before you make it half way across the room."

Reddy nodded weakly. "It's almost over. Do what he wants."

Jen did as she was told.

"Get some sleep, Nana," Freddy said.

Edith Gray swallowed the pill and the new future began.

CHAPTER 54

Bandon, Oregon
Last Night

As soon as she swallowed the pill, Edith Gray shuddered and went into convulsions. The room went cold, as if a stiff wind had blown open a door on a winter day. A mist rose around the old woman's body, enveloping her. Outside, a skyquake erupted, like gears grinding in an impossibly huge machine. The building shook.

"What's happening?" Freddy yelled. "This isn't supposed to happen!"

"It is as it was foretold," Reddy said, "with minor variations." He glanced down at his wounded knee and winced at the pain. "Not all the variations are minor to me."

A bolt of lightning shot through the window, shattering it. The arc of electricity took Edith gray in its grasp. What little hair she had stood out straight from her scalp. Her arms and legs contorted, folding up as her fingers curled into fists. Freddy was caught in the charge and thrown back against a cabinet. Glass shattered as he collapsed to the floor.

The overhead lights blew out. The room fell into darkness as the arcs of electricity disappeared.

After a moment, the hospital's backup generator kicked in. An emergency light from the hallway cast a beam into the room. Freddy lay bleeding near the door, the Glock 23 still in his hand.

Edith lay on the floor at Jen's feet. She smelled like burnt bacon, expelled urine and feces. The flexor muscles in her arms and legs were still triggered from the electrical charge that flashed through her. Her arthritic fingers were still curled. The remaining pill was still clutched in her palm.

"Edith?" Jen reached out and gently shook the old woman.

"Dead." Kallaste said.

"How? Was the pill poison?"

Reddy shook his head weakly. "The water."

"That was holy water, wasn't it? You...you drink holy water?" Jen asked.

"Ever since I began monitoring alien activities through the Choir Invisible, yes. Paranoia pays dividends."

Jennifer stared at him, disbelieving. "But how?"

"I ordered every water bottle we stored at Berkeley be thrice blessed."

"Tastes the same as regular bottled water," Kallaste said,

"To us," Reddy replied. "To the aliens — " he gasped in pain. "Possession by demons or other inter-dimensional beings is a capital offense according to a ruling by the FISA court."

"You told Edith not to take the pills!" Jen said.

"I deceived her."

"And now she's dead."

"So shall you all be," a deep voice rumbled from the broken window.

Still crouched against the wall, Jen, Kallaste and Thomas Reddy looked up at a massive monster in black armor.

"Cord, I presume?" Reddy asked.

"I am Cord."

Jen trembled as she recognized the monster. "That's the thing that branded me."

Cord ignored her outburst, looking to Reddy. "Your race is devious."

"For a moment, I thought my mission was over," Reddy said. "The oracle said you'd show up."

"Oracles are notoriously vague, almost useless. I wound up on the roof, thanks to you." Cord climbed in through the window, knocking more glass to the floor. The shards crunched under the monster's weight. The alien pulled a long, curved sword from a sheath on his back. "Did your seers tell you I'd kill you?"

"Yes."

"Yet you came anyway, instead of running from Fate."

"My business is fighting Fate."

"A warrior's answer. I shall allow you to die swiftly."

The monster looked to the still form of Freddy. "That vessel served us well. When he awakes, I shall be covered in your blood, Agent Reddy." The alien nodded to Kallaste. "And yours, doctor. Then Frederick Chambers will be our new key to the gateway. The invasion will continue."

"You don't have to kill us," Jen said.

"I won't kill you, Miss Daimler," the monster replied. "You bear my mark. You shall serve me."

"I'd rather die."

Cord shrugged. "If you prefer. Once we start the slaughter, there will be willing volunteers who prefer to serve. We shall mark a number of those who see the wisdom of obedience."

"There were slaves in my family once," Jen said. "I'm not going back to that."

Cord raised his sword, ready to cut her down.

"Don't kill her," Agent Reddy said. He slumped farther down the wall, close to losing consciousness.

Cord hesitated.

Trembling, Jen squeezed the agent's shoulder. "You can't save me, Thomas."

"No," the agent whispered, "but I was hoping you could save us."

"What?"

"I'm tired. Aren't you tired, Miss Daimler? Aren't you exhausted?"

"Y-yes."

"Get some sleep, Miss Daimler."

Jen's eyes widened in understanding. She reached out to snatch the remaining pill from the dead woman's hand. Cord's sword swung down, missing her hand by an inch, cutting through the corpses's arm and digging into the floor.

Jen swallowed the pill dry.

Before Cord could strike again, her eyes rolled back in her head and she slipped to one side. She collapsed into sleep on Agent Reddy's shoulder.

She woke in a white room. "Mindscape!"

"This is the White Space," said a disembodied voice. "Some of my people liked to call this the lobby to the Twilight Zone. Everybody's a clever little comedian, aren't they?"

Jen looked around. She knew that voice.

CHAPTER 55

The Unus Mundus
   Out of Time

"Captain Frist!"

"Harrison. Just call me Harrison."

The Psy Ops officer appeared in a pink and blue tie-dyed t-shirt. He looked younger. "Hello, Jen."

His hair was jet black. He looked more relaxed than the man she'd seen at Berkeley. "I didn't get a chance to speak with you much."

"I thought you were dead."

"I am. And I'm not. I read the reports from the Choir Invisible but I didn't really believe in ghosts until now. *Heh.* The term 'ghost' is an oversimplification, of course, but it suits our casual understanding of the supernatural. Even the term 'supernatural' is wrong. Turns out, it's all natural."

"What are you talking about?"

"I slipped into the *Unus Mundus* as the tank crushed my body. Maybe that's what happens to all of us when we die, I'm not sure. It turns out the universe is even more complicated than we thought. It's like I lived in a 2D world, never guessing it was 3D."

"I left Mik and Agent Reddy with one of the aliens in a hospital room in — "

"I know. There's time."

"But — "

"Trust me. Dr. Kallaste and Agent Reddy are unharmed for now. I have to show you something so you can help them."

Jen frowned but held her tongue.

"The *Unus Mundus* is much bigger than I had imagined. I thought of it as the collective mind of the human race. There is much more to explore. Fungi speak to other fungi. The trees of the forest communicate with each other through their root systems. The planetary energetic network is so vast that the *Unus Mundus* defies description. I haven't even looked to the stars to begin exploring beyond Earth yet. I never suspected how broad and deep the nature of consciousness is. In life, all we have is a few frames of the film and very little time to understand. Now that I see the connections between things, I'm beginning to understand the big picture. I saw a small part of the puzzle before. I thought my life was supposed to be a war movie."

"It's not? We are in a war. Several, it seems."

"I think the big picture, the big puzzle, might be a conversation. DNA is a code we're cracking but it's also an evolving conversation. Ideas are the genes of our culture. Ideas are the information that will shape what's to come."

"What is to come?"

"I don't know yet. I think that's kind of the point. All life hangs over an abyss of annihilation and non-existence. We don't know where we're going but every day we build a bridge out over Nothingness. We build it with what we think and feel and do. I don't know where the bridge ends for the human race. I'm sure ours is not the only bridge. There are lots of branches on the evolutionary tree. Many end in dead ends."

"Make sense."

"The aliens are facing extinction. So are we. Frederick Chambers wasn't all wrong, you know. Right now, our conversation with the Ra takes the form of war. If both our species are to survive, that conversation will have to change."

"Please — "

"The *Unus Mundus*, the Mindscape, the One Mind…whatever you choose to call it. I thought of it as a place."

"Freddy said it was a gateway between dimensions and one of the ways to accessing it was through dreams."

"But the *Unus Mundus* is not a place or a what. The Mindscape is a who."

"I don't get it."

"That's okay. Neither do I. Not yet. But we're part of it and it's part of us. I feel like I just found out my television carries an infinite number of channels and I've only been watching one all my life. I'm very grateful to have this chance to surf more channels."

Jen looked around nervously. This place seemed the same as the white nothingness where Cord had branded her with his slave tattoo.

"You are uncomfortable with this view," Frist said. "We have time to make you comfortable before you get back to your war movie. I'm afraid your comfort will not last long."

The whiteness melted away and Jen found herself standing atop a large rock in a park in a city at night. People walked around, oblivious to the young black woman speaking to the tall man. He was now dressed in denim.

She recognized the skyline and smiled. "Central Park!"

"I love New York," Frist said, "though I had no idea how many rats there are here. It's staggering. The *Unus Mundus* reveals a lot of things we'd rather not know."

"This is just an illusion, though, right? We're not in New York?"

"No, and yes. The distinctions between here and there are fuzzier than that. It's a Schrodinger's cat situation, dead and not-dead until you look, sort of like me. I do have something to show you that is not real. Not quite yet, anyway."

People began to move faster, as if Jen was watching a film speed up. Lights in buildings flicked on and off. As passersby moved faster, the effect was comical. Car headlights began to blur into long streams of light. As the sky lightened, the city slowed again.

"On our current trajectory, Cord is delayed but not stopped. This is what happens tomorrow morning in New York."

Jen winced as a bright flash washed the city white for a moment, obliterating every detail. She squeezed her eyes shut and covered her face with her hands. Jen could still see the bright white light. She could even see the bones of her hands through her closed eyelids.

"You are unharmed," Frist assured her. "Any mortal who sees this flash will be blind, burned and dead."

To the southwest, a massive mushroom cloud erupted.

CHAPTER 56

The Unus Mundus
Out of Time

"Prepare yourself," Frist said. "What you see is disturbing. In the *Unus Mundus*, the experience is richer."

Jen bit her tongue. She tasted blood as the shockwave hit, flattening everything. The roar of the explosion forced Jen to her knees. She covered her ears. Towers of glass shattered. More crumbled in the onslaught. Others tipped like dominoes as clouds of dust rose to blot out the sun.

"Boston's gone, too," Frist said. "And somewhere between here and there, the invasion has begun. When the rift opens, millions of the Darkness Visible will pour in."

"The same will happen to San Francisco and Los Angeles, won't it?"

Frist nodded sadly as he surveyed the darkening day, "New York is a forest of towers. Every neighborhood will burn. The aliens will range all over the country and the world. The Ra will rebuild and make new cities one day, but not here. This place, once so alive, will be called Never York. Ba'al will allow no memorials or markers. This city will remain a graveyard until the Ra come to their own extinction. The aliens will leave these four cities forever in ruins as a reminder to us of their domination, as a monument to their contempt for the human race."

"No immortality."

"In another timeline, Freddy's happy, cooperative vision might have taken place. That's not our current trajectory. We might have escaped to the stars, immortal and ready to populate other galaxies."

Jen watched as waves of heat melted metal and plastic. Fires ignited everywhere. The few remaining trees that had withstood the shockwave became torches as the black mushroom cloud darkened the sky further. The dawn sky curdled, retreating to night.

But what she saw was not what drove Jen to her knees again and made her cry out. The heat and destruction had left her untouched. It was the screams, the terror and the anguish of every living thing in New York that obliterated the boundary between herself and the pain that burned across the *Unus Mundus*.

Jen curled into the fetal position, squeezing her knees tight to her chest.

Harrison Frist crouched beside her. As he touched her shoulder, she stirred. "I wonder if that's why unborn babies are always in the fetal position," he said. "A part of them is still in the *Unus Mundus*. They see all that's headed their way. They know the future of the world and all its pain."

"All I feel is pain."

"You can change our trajectory, Jen. Maybe when this mess is over, you could change a lot of things that need fixing. I've learned a lot here. The most cruel fact I know is that death, no matter how swift, is never truly instantaneous."

"Peachy," she said.

"For the dying, the end always comes too slowly. It's true for everyone. Before we can move on, Whoever is in Charge wants us to feel the full weight of the period at the end of our life sentence. Despite the fact that my consciousness has survived my body, the vastness of death remains a horror. It reminds us to make the good moments of life happen more often and to savor them."

Jen looked up. "Harrison?"

"Yes?"

"When I came here the first time, I thought this was Hell. I was right. The *Unus Mundus* is Hell, isn't it?"

Frist offered his hand and pulled her to her feet. He embraced her gently, with compassion. "It's a mind, Jen. It's what you make it. This could be paradise. Everywhere could be paradise with a push in the right direction."

"Why have you brought me here?"

"I didn't bring you. Freddy's pill did. I'm a bit jealous. If I could have taken a single pill instead of training in hypnotic induction, breathwork and meditation, I could have better known the *Unus Mundus* while I was still on the Earth plane."

He stepped back to wipe her tears and chuckled. "Earth plane. Ha! Sounds pretty crunchy granola hippie dippy, doesn't it?"

"Why am I here?"

He smiled. "I think I'm supposed to arm you for battle, before you go back. Take a bit of the power of *Unus Mundus* with you. That's how Cord has been making so much trouble, in Dreamland and beyond."

"Back in Oregon, Edith's dead. I don't see her here. I can't act through her while she's sleeping like Cord did."

"Jen, you don't have to be asleep to use your power. You just have to plug in. Do that and what happened to New York tomorrow morning won't happen again."

"It's happened and it hasn't happened yet?"

"Time is a slippery concept in the *Unus Mundus*. Right now, back in real time, you're still collapsed on the floor. Reddy is still alive."

"This makes no sense."

"It makes perfect sense once you step out of your prejudices and go with the flow. Everything makes sense but, so far, the sense it makes is outside of your expectations and experience. You expect one story. I'm giving you a better one yet you cling to your original expectations. Time to let that go, right? Back in the world, you are running out of time."

"Running out of time for what, exactly? What's the plan?"

"In the time you've spent with me, only a second has passed in that hospital room in Oregon."

"That can't be. It feels like I've been talking to you for an hour."

"But we haven't been talking, Jen. You've had this conversation at the speed of thought. Not the kind of thought that requires chemical reactions, either. This has been an energetic exchange so all that has transpired here has been happening at great speed. Our speed and breadth of perception varies widely. Even on Earth, that's true. Imagine how differently a hummingbird, a bee or a housefly sees the world, compared to humans. We move and see very differently compared to how we perceive the world."

"Watching New York get nuked felt like it lasted a month. What I saw and heard...the babies — "

"*Sh.* New York's destruction hasn't happened yet, not where you're from. You can save those babies and everyone else but time still passes in the *Unus Mundus*. If it didn't, everything would happen at once and we'd be overwhelmed with information. The procession of time, though not exactly a constant, is necessary for the gears that turn the universe to work properly. Think of Time as not one constant, but a pile of gears of varying sizes within a watch."

"It's all a bit much to process."

"We should hurry now. Mik is beginning to react."

"React how?"

"He's about to throw himself between you and Cord. Mik is trying to save you. Cord is swinging his sword down as we speak. The doctor means well but his attempt will fail. The tip of the alien's sword will drive through his chest and continue into your body, penetrating your belly. On your current trajectory, you both will die in a few moments. If that happens, the tragedy you have seen will occur. I don't see any other variables to dissuade Fate. You are the last variable, Jen."

"On my current trajectory? This is how the oracle works, isn't it?

Reddy said the oracles make prophesies but they aren't always accurate."

"The seers are not sufficiently dead to be more precise. Like me, back when I worked in Psy Ops, I could touch the *Unus Mundus* and get snapshots. The Remote Joes couldn't raise their consciousness enough to actually live here. If we could have managed it, there would never have been another surprise terrorist attack. We could have stopped them all before they began."

"So you're saying I'm about to die and that's certain? And it's going to be horrible and it's going to feel like it lasts a long time?"

"Your trajectory is already changing, Jen. By now, you understand the power of lucid dreaming. To defeat Cord and to stop the Ra, it's time for lucid waking."

"How do I do that?"

"Take a lesson from what Cord and Edith Gray managed to do. You don't have to be asleep to dream big."

"Can you do it?"

"I've got no body to return to, Jen. But you can do great things back in your world. "

"I'm sorry you can't come back with me, Harrison."

"I'm not. I'll stay and make my own little heaven. I still have purpose. I'll make it my business to stop further incursions by the aliens on the dream plane. My work continues. Deal with Cord and I'll keep this gate closed. They won't come back through this way. I'll make sure of it."

"You're stuck here then?"

"I'm where I'm needed. And I can do whatever I want to do without consequence. I'll live in a cozy cabin at the foot of Mt. Fuji and every day it will rain cherry blossoms. I'll finally have peace. I'm the lucky one."

"And I'm — "

"Not."

CHAPTER 57

Bandon, Oregon
  Last Night

The tip of Cord's blade was just about to pierce the doctor's chest when the sword shattered like glass. Wide-eyed, Kallaste stared up at the monster. The monster stared back.

Both human and alien froze in surprise until Jennifer said, "Mik? Get off me. You're on my leg."

Cord threw his sword's hilt in the doctor's face. Kallaste cried out as the pommel cut his forehead over the left eye. The doctor struggled to his feet but, with one sweep of his huge arm, Cord batted him to one side. He fell over Agent Reddy's still form and hit the floor hard.

The alien grabbed Jennifer by the throat and stood her up, pinning her fast to the wall. "What did you do, slave? What did you do?"

"The same thing you did," she croaked. She tried to kick him but the monster's arm was longer than her legs. She pawed at Cord's wrist and tried to break his grip. The monster laughed as he began to strangle her. She felt like a small child trying to fight off a huge man.

Jen closed her eyes. She'd either live or die in the next few moments. For a fleeting second, she considered that neither option was measurably better than the other. Not for her. She had wanted to stay in the *Unus Mundus*. But if she died at the monster's hands, she'd perish as Cord's slave.

"You're mine," Cord said.

"Never."

In her mind, Jennifer pictured a clock's hands, turning.

Cord squeezed her throat and, when Jennifer tried to gasp for air, she found she could not. She pictured the second hand of a clock rushing around its radius. Then she envisioned a spinning wheel, gaining speed.

The monster eased his grip slightly and Jennifer coughed and wheezed. She managed to take in a sip of breath.

"Ready to be my slave in the new world? Last chance, Jennifer Daimler. I think your new name will be Thing. I will call you Thing One."

"I think that's Dr. Seuss."

"What?"

"Never mind."

Cord sensed movement behind him. Edith Gray's long-term care bed weighed over two hundred pounds. It turned slowly in the air as it lifted from the floor.

"*Ha!*" Cord crowed. "Is that the best you can do?"

"What the hell is this?" A police officer appeared in the doorway, face pale and jaw slack. His eyes darted from the bodies on the floor to the spinning bed and the giant in black armor. The officer drew his pistol.

Still holding her to the wall, Cord looked back and laughed. "That won't work."

"This will." Jennifer closed her eyes and pictured a blender, then helicopter blades. The hospital bed exploded into a blur of motion. Its steel frame crashed into Cord. The monster was thrown across the room and out the window. The bed skittered across the room. It narrowly missed the police officer and, with a crash, embedded itself in the wall by the door.

"Man down!" Kallaste said. "I need a gurney!"

The officer did not move. "What...what was that thing?"

Jen pushed herself off from the wall. "Halloween came early this year. Help them." She staggered toward the broken window.

"Jen! C'mon!" Kallaste called. "Let the authorities deal with Cord."

"Go, Mik. Save Agent Reddy."

"You sure?"

"I got this."

Kallaste ran for the door, pushed the officer out of the way and yelled down the dim hallway for help. A doctor and two nurses ran in, wheeling a gurney.

Satisfied that the NSA agent was getting the aid he required, Jen turned all her attention to stopping the alien's escape.

Below, Cord had fallen into the parking lot. The alien had only fallen two floors but the bed's steel frame had crushed in part of his armor. Disarmed and in pain, Cord struggled to his feet. He began to limp through the parking lot.

"Cord! We're not done here!"

The monster turned in fury, caught in the glare of the xenon light that illuminated the parking lot. Even wounded, Cord hardly looked less formidable. He crouched between two cars to catch his breath. "What is it, slave?"

"Give up?"

Cord chuckled but his laughter turned into a ragged cough. He removed his helmet to spit black blood. Jen gasped. The monsters horns looked sharp and deadly, but the monster's face was a burned wreck on one side. The sharp angles on the right of Cord's face, though alien and unsettling, devolved into a mass of scars on his left.

"Your people burned me." Cord said. "Your bomb killed millions and burned thousands of my people. I've burned some of your kind, but...heh. You dare to ask me if I surrender. Would you?"

"No, I guess not."

"You don't know what you're dealing with."

"I don't think you do, either."

"Telekinesis," Cord said. "I did much more than that. I'll do much more. We'll meet again, Jennifer Daimler. You bear my mark. You are mine to own and mine to kill. I will look for you on the battlefield!"

"The mark you gave me doesn't mean what you think it means!" Jen called. "Your symbol is my prize! It shows everyone I am not your slave. It'll tell everyone the name of the first demon *I* owned, the first one I killed."

"Brave speech," Cord said, "but, even from here, I can smell your fear. You are exhausted. When I come back, I'll bring another sword. I'll cut out your tongue, grind it up and feed it to you through a straw. You will bow to me. I will savor your screams for mercy."

"Everybody dies slow," Jen said, "but good speech, I guess." She began to applaud him. As she did so, a shudder went through the parked cars on either side of Cord and their alarms began to shriek.

The alien almost got away. As she clapped her hands, on the third attempt, the cars smashed together.

Her attack took the monster to his knees. The fenders crushed around him. As she pulled her hands apart, the cars slid aside. Jagged metal hooked metal and Cord's gauntlets spun away into the darkness.

Jen brought her hands together again. Cord howled in pain as the engines smashed together, crushing him. Metal screeched against metal. As she brought has hands apart, more armor was ripped away.

"S-s-stop!"

Jen paused. "Sorry about the burns and your losses, dumbass, but you came at us. You started the fight. The bully doesn't get to complain when he loses."

The alien struggled back up to his knees, bloody and naked. He panted, shallow and fast. "I am beaten. I am not your master." He bowed his head.

Jen didn't stop her applause until the alien invader was pulp and both cars were useless wrecks.

CHAPTER 58

Bandon, Oregon
Last Night of the Invasion
First Night of What Comes Next

Jen stood in the shattered window. She watched two police cars arrive, lights flashing and sirens wailing. "Oh, sure. Now you show up."

She turned to find that Kallaste and Reddy were gone. Edith Gray lay where she'd fallen on one side of the bed. Freddy Chambers lay near the door. He stirred but was in no shape to run. That left the police officer whom she'd nearly killed with the spinning bed. He'd tucked Reddy's Glock 23 into his belt. His service revolver was trained on Jen.

"Police!" the man announced nervously.

"You're wearing the uniform. I get it."

"Hands behind your head!" The officer's voice shook, almost as much as his hands.

"You've got to be kidding me."

"I said, hands on your head! I need you on your knees. Lace your fingers and cross your ankles behind you."

"I'm not much for yoga. Or Simon says. That monster out there wanted me on my knees, too."

"I'm not joking. Do as you're told! You want to argue, we'll figure this out later! Right now I need you to — "

"Don't you want to wait for more backup? There's only one of you and I just took down a badass alien slash demon in armor. Did you... you saw that right?"

"Look, I don't know what's going on here, but I got damage everywhere, a dead old woman on the floor, this guy's out cold — "

"And your first instinct is to arrest the only black person you see."

"Ma'am, lots of backup is on the way. If you don't plan to cooperate with me, five or six more cops will make sure you do."

"Stop." Jen closed her eyes and raised her hands. She imagined her right hand on the officer's gun hand and the other cupping his elbow. She could feel the ghostly weight of his arm in her empty hands.

"Ma'am? I will shoot you if you don't get on your knees — "

"I've already had that discussion once tonight. I'm done with that, for now and forever. I just saved the world. Everybody owes me one." She crossed her hands sharply in the air in front of her. The gun went off before it was ripped from his grasp. The round narrowly missed her. The officer's elbow snapped and he moaned.

Jen imagined a giant hand pushing down. The officer sank to his knees. She bent, scooped up his weapon and casually tossed it through the window. Then she did the same with the Glock 23.

The officer tried to stand but he stopped when she quirked an eyebrow at him. "You really think you're up to it? You couldn't take me down with a gun. You try that pepper spray shit on me and I'll make you eat the whole can. If you run after me with your baton, I'll spank you with it."

He nodded and wisely stopped struggling.

Cradling his broken arm, the policeman looked at Freddy Chambers and Edith Gray. "What happened?"

"*Now* you ask politely? Nice."

"Well?"

"It's an issue of national security. It's classified. I think, from now on, I'm classified. Sorry if I sound grumpy, officer. I'm not usually like this. Everybody likes me and I'm always so nice...but I think I was nice because I was always a little bit afraid. I'm not feeling that now. In fact, I'm kinda pissed about the whole deal."

"They'll be forming a perimeter around the hospital. You need to give yourself up."

"You think a little yellow tape and men with guns are going to stop me from walking out of here?"

"N-no. I guess not. Please don't hurt them."

"Hurting people is not what I'm about." She glanced out the window at Cord's remains and added, "Usually. Sorry about your elbow, too, but — "

"How did you do that? I mean, with the bed and my arm — "

"Never underestimate the importance of a good sleep. Or the right pill at the right time."

He watched her go but called after her, "*What are you?*"

Her reply echoed down the corridor. "I'm a physiotherapist!"

CHAPTER 59

Walter Reed National Military Center
  Bethesda, Maryland
  One Week Later

Kallaste was back at his desk at Walter Reed. Agent Reddy was recovering from his wound at the Washington DC Vet Center. The doctor didn't know what had become of Freddy Chambers. He presumed the evil genius was locked up in Guantanamo Bay or someplace similar. Maybe he was locked up in a lab creating more super psychonautic drugs.

Cahill had called to meet but the doctor had begged off. "You're sad, huh?" Cahill asked over the phone.

"More like, recovering. I slept for days after the drugs wore off. Now I'm having trouble sleeping again."

"A sleep doctor with sleep troubles. What will your patients say?"

"I dunno. All the time I was working the problem at Berkeley, I was exhausted. I wanted nothing more than to come back home and to get back to work. Now that I'm here — "

"You realize it was the best time of your life?"

"Not the best, but most memorable. Coming back to work, each day feels like every other day."

"Just another day in the life of the average human, Doc."

"Mm. Yeah. Life feels more precious now. I remember feeling the same way in Iraq. I hated it. Then I sort of missed it."

"Well, you've been to two war zones and you didn't die. That was unexpected, all things considered."

"Yeah."

"You didn't get the girl."

"I know. Thankfully, neither did you."

Cahill sighed. "I didn't get the guy, either."

"Jen is still missing," Kallaste said.

"She's not missing, dude. I'm sure she knows where she is. I keep expecting to see her picture on a supermarket tabloid, wearing a cape and stopping a bank robbery or something."

"I hope she turns up. I just want to thank her for saving my life."

"You don't just want to thank her, man."

"No, I suppose not."

"You talk to Reddy about tracking her down?"

"No, but Agent Shin came around. If I don't let her know when Jen calls, I'll be in big trouble, apparently."

"Perfect!" Cahill cackled. "And a grateful nation thanks you for your service."

"This phone call is probably being recorded."

"Undoubtedly. I think I'll go surf some grandpa porn on my computer. Whoever's assigned to watch me at the NSA will have to watch with me."

"My mother would call you a special pumpkin. You're a special pumpkin, Eugene."

"It's kind of a turn on, actually. I think I've discovered a new fetish. Think of it: some big burly guy with a gun in a darkened office watching me watch — "

"Bye, Eugene."

"Friend me on Facebook! If you change your mind, you'll notice my relationship status is still single."

"Thanks."

"In case you come to your senses — "

"Got it, Eugene."

"Catch you at the next apocalypse, Doc!"

CHAPTER 60

Bethesda, Maryland
One Month Later

Jen showed up in the back seat of Kallaste's car. He was three blocks away from work before she sat up. He caught her reflection in his rearview mirror. Startled, he almost ran into a tree.

Jen giggled. "How about you take me out to breakfast as an apology for your terrible driving?"

"I drive better when I don't crap my pants. How'd you get into my car?"

"Sweetie, I crush demons with cars. You think I couldn't pop a lock?"

"I heard you went all *Firestarter*, only in this scenario, you're the telekinetic dad, not the little girl who burns everybody alive. Where have you been? Eluding the FBI?"

"Oh, that's all called off. The NSA knows where I am. I had a chat with Agent Reddy. Agent Shin and her friends won't be watching you anymore, either. I got a new job."

"Where?"

"You remember that super secret base in New York that's trying to stop the alien invasion and save our dimension, etcetera, etcetera?"

"Yeah. Team People. That's the super secret base I'm supposed to forget? The Choir Impossible. Never heard of it. Already forgotten."

"The Choir *Invisible*."

"Right. What exactly do they do there?"

"Swords and sorcery, but not the kind of movie sword and sorcery stuff you see with nearly naked dudes walking around in the desert in sandals. Do you believe in ghosts. Mik?"

"Given all I've seen, I'm prepared to be more flexible about my worldview. I still think all magic will be explained by science. Then it won't be magic anymore."

"That's a start. I'll take it. I want to introduce you to my boss. When you see her, you'll freak."

"Why?"

"She's got horns growing right out of her head."

"Um...are you sure she's not one of the bad guys? The only person I've seen with antlers tried to impale me with a sword."

"Hers is a complicated, long and entertaining story, but no, the boss is on Team People."

"Should you be telling me this? These are state secrets, right?"

"You're probably right. I'm going to have to kill you unless you join up."

"Join up to do what?"

"You're a combat veteran and the Choir Invisible needs a new doctor on their staff."

"What does it pay?"

"They're military contractors, Mik."

"So, more?"

"Much, especially with the danger pay."

"I don't know if I like the sound of that."

"You'll get to see me all the time and possibly help stop aliens from eating us."

"I don't want to sound like a coward but can I ask what happened to their old doctor?"

"Impaled on a demon's spear outside a bodega in Brooklyn. He stepped outside the fortress and the Darkness Visible got him. They've got a new trick now. They're impersonating a lot of humans."

Kallaste contemplated this news. "So the war is still on, despite everything we did?"

"The fronts on which war is fought move around sometimes. Nobody's safe until we shut down all the alien plots to invade."

"And you need me?"

"The Choir Invisible needs you."

"What about you, Jen?"

"I don't need you. I want you."

"Well, that's all right."

"This isn't going to get weird, is it? You won't be intimidated going out with a woman with telekinetic powers?"

"As long as you promise not to turn me inside out when we have an argument."

"Deal...but god help you if you ever leave the toilet seat up."

"Understood."

"Dr. Kallaste, I think we're going to get along just fine."

"Battle demons together?"

"And saving the whole messed up world. Yup."

"Do you imagine this will end well?" he asked.

"I don't think about tomorrow. I've learned to enjoy the moment more. No happiness that ends, ends well. Time is too slippery a construct and reality has too many variables to try to control it all. I'm looking for a good now. We all need a good now."

"Um, so...breakfast?"

"Turn around. Your place, first. Breakfast, after."

"After what?"

"After a good now."

CHAPTER 61

Austin, Texas
What Comes Next

The girl with spiky blue hair sat in a small booth at the Comic Con. For a few bucks, she drew caricatures of attendees. For a few bucks more, Crystal Perry would draw a proper portrait.

To her right, Levar Burton signed autographs. Depending on the age of the fans who approached the actor, some talked to him about *Reading Rainbow*. Most wanted to discuss *Star Trek, The Next Generation*. A couple of his oldest visitors talked to him about getting chased by OJ in *Roots*.

To Crystal's left, the Smoking Man from *The X-Files* signed autographs and bantered genially with his fans.

The girl looked up from idle doodling to find a thin man in a purple suit sitting on the stool opposite her. His make up was perfect. He looked like Heath Ledger's version of the Joker.

"Wow," she said. "Are you gonna kill me, Mr. J?"

"Not yet."

"Impressive costume. The green hair is stellar, man. Did you do your own makeup?"

"Yes. You used to have green hair, too, not so long ago."

"Um...aren't you going to ask me if I want to know how you got those scars?"

The clown looked at her for what seemed a full minute. "I'm more concerned about your scars, Crystal."

"My name's Julie."

"Don't."

"Julie Barnes."

"You are Crystal Perry. You think changing your address and your hair color would deceive me?"

"How did you find me?"

"You only ran away as far as Austin. Strange."

Crystal stiffened. "Not so strange. A girl with blue hair can get lost in Austin. I didn't have enough money to get farther. So I got a gig."

The clown leaned forward and looked at her drawings. "Teddy bears doing battle with...who is that fellow in white?"

"Moon Knight. And those are Care Bears."

"No dragons, hm?"

Crystal's eyes were wet. "I don't draw anything scary. Not anymore."

"Pity. A girl with your talents shouldn't hold herself back."

"I have to."

"Why?"

"Because of what I could do."

"But the Woman in White showed you what you are capable of."

"I know."

"Are you eating enough? You look awfully thin."

"The job doesn't pay much. I'm saving up to get off the streets."

"I can help you with that. You can still do it, yes?"

"The power? I've still got it."

"Why not use it? You could be living anywhere you want, couldn't you?"

"It's too dangerous."

"Danger interests me. Doesn't it interest you? I think it does."

She looked at the floor and the man reached out to lift her chin.

Crystal relented and looked into the man's eyes. "I can't. I can't do it again."

"Why?"

"Because I'll get caught. Or I'll have to keep on running."

He regarded her for another few beats before scooting his stool closer. "You are an interesting young woman."

"Thanks…I guess."

"You have the power to bend the world to your will but you still live the way you do."

"I'm just trying to do the right thing."

"No, no. Don't start lying to me now."

"What?"

"You don't use the power you so ably demonstrated in Houston. Imagine that! Fire from the sky! Dragons! Death and satisfaction — "

"Satisfaction?"

"Crystal! Darling! When I asked you why you didn't use your power, you didn't say you were holding back because it was wrong. You're not worried about hell and damnation and the fate of your eternal soul. You said you didn't want to get caught."

She looked down again. "I killed my dad. I didn't want to do that."

"But the others?"

"The teacher…the teacher didn't really deserve to die." Her lips betrayed her. She let a crooked smile rise.

"There's my girl. There's the girl who was bullied all her life. You don't like bullies, do you?"

"Nope. I sure don't."

"And, my Southern belle, you despise injustice, am I right?"

"You're not wrong, Mr. J."

"What if I told you that there was a cause, a righteous cause, that could save the world? What if I told you that cause needs a person with your power?"

"I'd say you were crazy?"

"Crazier than spending your days drawing pictures for strangers? Crazier than sleeping under bridges? Crazier than sleeping in a shelter and someone stealing your shoes and your sketchbooks?"

Her eyes were wet again. A hot tear slipped down her cheek.

"A warrior with your talents should never be without her sketch-book, Crystal. That's like a warrior without a sword."

The clown reached out and wiped her tears away with a purple glove. "With me, you'll be safe from those people who hunt you down. There are people who are looking for you, Crystal. If I found you, they'll find you, too. They'll want you in jail...a special jail. Or maybe they'll just kill you."

"What do you want?"

"Like I said, I want you to save a world."

"Um...not *the* world? You said, *the* world before."

"We can talk about details later. Here, you look hungry. Have an apple." A bright red apple appeared, as if by magic, in the clown's palm.

"You don't want a caricature done?"

The clown looked down at himself. "This is already a caricature. I want you to capture the real me. You have already captured my heart."

Crystal gave a weak smile and nodded. "A portrait, then?"

"Yes, please," the clown said, "just like this."

When she looked up again, the man in the chair still held out the shiny apple. However, he was no longer a clown. He was a large creature clad in shiny black armor. Antlers protruded from his head. A long curved sword rested across his lap.

Startled, Crystal gasped. Cosplayers ambled by. No one seemed to notice the thing in the scary mask. Crystal was unsure if they could see the horned beast or if the passersby simply accepted he was another cosplayer in remarkable armor.

"Don't scream," the creature said in a deep rumbling voice.

"I wasn't going to."

"Then you're just the person I thought you were. We have plenty of time now. Please, eat your apple."

"But what happens next?" Crystal asked.

"Have you ever been to New York?"

"I've never been anywhere."

"New York, New York. It's a hell of a town. At least...it will be. You'll need to choose a warrior's name. I think you already have one in mind, don't you? Didn't the Woman in White — "

"I know what I want to be."

"Wonderful. You are ours now. You are our family and we are your tribe. You stand among the Darkness Visible. We will protect each other. Welcome to the Dimension War. What warrior name will you choose?"

"Call me Deathless." The girl took a bite of the apple.

ABOUT THE AUTHORS

Best known for *This Plague of Days*, Robert Chazz Chute is a multiple award winning suspense writer living in Other London, Canada. Find him at AllThatChazz.com.

When she's not writing scary stories, Holly Pop studies biology. She's taking a break from writing while Robert continues the *Dimension War Series*.

COMING IN SUMMER 2018

The AFTER Life Trilogy
Inferno
Purgatory
Paradise

When a terrible new technology is unleashed from a research lab in Toronto, it's up to ETF officer Daniel Harmon and his team to secure the facility. As the action unfolds, Dr. Chloe Robinson attempts to save us all. The epidemic that threatens a city could soon take over the world and destroy our future.

Come for the twisty action. Stay for the snappy dialogue.

Do not miss *The NEXT Apocalypse Series*!

ALSO BY ROBERT CHAZZ CHUTE

Haunting Lessons, Book 1 of The Dimension War

Death Lessons, Book 2 of The Dimension War

Fierce Lessons, Book 3 of The Dimension War

~

This Plague of Days, Season 1

This Plague of Days, Season 2

This Plague of Days, Season 3

This Plague of Days, Season, Omnibus Edition

~

Robot Planet, The Complete Series

~

Wallflower, A Time Travel Novel

~

Brooklyn in the Mean Time

~

Bigger Than Jesus, Book 1 of The Hit Man Series

Higher Than Jesus, Book 2 of the Hit Man Series

Hollywood Jesus, Book 3 of the Hit Man Series

~

Murders Among Dead Trees

Self-help for Stoners

~

Do the Thing: The Last Stress-busting Book You'll Ever Need

ALSO BY HOLLY POP

Ouija

www.ingramcontent.com/pod-product-compliance
Lightning Source LLC
Chambersburg PA
CBHW020409260626
47156CB00007B/2298